Doomsday
In The
Capital

Doomsday
In The
Capital

Rob Shumaker

Copyright © 2023 by Rob Shumaker

This is a work of fiction. Names, characters, places, and incidents either are the products of the author's imagination or are used fictitiously. Any resemblance to actual persons, living or dead, events, or locales is entirely coincidental.

All rights reserved, including the right to reproduce this book or portion thereof in any form whatsoever.

Cover design by Cormar Covers.

Also by Rob Shumaker

CAPITAL SERIES

Thunder in the Capital
Showdown in the Capital
Chaos in the Capital
D-Day in the Capital
Manhunt in the Capital
Fallout in the Capital
Phantom in the Capital
Blackout in the Capital
Justice in the Capital
Firestorm in the Capital

—

The Way Out

—

HURON COVE SERIES

The Angel Between Them
Turning the Page
Christmas in Huron Cove
Learning to Love Again
The Law of Loving You
The Fire of Love
Love on the Diamond

Acknowledgments

A special thanks to Mom and Dad for offering their editorial assistance. Thanks also to Special Agent Dave for his invaluable assistance and expertise on my law-enforcement questions.

Self-defense is not only our right, it is our duty.
President Ronald Reagan

CHAPTER 1

The White House – Washington, D.C.
"Mr. President, we have to evacuate!"
The male voice was adamant and direct. It was a command, not a suggestion. No time to waste.
"Now!"
In the darkness of the bedroom, President Anthony Schumacher saw two figures moving toward him. The first thing he reached for was not his wife lying next to him, but his eyeglasses on the nightstand. He knew a Secret Service agent or maybe two would grab the First Lady from the other side of the bed, and he needed to be able to see. The contact lenses would have to wait.
The next things he remembered were the covers being yanked off and two sets of hands lifting him by each arm out of the bed. He felt like he was floating, propelled into weightlessness, but he knew it wasn't a dream. The race was then on.
An agent in the hall raised his wrist mic and radioed, "Shadow and Sunshine are on the move."
"What's going on?" the President asked, now upright and on the move, his feet only touching the carpeted floor of the White House Residence every so often. The bright lights of the hall caused him to squint, and he could feel the rush of cool air from the speed of the two men who were hustling him through the air-conditioned hall toward the waiting elevator.
"Russian bombers, sir. They've crossed into U.S. airspace."
The President repeatedly opened and closed his eyes to focus. He thought he could faintly hear people yelling orders through the agents' earpieces. *Russian bombers. In the United States?* "Where are they?"
"Near Baltimore and Virginia Beach."
"How many total?"
"Two."
"Son of a . . ."
"Both of them heading this way, sir."
The elevator doors shut and down they went. The President blinked

the tiredness from his eyes, trying to focus. Thirty seconds ago, he was asleep. Now the fate of the country was front and center in his mind. What the hell were Russian bombers doing over the U.S.? He knew the bombers would soon be met by jet fighters and defense systems surrounding the Beltway would be on high alert. But was it a diversion? Or was it the start of a coordinated attack on the U.S. mainland? He needed to contact the Defense Secretary and the Chairman of the Joint Chiefs of Staff ASAP.

The doors opened and the four Secret Service agents hurried the President and First Lady down the long hall until they reached the doors to the bunker underneath the East Wing of the White House. They were met by a Secret Service tactical team ready to repel any invasion or evacuate the President off the grounds. The First Lady was whisked into the presidential suite, and the President entered the Presidential Emergency Operations Center (PEOC).

"Get Secretary Javits and Chairman Cummins on the line," the President said to the watch officer.

The voices came from the speakers above. "We are here, sir," Russ Javits and General Hugh Cummins both announced.

"Russ, where are you?"

"I'm at the Pentagon, sir."

The President looked at his wrist to check the time but realized his Timex Ironman was still on the nightstand. The clock with the red digital numbers on the wall showed the time in Washington, D.C. was 3:10 a.m.

"Did you sleep there, Russ?"

There was no hesitation. "Yes, sir."

The President managed a smile. Javits was certainly dedicated to his job. "I'm in the PEOC, guys. What's going on, Russ?"

"Two Russian long-range bombers crossed into U.S. airspace five minutes ago, sir. One of them came in from the northeast over Atlantic City. The other one came from the southeast near Virginia Beach. Both of them are heading in the direction of the capital."

Someone handed the President a can of Diet Coke. Despite the early hour, the President popped the top and took a good sip. "Get me my clothes," he said to a military aide before returning his focus to Javits. "Have we been watching them, Russ?"

"Yes, sir. They took off from Cuba about four hours ago. We've had eyes on them the whole time, and we thought they were out on maneuvers or were messing around. But they took a turn toward the U.S. and crossed into our airspace."

"What type of bombers?"

"Two Russian Tupolev TU-ninety-fives. Four-engine turboprops, long range."

"What can they carry?"

"Air launched cruise missiles mounted under the wings."

"Range?"

"Nine-thousand miles."

"You think they're hostile?"

"I think we have to take it for granted that they are."

"What's their altitude?"

"Both of them are steady at thirty-thousand feet."

"And neither of the aircraft received diplomatic clearance?"

"Correct. I checked with the State Department, and the planes have no routing authorization from the FAA."

"Okay, keep me posted if there's any change."

The President's spare set of dress clothes kept in the bunker for such an occasion was handed to him. The last thing he wanted was to make a decision to shoot down Russian planes in the middle of the night in his pajamas. He put his dark pants on over his shorts and his white dress shirt over his white T-shirt. The red tie had already been knotted so he slipped it over his head and around his neck and secured it under his collar. When the White House photographer inevitably arrived to document the emergency, the American people would see their President being presidential. Any glimpse of the President's bare feet could be edited out later.

The PEOC conference table could seat fourteen, and members of the National Security Council and President's staff hurried in. Deputy Chief of Staff Tim Durant was the first to arrive. Military aides were next, bringing in carafes of coffee, paper cups, and bottled water.

TVs on the wall started popping to life, men and women of various government agencies appearing on the screens. The President waved at one of the screens, acknowledging Javits, who was also wearing his white dress shirt and red tie. A second screen showed radar images of the bombers heading toward D.C.

"General, what do we have in the air?"

Cummins cleared his throat. "We have six fighters on each of them. The Russians have so far failed to respond to our orders to leave the area. Combat air patrols have gone up across the country."

"What about on the ground?"

"Warning lasers are in use. The Avenger missile defense system is up and running across the street from the White House and around the Capital region. They're hot and ready."

"Anything else?" the President asked, his mind racing through the possibilities. "Any Russian missiles or subs detected?"

"Negative, sir. NORAD says there are no other threats at this time. We're still monitoring."

"Russ, what defense condition level are we?"

"We're at DEFCON Five, Mr. President."

"Any change?"

Javits suggested the level be raised to DEFCON 4. It would increase intelligence and ramp up security procedures across the country. Cummins concurred.

"Then do it," the President said.

After a pause, Javits chimed in. "Sir, we need your authorization to take out the bombers . . . if necessary."

"You have my authorization, Russ."

"Roger that."

The President stopped long enough to think that he had gone to bed last night watching the Cardinals game. Now, five hours later, he was authorizing the shoot-down of enemy planes over U.S. soil. He shook his head. What a messed-up world. He took another sip.

"Where's Ty?"

"I'm right here, sir," Vice President Stubblefield said as he walked into the room.

The President looked at the big man. "They got you out of bed, too."

"Yeah. They said it was important, and I didn't want to miss out on the fun. I didn't think the limo could move that fast."

"And Tina?"

"She's in one of the suites down here."

The President brought Stubblefield up to speed and they discussed options.

"Get Bill Parker in here or on the line," the President said to the watch officer regarding the CIA Director. "He might have something to offer. We're going to need the Secretary of State, Homeland Security, and the National Security Advisor, too."

"Secretary Arnold is on the way," somebody said.

"How close are they?" Stubblefield asked, looking at the screen with the radar.

"Forty miles and closing," Javits reported. "They're not traveling in a straight line. They're all over the place but they appear headed toward the capital."

Those in the PEOC watched the blinking lights getting closer to the bull's-eye that was Washington, D.C. A military aide brought in the President's shoes and socks, and he took the time to get fully suited up. Now he could pace the floor in thought.

Secretary of State Mike Arnold hustled into the PEOC. He looked out of breath, like he had run from his armored SUV down to the bunker.

The President stopped his pacing and gave Arnold an order. "Mike, get the Russian Ambassador on the phone. If we have to get out of bed for this, so should he."

"I'm on it," Arnold said, picking up the receiver for one of the phones on the conference table.

A thousand thoughts were racing through the President's mind. Becoming President didn't include training for situations like these. In that frenzied atmosphere, he had to consider the consequences of shooting down Russian bombers over the U.S.—not only to the American citizens on the ground who might be in the path of the wreckage but also the world at large that would have to deal with the aftermath.

The President had yet to meet with Russian President Yuri Volkov. The man was a former KGB agent, a man obsessed with amassing as much power and wealth as he could. It was difficult to anticipate the man's next move, but the stakes could not be any higher. There had been signs Volkov was growing increasingly hostile, but sending bombers to the United States was beyond hostile.

It was an act of war.

Interrupting the President's train of thought, Stubblefield leaned closer toward his ear. "You're going to have to decide how close you're going to let them get to D.C. before you give the order."

The President nodded. The time for thinking was over. It was time to act. "General, where's the best place to shoot 'em down."

Having left his office and made his way to the Pentagon command center, General Cummins appeared on the screen next to Javits. After a quick look at the radar, he said, "Mr. President, the best place for the southern plane is the short period of time it crosses the Potomac. A lot of wooded territory and not much else."

"And the northern one?"

"There's some forest area south and east of Fort Meade. After that it's more densely populated. If both planes continue on their current courses, those would be the places I'd recommend."

The President cursed. "They still ignoring our warnings?"

"Yes, sir," Cummins said. "We've done everything we normally do. Radio communication, flares, lasers, divert maneuvers with afterburners. No change."

"Can we get our pilot communication?"

"Yes, sir," Cummins said.

"Get it up."

Cummins motioned to someone off screen and then said, "This is the lead pilot shadowing the northern plane."

After a few seconds of static, the voice of U.S. Air Force Major Rick Dunigan, call sign "Popeye" because he liked to show off his muscles, reverberated through the PEOC. "Russian Tupolev. This is the United States Air Force. You have entered U.S. airspace. Alter your course eastward toward the Atlantic."

Video from Popeye's F-16 came to life on the screen. The bomber was difficult to make out in the darkness, the red lights on its fuselage blinking every three seconds. Popeye was asked if he could see into the Tupolev's cockpit, but he said the windows were darkened. He radioed the Russians on the emergency frequency but received no response. He also reported the Tupolev was carrying four missiles under its wings.

"Russian Tupolev. This is the United States Air Force. You have entered U.S. airspace. Acknowledge this transmission by rocking your wings."

Five seconds passed, but the bomber remained level and on course.

Popeye gave it another shot by telling the Tupolev to flash its navigational lights at irregular intervals.

Still nothing.

Mike Arnold held his hand over the phone receiver. "Mr. President, I have Ambassador Grigorov on the line."

The President punched the button for the speakerphone and then put both hands on the table as he spoke. "Ambassador Grigorov, this is Anthony Schumacher. What the hell is going on? I have two Russian bombers in my skies and I'm about to shoot 'em down. You want to explain what your military is doing?"

Groggy and perhaps hungover, Grigorov struggled to find the right words. Something about having to contact Moscow and that it would take time. It was clear he had no clue what was going on so the President motioned for the call to be silenced.

Javits spoke up. "They've entered the thirty-mile restricted zone, Mr. President. Altitude twenty-eight thousand feet. NORAD's Visual Warning System has been activated."

Popeye reported he could see the alternating red-and-green laser lights of the Visual Warning System. "If I can see them, they can see them."

"What about the second plane?" the President asked. "The one from the south."

Javits looked off camera before stating, "It too has entered the restricted zone. Altitude twenty-seven-thousand feet."

"Russian Tupolev," Popeye said again to the plane southwest of Baltimore. It was time to give the Russians the cold hard truth. Turn back or face the consequences. "You have entered restricted airspace. Alter your course immediately or you will be shot down."

Those in the PEOC and at the Pentagon zeroed in on the screen and held their collective breath, wondering if the Tupolevs would finally take the hint and get out of Dodge. They didn't, and the radar showed their course heading for the capital like two arrows zeroing in on the target.

"You're going to have to shoot 'em down, sir," Stubblefield said quietly. "Both of them. We've given them enough warning. We shouldn't even need to give them a warning. They know better. They have to know we will respond with force."

Javits felt the need to add his thoughts. "We need to take them out before they get anywhere near the capital, Mr. President. We can't have the flaming wreckage of Russian bombers raining down on the streets of D.C."

"He's right, sir," Stubblefield said. "Any closer and it creates even more problems."

The President looked down at the conference table. It had come to this. Thirty minutes ago he was asleep in bed. Now he had to make the decision to send Russian airmen to their deaths, not to mention the possibility of causing American casualties on the ground. *Will this go down in history as the start of World War III?* He closed his eyes, inhaled, and then let it out.

"Twenty-five-thousand feet and dropping, sir," Javits reported.

Stubblefield turned his head and whispered, "Mr. President?"

The President looked up at the screen and focused on Javits.

"Shoot 'em down, Russ . . . Both of them."

CHAPTER 2

The White House – Washington, D.C.

"Missiles are hot," Popeye reported. "I've got good tone."

An unknown voice echoed from the speakers in the PEOC, giving Popeye the go-ahead to fire. "You are cleared hot."

The President gritted his teeth. He could feel the heat rising on the back of his neck. He felt like kicking President Volkov's ass right then for putting him in this position. But he had no other choice. There was only one option left, and he couldn't risk doing nothing. It was time for America to defend herself.

"Stand by," Popeye said.

Everyone in the PEOC and at the Pentagon waited for the Maverick missiles to light up the sky and smash into the Tupolev before it plummeted to the earth in a ball of fire. Nothing happened. Eyes focused on the screen strained to see anything.

"What's going on?" the President asked.

"The Tupolev is turning," Popeye reported. "Repeat the Tupolev is turning. It is banking left." After a few more seconds, he added, "Now heading east."

The President adjusted his glasses and squinted at the radar screen, his eyes zeroing in on the red image of the Tupolev as it altered its course and headed straight east toward the Atlantic. The screen also showed the second Tupolev south of D.C. banking right and heading away from the capital. The pilots shadowing the bomber confirmed the change in direction.

"Request further orders," Popeye said.

"Russ," the President said to Javits. "Hold your fire. Hold your fire."

The command was passed up to Popeye and the rest of the fighters, all of them instructed to follow the Tupolevs out of U.S. airspace over the Atlantic and make sure they didn't come back.

"I think we dodged a bullet there," Stubblefield said under his breath. "Maybe more than one."

The President concurred and then asked Javits, "Any other threats, Russ?"

"None at this time, sir."

The sudden turn of events enabled everyone in the PEOC and at the Pentagon to breathe easily for the time being.

Once the Russian bombers left U.S. airspace, the President sighed and said, "Well, that's a heck of a way to start the morning."

There were a few tired smiles but little small talk. Everyone was too busy wondering what in the world the Russians were thinking. The President was first among them. It was such a reckless and dangerous act that it was almost beyond comprehension. The thought of American bombers heading toward Moscow was unfathomable.

"Thank you everyone for your efforts this morning," the President said to those in the PEOC and those on the screens. "You all did great work. Russ, please pass along my praise to the military for being ready. I want everyone in the Situation Room for a meeting at eight o'clock. We need to figure out what Volkov is up to and how to respond the next time he does something this stupid. Start thinking of options."

The President left the PEOC and found his wife lying half-awake on the queen bed in the bunker's presidential suite. A table lamp was on low, and the First Lady hadn't even turned back the covers. The President sat on the bed beside her and saw her eyes blink awake.

"It's all over," he said quietly. "The Russians tried to put a scare into us for some reason. Both bombers turned and headed toward the Atlantic just before they were going to be shot out of the sky." He winced and shook his head in disgust, telling her without words that it came close to happening.

"Why on earth would the Russians do that?"

"I don't know. Hopefully the light of day will help us figure it all out."

The First Lady sat up and then yawned. "Are you going back to bed?"

The President quickly considered it but knew it would be useless. He was wide awake and in a foul mood. Going back to bed would only lead to staring at the ceiling and cursing the madman currently in control of Russia. He shook his head. "I'm too wired to sleep." He stood and reached out his hand. "Let's get you back upstairs." Once out in the hall, he turned to a Secret Service agent. "I'm going to take a shower and head to the Oval."

"Yes, sir."

* * *

Sitting in his usual high-backed leather chair at the head of the conference table, the President was the first in the Situation Room later that morning. He read through the President's Daily Brief, the day's classified intelligence material highlighting the threats that were tracked across the world—everything from Iran to North Korea to China and any other terrorist organization looking to do harm to the United States of America. He was impressed that there was a section on the Russian bombers from several hours earlier, giving a minute-by-minute breakdown of the whole episode.

The one thing it couldn't do was tell the President what Volkov's intentions were or predict his next move. That was the President's job to figure out and come up with a plan to deal with it. He hoped those entering the Situation Room had some ideas.

Vice President Stubblefield took his seat on the President's right, and the conference table soon filled with classified folders and top-secret binders from Secretary Javits, Chairman Cummins, CIA Director Parker, Secretary of State Mike Arnold, Homeland Security Director Bradley Michaelson, and National Security Advisor Carl Harnacke.

Kimberly Carmi, the President's long-time spokeswoman, entered carrying a black portfolio and looked at her boss.

"Sir, I have the press release," she said, handing him a copy.

"Read it out loud. Let's hear how it sounds."

Carmi cleared her throat and read the release.

The White House
Washington, D.C.

For Immediate Release:
At approximately 3:05 a.m. (EST), the Continental Region of North American Aerospace Defense Command (NORAD) detected two Russian Federation long-range TU-95 bombers, having taken off from Havana, Cuba, entering the sovereign airspace of the United States near Atlantic City, New Jersey, and Virginia Beach, Virginia. They proceeded on a course toward Washington, D.C., and were quickly intercepted by NORAD aircraft, including F-16 Fighting Falcons and F-22 Raptors.

President Schumacher was notified and safely evacuated to the Presidential Emergency Operations Center (PEOC) in the White House. Repeated attempts to contact the Russian pilots were ignored. After consultation with Vice President Ty Stubblefield, Secretary of Defense Russ Javits, the Chairman of the Joint Chiefs of Staff Hugh Cummins, and members of his National Security team, the President authorized the shoot-down of both Russian aircraft. Prior to the execution of the President's order, the Russian aircraft altered their course and proceeded to exit U.S. airspace. No further action was taken, and no other hostile activities were or have been detected. The President and the First Lady remained in the PEOC until the Russian bombers left U.S. airspace.

This morning, President Schumacher will meet with the National Security Council to discuss the United States response to this unprovoked act of aggression. The United States will take any and all necessary measures to protect the American people and their homeland.

Once Carmi finished reading, the President reached his hand toward her. "Give me your pen."

After another second of thought and with a swift swipe, the President crossed out the words "safely evacuated to" and handwrote above it the words "took command in" the Presidential Emergency Operations Center.

"There," he said, returning the pen and paper to Carmi. "No sense giving President Volkov the satisfaction in a written White House statement."

"Yes, sir. Shall I release it?"

"Yes."

Opening her portfolio again, Carmi reached in and grabbed two pictures from the White House photographer. "Casey has two photos that could be released along with the statement."

The first one showed the President seated at the PEOC's conference table looking at the bank of screens on the wall. The second showed the President, dressed in dark slacks and a white dress shirt with red tie, standing, pointing his finger at someone off camera, making the tough call and giving the order in the heat of the moment.

The President tapped the second picture. "Use this one."

"Yes, sir." Carmi took the pictures and then left to notify the world of what went on early that morning.

The President looked out at the assembled crowd, all those in attendance sufficiently caffeinated after a long and intense night. "Good morning, everyone. Thank you all for being here. And thank you all for your work this morning. If nothing else, the Russians provided us with a good training exercise and I think you all proved yourselves up to the task." The President paused to take a sip of his Diet Coke. He had lost count of the number he had that day. "But there's more work to be done. We need to figure out what Russia is up to—militarily, politically, economically—and what to do about it. I want everything out in the open. Give me your thoughts, ideas, and suggestions."

After the President finished and looked around the table, Secretary Arnold, America's top diplomat, spoke up. "I guess I'll start, Mr. President." He opened his black leather portfolio and turned to the second page. "President Volkov . . . For some time now, we have had many concerns about his mental stability. There are rumors, unconfirmed at this time, that he has serious health issues. One of those rumors is that he has stage four lung cancer. He has long been a smoker, so it is a very real possibility. There are some in the intel community who think he knows he doesn't have long on this earth and wants to go down in a blaze of glory."

Director Parker nodded and confirmed the thought. "We have heard that, Mr. President. I think there might be some merit to it. There's some talk he might have four to six months."

Secretary Arnold continued. "Volkov is an old-school hardliner from the old Soviet days. He wants to be in the same league as Lenin and Stalin, celebrated by Russians from now until the end of time."

"And attacking the United States would do that for him?" the President asked.

Arnold raised his hand. "Not just attacking the United States, sir, destroying it. Volkov has long held the belief that Russia has the world's most superior military with nuclear weapons capable of annihilating the U.S. The concerning thing is he might be crazy enough to use them."

"Mike, he has to know that the U.S. would immediately respond with overwhelming force. Our NATO allies would respond, too. He might get a strike in, but we would decimate his capability to do catastrophic damage. And, in the end, we would destroy Moscow, every military base in the country, and ultimately set Russia back a hundred years."

"He doesn't believe so, sir. He thinks he can take out D.C., New York City, Los Angeles, and other major cities before we can retaliate. This morning's bomber flights might have been a dry run at a first wave of attacks. With long-range nuclear missiles and sub-launched nukes, it could incapacitate us to the point that we would be defenseless." Arnold held up a finger to make a final point. "And all this is not taking into account if Russia has help from our enemies—China, North Korea, Cuba, Iran, Venezuela. If any one of them coordinated with Russia to launch, for example, a cyberattack at the time of a Russian nuclear launch, it could be a big problem."

The President nodded. He had his issues with China, and he knew those in charge in Beijing were never up to any good. And if the Chinese communists teamed up with the ex-Soviet hardliners, it could be a problem. Two superpowers against one might not end well for the United States. The President knew the U.S. could be in for some rough waters ahead.

"Russ," the President said. "Does the Pentagon share these concerns?"

"Yes, sir, we are very concerned. If he only has four to six months to live, he might feel emboldened to lash out, to strike the United States and show everyone that Russia is the preeminent superpower in the world."

"What about Russia's nuclear arsenal? How formidable is it?"

"It's aging, sir," Javits said. "But it's still a problem. As the Russians like to say, their nukes might be rusty, but they still work."

"Well, how are we with the military? What's our readiness?"

Without hesitation, the Defense Secretary said, "We are ready to go, sir. You give the order and it will be done. Bombers, subs, missiles, it's all ready. Conventional and nuclear."

"You have everything you need?"

"Yes, sir."

The President looked across the table at Chairman Cummins. "General, you concur?"

"Yes, sir. One hundred percent."

"How much time will it take for our nukes to reach Russia?"

Chairman Cummins thought for a second, his mind finding the right description of the military's capabilities. "You know Saint Basil's Cathedral in Red Square? The one with the multi-colored flame-like domes?"

"Yeah."

"Once you give the order, I can reduce that to a pile of ash in twenty-eight minutes."

The room fell silent as everyone conjured up that mental image in their minds—Red Square reduced to rubble. The frightening thought of what was being discussed made a handful of them shudder in their seats.

"What about the others in Russian leadership?" the President asked. "Who do we have to keep our eyes on?"

Opening his laptop and making a few clicks, Javits took the lead. "Two men especially, Mr. President. After President Volkov, who is the Supreme Commander-in-Chief, our focus is on the Defense Minister Dmitri Balakin as well as the Chief of the General Staff Sergei Dernov. Both of them, along with Volkov, are the decision makers when it comes to launching nuclear weapons. Nothing can happen without those three."

Pictures of Balakin and Dernov appeared on the screen. Some in the room recognized the men, but others knew little about them.

"Tell me about Balakin," the President said.

"Balakin, the Defense Minister," Javits said without looking at his notes, "is a long-time friend of Volkov's and part of his inner circle."

With a tap on his laptop, a new picture of Balakin appeared on the screen. He didn't look like a Defense Minister, maybe a diplomat, but not someone in charge of a country's defense. He had the air of an actor or a TV news anchorman. Someone who knew how to look good in front of a camera. The smile was polished, the clothes stylish, and his dark eyes had a hint of flare.

Javits continued. "Fifty-six years old. He and Volkov go way back–all the way back to their days in the KGB. Through the years, Balakin has been a loyal confidant who carries out Volkov's wishes, and many are saying, if he plays his cards right, he will be Russia's next president."

The President nodded. "And Dernov?"

A new picture popped up on screen. Unlike Balakin, Dernov would strike one as a man born to do his job—striking fear into the enemy or even his own countrymen. With his bulbous nose and bleary-eyed look, he looked like he had been out late the night before the picture was taken. The smile was smug and sinister, the eyes beady and untrustworthy. The look on his face indicated he was not afraid to lie, cheat, and steal, with force if necessary, to get things done.

"Sergei Dernov is the highest-ranking officer in the Russian Armed Forces. He was appointed by Volkov and is a dyed-in-the-wool Soviet communist. He longs for the day of Mother Russia's return to prominence and he always has his eyes on expanding Russian territory."

"Is he older than Volkov?"

"Yes, about ten years older," Javits said, looking at the screen on the wall. "Although he looks older than that. Sources tell us Dernov loves his vodka and can go through a pack of cigarettes in a day. He and Volkov get along quite well, and Volkov appointed him because he knew they shared the same dreams of Russian prominence. I would imagine he is feeling proud of himself right now for what the Russian military pulled off this morning."

"Are they all corrupt?"

Javits' head turned toward the President. "They're ex-Soviet communists, Mr. President. So yes, they're all corrupt. Some more than others."

"So these are the three men we need to be worried about?"

"Yes, sir. If the Russians launch nuclear weapons, these are the men who will make it happen."

The President sat back in his chair, his eyes looking at the pictures of the Russian leaders on the screen. These were the men he would have to do battle against in the days and weeks ahead. He knew he had to be ready.

"All right, thank you all for your input this morning. We'll see what the Russians have to say. Let's go forward with the thought that Russia is looking to conduct an attack in the very near future. Get all your people in place and all your hardware where it needs to be."

Those seated around the table nodded, all of them knowing they would have to clear their schedules and focus on little else in the coming days.

"Anything else?" the President asked.

When no one spoke and as the President pushed back his chair, CIA Director Parker raised his hand. "Mr. President, if I could have a word with you in private."

CHAPTER 3

Severodvinsk, Russia

The fierce wind blowing in from the White Sea did little to mess up Dmitri Balakin's perfectly coiffed hair as he exited the armored limousine. He stood tall, straightened his Armani suit, and tugged at the cuffs of his white dress shirt to make sure they were the appropriate length.

On every public occasion, from his styled hair to his high-end footwear, Balakin definitely had the look of someone in charge—confident, fashionable, recognizable, and ready for any camera that was pointed his way. In contrast to many of his predecessors wearing their dress uniforms laden with medals, his choice of clothing was a fine tailored suit from Italy.

Balakin had been the Defense Minister for five years now, and he traveled the world on behalf of a superpower. Or at least a country that had once been a superpower and was now desperately trying to stay relevant on the world stage behind the United States and China.

Volkov had handpicked him from a cadre of well-connected men he had known since his days with the KGB and then its successor, the FSB, Russia's internal security service. Volkov wanted Balakin to crack down on fraud in the Russian Defense Ministry, since any corruption had better line the pockets of the Russian President before anyone else. Although Balakin was not greeted warmly by those in the Defense Ministry, since he had not served in the military, it didn't matter. He had the support of the President, and nobody dared speak out against him.

Volkov knew he could trust Balakin, at least as much as any former KGB agent could trust another former KGB agent. But he also knew he could control him, that Balakin would be a team player and back him up whenever and wherever he needed it.

Balakin was willing to play along. Kiss the ring until it was his turn when Volkov finally relinquished power—voluntarily, which was unlikely, or involuntarily, either by death or coup. And Balakin thought one of those possibilities could happen sooner rather than later. As a proud and committed Russian, he was eager to take command, the promise of wealth and power on the horizon and well within his grasp.

He waved at a cameraman capturing those arriving, most of them higher-ups from the three branches compromising the Russian military. With his hand, he nonchalantly patted the right pocket of his suit coat. He felt the plastic card through the Armani. It reminded him that, not only was he the superior of the men in uniform, he was also one of the most powerful men in all of Russia, in all of the world for that matter. With the card in his pocket, he was one of the three men who could launch nuclear weapons and destroy any country on the planet.

Although the Russian President is the Supreme Commander-in-Chief of the Armed Forces of the Russian Federation and although he has a nuclear briefcase called the *Cheget*, much like the "nuclear football" that accompanies the President of the United States, he cannot launch an attack on his own. The Russians took that power away after the fall of the Soviet Union. But it does not prevent the President from executing his will, so long as he has his trusted allies where they needed to be.

Upon making his decision to unleash nuclear war, the Russian President's *Cheget*, which is connected to the Russian command-and-control network, would be used to transmit encrypted launch orders to the Defense Minister, who uses his card to identify himself and send his codes to the Chief of the General Staff, who does the same and issues the targeting plans.

Only then, after all three players have taken part, can the Russians launch their nukes.

Balakin patted his pocket again. It was like his American Express card. He never left home without it. The military aide with Balakin's black Samsonite briefcase stood off to the side, always avoiding the cameras but always ready in case Balakin needed him.

Balakin turned around in time to see another armored limousine rolling to a stop outside the headquarters of Russia's Northern Fleet. One of the other members of the nuclear trio had arrived. The door flew open and Sergei Dernov barreled out of the back seat like it was on fire. With a chest full of medals on his olive-green uniform, the Russian Chief of the General Staff made no attempt to straighten his jacket before hurrying toward Balakin.

"Dmitri, my friend," Dernov said, his meaty right hand with sausage-like fingers outstretched. "So good to see you."

Almost overcome by the stench of cheap Russian cigarettes from Dernov, Balakin kept from choking long enough to extend a hand and say, "General, always a pleasure."

The two men kept their gaze on the other, both knowing full well that the other was lying. They weren't friends. Never had been and never would be. And neither would privately ever say it was good to see the other. The only reason they were even shaking hands was to keep the other from having one hand free to stab the other in the back.

"It is a beautiful day, Dmitri," Dernov said, motioning toward the building behind them. "It is always a beautiful day when Russia shows the world its mighty power." When Balakin didn't respond fast enough, Dernov turned and said, "Don't you agree?"

Balakin kept from rolling his eyes. Dernov was testing him. If he responded in any way that might disagree with Dernov's views, the response would be reported up and down the chain of command to be used against the Defense Minister and for Dernov's benefit. Balakin knew better. "Of course, General. It is a wonderful day. Any time that Russia can launch another submarine, it is a good day."

"Oh, but it is not just 'another' submarine, Dmitri," Dernov corrected. He was the highest-ranking officer in the Russian Armed Forces, and this was his baby they were talking about after all. "This is the most powerful submarine in the entire world. It will strike fear into the hearts of everyone on the planet." He reached out and grabbed hold of Balakin's arm to emphasize his point. They both stopped walking to look at each other. "And it will return Russia to the mighty superpower it once was. One that will again be feared around the globe."

Balakin released himself from Dernov's grasp and tugged at the cuff of his shirt to return it to its proper length beyond the sleeve. He smiled at Dernov, knowing the man had slipped up. The Defense Minister never missed an opportunity to point it out.

"General, you make it sound like we are not a feared superpower now." Balakin grinned. "I do hope you haven't lost confidence in President Volkov's leadership. He would not be happy with his top general if you weren't totally committed to his agenda."

Dernov's eyes widened and he fumbled for a response. "Of course I am committed. Any thought otherwise is preposterous. We are feared now. I just meant we will be even more feared when the *Belgorod* is unleashed on the world."

Balakin smiled and thumped the General a couple times on the shoulder. He'd keep that little slipup in the bank and use it when necessary. "That's what I thought you meant, General. You have served Russia for many years."

"Try my entire life, Dmitri," Dernov said, hoping to provide the reminder that he had paid his dues.

"Yes, you have, General." The door to the headquarters opened and the principled gentleman Balakin allowed Dernov to enter first. "Now, let's go celebrate."

Located nearly 800 miles north of Moscow, Severodvinsk had become known as Russia's premier shipbuilding port. From its docks, it had seen the launch of hundreds of subs and battlecruisers that had prowled international waters and menaced foreign countries for sixty years.

But today was a big day. Some might say the biggest day in the long and glorified history of Russia. A return to its former glory was just around the corner . . . unless the people in charge screwed it up again.

As they entered the vestibule, Balakin's phone buzzed in his jacket pocket. He took it out, looked at the screen, and smiled.

"Excuse me, General, it is my daughter. I must take this."

With the large crowd gathering for the ceremony, Balakin's security team directed him to a holding room where he could have some peace and quiet.

"My darling, Katia," he said. "What a pleasant surprise."

"Hello, Father. I am sorry that I didn't call to wish you a happy birthday yesterday. I was terribly busy, but I should have called."

The concern in his daughter's voice warmed his heart. She was his only child, the daughter he had with his ex-wife, a former Russian underwear model. He had been the reason for the divorce. With his wandering eye and world travels as he rose the ranks to eventually become Defense Minister, it was all too easy to have a mistress on multiple continents. His ego got the best of him once, though, as his wife caught him fooling around with his secretary in his office. She knew it wasn't the first time and wouldn't be the last. She threatened to tell the world that he was a cheating scumbag, but she quickly thought better of it when she considered he had very powerful friends in very high places who would not hesitate in making her life difficult.

So the divorce was quiet and without fanfare. The ex-wife received a sizable nest egg and custody of their only child. To Balakin's surprise, Katia, who was sixteen at the time of the divorce, did not blame him. It was as if she knew that her dad's philandering was what was expected of Russian men who occupied the seats of power. It certainly was not a surprise. Even though he cheated on her mother, Katia still revered him.

And despite having multiple women on his arm since the divorce, including the night before, he always had time for his beloved daughter.

"Well, that is kind of you to think of me, my darling. But it is just another day when you get to be my age. And I know you are busy. Where are you now?"

"Vancouver."

Balakin stopped pacing, his mind going through the world maps that he had memorized as a young boy and trying to picture where she was. "Washington?"

"No, north of there. British Columbia."

"Ah, Canada."

"Yes, we're on location. Canada has a vibrant film industry. It's cheaper and easier to make movies here than in the U.S. so many of our scenes are filmed up here."

Balakin grunted. Just another thing wrong with America. When she was twenty-one, Katia left Russia to pursue a film career, much to the chagrin of her father. But she had the looks of her mother—blonde and beautiful with legs long enough that made her stand out in a crowd. She also had her father's brains—enabling her to learn English and French with relative ease—and his prowess in front of a camera. She could have joined her dad in government work, turning heads on the world stage on behalf of Russia.

Instead, she had her sights on the big screen and the glitz and glamor that came with it. She started in Paris and had a few small parts. But she knew she had to find her way to America. Hollywood was calling her, and it didn't take long for her to make her mark. She starred in a few action flicks and then made the cover of a gossipy magazine. Her big break came when she won the role opposite screen legend Michael Hawthorne, a performance that some say should have landed her an Oscar nomination. With her looks and growing popularity, the paparazzi were known to stalk her at all hours of the day. Oftentimes the trending celebrity on social media, she was well on her way to superstardom.

Despite the fact that her recent success occurred in America, it all made her dad immensely proud.

"How long will you be there?"

"It's a two-week shoot. An action film. I'm the lead character, and they're even letting me do some of my own stunts. It is very exciting."

Balakin could indeed hear the excitement in her voice. It had been a year since he had seen her. Too long for him. "It does sound exciting. I hope you are not doing anything dangerous."

"Of course not. We always take precautions."

"Maybe when you are finished, you can come home to visit. I would love to see you."

"I will try, Father. I have a few other movie opportunities on the horizon, but I will try." There was a pause in the conversation. "I forgot to ask. Where are you?"

"I am in Severodvinsk. We are celebrating the launch of Russia's newest submarine. The President is about to arrive and give a speech."

"What happened last night, Father? I am seeing things about Russian bombers over the United States. People are reporting that they were going to attack Washington, D.C. Is it true?"

Balakin looked left and then right. He was amazed at how he could forget all about the power that he had as Defense Minister when talking with his daughter. Her question brought the stark reality of his work life back to him. "Katia, you know I cannot discuss such matters over the phone." He lowered his voice. "The Americans could be listening."

"Father, the Americans are freaking out. It was all over the news. Some are calling it an act of war. They said something like this has never happened before. Should I be worried?"

Balakin didn't respond. The thought of his daughter's security had not occurred to him when President Volkov ordered the bombers to fly into U.S. airspace. The thoughts now racing through his mind were not pleasant. What if something happened to her? What if a Russian bomb meant for the Americans injured or killed her? He was going to have to get Katia out of the United States before it all went down. He couldn't risk losing his daughter. She was everything to him. He patted his suit coat and felt the nuclear authentication card in his pocket.

"Father, are you still there?"

Shaken out of his thoughts, he said, "Yes, yes, I'm still here, Katia." He then lied and said, "No, you don't have anything to worry about, darling. Everything will be all right."

"Okay."

"I do hope you will come home soon for a visit, though. I would love to see you."

"I will, Father. I'm sorry to cut this call short, but I need to go over my script again. I hope you have a safe trip back home."

No matter where he was, a feeling of somberness came over him when his daughter ended a call or left on another journey. She seemed so far away. "Thank you for calling, my darling. I love you very much."

"I love you, too. I'll talk to you later."

Balakin put the phone back in his pocket. Sometimes he thought he'd give up everything just to have a few minutes with his daughter. Someday she might have his grandchildren, whom he would spoil and teach all about the wonders of Russia.

But would that even occur if Volkov's dream of nuclear war came to fruition? He closed his eyes at that unhappy thought. His eyes shot open when he heard the commotion outside.

The guest of honor had arrived.

CHAPTER 4

Severodvinsk, Russia

Balakin made his way across the hall to the larger holding room. Those in the room snapped to attention as the doors flew open and Russian President Yuri Volkov strutted in with a purpose. He always did. As the Supreme Commander-in-Chief, there was never anything lackadaisical about any of his movements. He was always moving, almost charging, as if ready to bulldoze anything and anyone in his path. Those in attendance gave him a wide berth and hoped he didn't stop to berate them, or worse, hand them a first-class ticket to Siberia.

It was a rare occurrence when the three men of Russia's nuclear triumvirate were in the same place at the same time, but there they were.

General Dernov was the first to salute, although he waited a second to make sure the President was looking at him before doing so.

"President Volkov, welcome to Severodvinsk. I know the men of the Northern Fleet are honored that you would join us today to celebrate such a momentous occasion."

Volkov coughed and nodded. "Thank you, General." The weakness in his voice was evident, but he continued. "It is indeed a glorious day for Russia."

An aide leaned in and whispered something in Volkov's ear. The man then handed him a cell phone. Volkov held up a finger and walked away from Dernov and Balakin to take the call. The whole room went rigid when Volkov started barking orders into the phone. Something had not met Volkov's standards, and there was going to be hell to pay if it wasn't fixed immediately. The tirade seemed to dislodge the phlegm in his throat and he was like his old self.

As he stalked the room from one end to the other, a few people scurried toward the doors wanting no part of the President's wrath. Volkov ended the call and threw the phone at the aide. He yelled at him and gave him his orders. The man nodded and left in a rush.

Volkov then turned, his bloodshot eyes focused on the two men approaching.

"Idiots," Volkov said, referring to whoever was on the call. "I tell them to do something and expect them to do it. No questions asked."

"Yes, sir," both Balakin and Dernov said.

Balakin continued. "About last night, Mr. President."

The call that had made him so angry was quickly forgotten. Last night. Russia's latest moment of glory. A sign of even better things to come.

A smile crossed Volkov's ashen face. "Yes . . . my congratulations to both of you. It is the first time Russian bombers have invaded the United States. Our military performed flawlessly."

"Thank you, sir," Dernov said.

"General, I want to make sure the pilots are rewarded with medals for their bravery."

"Yes, sir. An excellent idea."

Volkov struggled to take a breath, his scarred lungs sucking in the air as best they could. "I'm sure the Americans were pissing themselves all night long."

"The White House said the President and the First Lady were in the bunker," Dernov said smiling, broadcasting his arrogance for all to see.

Volkov laughed and then suffered through a coughing fit. Once he recovered, he said, "I bet his security team carried him down the stairs like a baby." He gave it some more thought. "I wonder if his wife was naked when they hauled her out of bed in the middle of the night." The thought of the American First Lady being violated because of the Russian President's actions aroused him.

"They said President Schumacher gave the order to shoot down our planes," Balakin added, almost as the voice of reason in the trio.

Having none of it, Volkov held up his right index finger, steady as a rock. "But they didn't shoot them down, Dmitri. They hesitated. We surprised them in the middle of the night and they were too scared to act. The Americans see war as a last resort. Russia sees it as an opportunity. We could have unleashed our missiles on Washington, D.C. and destroyed it. Last night was just the beginning."

"When will the next phase take place?" Balakin asked.

"Soon. We must meet in Moscow to finalize the plans. I want everything to go off without a hitch. It must be planned to perfection—everything from the weapons to the timing."

Dernov nodded, already thinking of the forces he would deploy.

Balakin turned to Dernov. "General, could I have a moment in private with the President?"

General Dernov eyed the man suspiciously, as if the Defense Minister was going to tattle on him that he had not been sufficiently bellicose in his love for Russia in their earlier conversation. Neither trusted the other, for good reason.

Balakin noticed and lied to put him at ease. "It's a personal matter, General. Nothing important. Just something private."

President Volkov didn't give Dernov a chance to protest. "Give us a minute, General." He dismissed him with a wave of his hand.

Dernov, knowing he had no other choice, nodded in deference. "Yes, sir."

Balakin waited until Dernov and any other stragglers left and the door closed behind them.

The two old friends eyed each other before Balakin said, "You look good, Mr. President."

Volkov's eyes narrowed. "You are a liar, Dmitri. You have been since we first met." He winked. "That's why I always liked you."

For a few seconds, the two men were lost in thoughts of better days, back when the two strapping young KGB agents ruled the streets with iron fists and dominated the bedrooms of any woman they wanted. Those were the real glory days in their lives. Nothing but booze, sex, and, most important of all—power. They still had the power, and both men could snap their fingers and beautiful Russian women would appear to let the men have their way with them.

But time was running out—at least for President Volkov.

The President coughed into his hand. Only his doctor and his old friend Balakin knew he was dying of cancer. Speculation had run rampant around the world that something was amiss with Volkov's health—the coughing fits, the purplish marks on the back of his hands, the cancelled in-person meetings. It had people worried, especially those in Russia.

"How are you feeling?"

Volkov shook his head, like there was no point in even saying it. "Awful."

"Is there anything that can be done?"

Another shake of the head. "No. There is nothing. The end is near." The President looked at himself in the mirror on the wall. He buttoned his suit coat, which he had to get tailored on a near weekly basis to hide the weight loss. He centered the knot in his tie and then looked at both sides of his face, his cheekbones becoming more noticeable.

"Maybe you should cancel. The people would understand. We'll tell them that you had to rush back to Moscow to take care of an important matter. I can step in for you."

Volkov turned to look at Balakin and managed to grin. "I might be dying, Dmitri, but I'm not dead yet. I still have a lot to accomplish before I'm gone and I want to let the people of Russia know that we will once again become the world's greatest superpower." He grinned again. "Soon."

"I talked to Katia just before you arrived."

The name brought another smile to Volkov's face, although Balakin thought there was something more to it than the joy of remembering another man's daughter. Volkov had no family. He never had any kids either, at least none that he would claim. He had doted on Katia as a child, even giving her the name of *kotenok*, Russian for "kitten," and always lavished her with gifts for Christmas and her birthday.

But Balakin saw the way he looked at Katia as she grew older. The innocent doting morphed into kissing and fondling. As she blossomed into a grown woman, he often made comments to him about her beauty, not to mention the size of her breasts and her "tight ass." He wanted to know whether she had any work done, who she was dating, and when she was going to start doing nude scenes. Balakin caught him on more than one occasion looking at racy bikini photos of Katia on his computer. As the years went on, he made sure to never leave the two alone together, and it was one of the few reasons he was glad that she stayed away from Russia.

"How is my beautiful *kotenok*?" Volkov asked.

"She is well, thank you for asking. She is in Canada filming. She said the Americans were up in arms about our bombers. They said it was an act of war."

Volkov looked at Balakin. The look of lust for Balakin's daughter was replaced with visions of a madman intent on unleashing hell on earth. "It was, Dmitri. The war has begun and we are going to win it. I am going to go down in history as the man who destroyed the United States once and for all."

Balakin swallowed and nodded.

His spirits buoyed by what the future held, Volkov slapped Balakin on the arm. "Let's go celebrate."

The two men walked out toward the podium set up near the shipyard. The Northern Fleet had come out in full force, the Russian Navy men in full dress and ready to show their pride and admiration for their leader. While Volkov waited to be introduced, Balakin and Dernov took their places behind the podium.

Off in the distance sat the *Belgorod*—the world's largest and most powerful nuclear submarine—finally completed and ready for launch. Nearly 600 feet long and weighing in at nearly 30,000 tons, the sub had the ability to carry nuclear-powered Poseidon drones capable of unleashing conventional and nuclear warheads to destroy coastal targets. With its stealth technology, it was believed to be able to sneak past enemy defenses like no other submarine on the planet. And Volkov thought the *Belgorod* was the final piece that he needed to attack the United States and destroy it for good.

The applause was thunderous when President Volkov marched onto the stage. The Russian national anthem fired up the crowd some more before Volkov strutted up to the microphone.

"Thank you," he said, his voice strong. "Thank you. It is a glorious day for Russia. Today, we will launch one of Russia's most powerful superweapons, capable of securing our great country from the depths of any ocean. The *Belgorod* will protect us from our enemies, and generations of Russians will live in safety and security."

The television cameras would show General Dernov over the President's left shoulder, beaming with pride in knowing it was "his baby" that would be prowling the oceans on behalf of Mother Russia. He had the look of a man who desperately wanted to put the *Belgorod* through its paces and annihilate Russia's enemies.

As President Volkov let the world know that the *Belgorod* would soon return Russia to its place in world prominence, Defense Minister Balakin could be seen over the President's right shoulder. He was not smiling. He had the look of someone who knew death was right around the corner, and it worried him what it meant for his friend and, more importantly, the future of his homeland. He wondered what the next decade would look like for him and his daughter. As his friend thundered to a close, the thought of his daughter brought a smile to his face, the cameras capturing his apparent joy at the fiery speech.

If they only knew.

CHAPTER 5

The White House – Washington, D.C.

"You were kind of quiet in there, Bill," the President said, taking a seat behind the Resolute Desk. "I was wondering if you might have something more to say."

"Yes, sir," Parker said, placing a briefing binder and a leather portfolio on the chair next to him. "I have a few things to run by you."

Ty Stubblefield took a seat on the right side of the President, the two men facing the CIA Director who took a chair in front of the desk.

William "Bill" Parker did not have the look of an international spymaster, someone who knew all of the secrets and clandestine operations of the United States Government. Instead, he would strike most people as an accountant, someone you could trust to do your taxes every year for a reasonable fee. Brown hair brushed to one side and a tan-colored suit covering a pudgy frame, he looked like he wanted to ask the President if he had any capital gains or losses to report for the prior year.

But he was not an accountant. As a young man, he had dreams of joining the foreign service in the State Department, working behind the scenes of diplomatic relations on a global scale. But his time at Georgetown University caught the eye of the CIA, which was always on the lookout for new recruits. After some thought, he signed on shortly after graduation.

Starting as an intelligence analyst, he had risen up the ranks at Langley, learning the ins and outs of international spying and getting to know the players around the world. He had focused most of his career on Russia until the end of the Cold War when he moved on to the Middle East. He thought his days worrying about Moscow were over. They weren't, and this was his opportunity to put his years of experience to good use.

Although the President had serious concerns with the CIA when he took office, the highly respected Parker had been a reliable leader and someone who gave the President what he needed and always wanted—options.

"What's on your mind?"

"First off, Mr. President, I want you to know that I respect everyone in that room. And I trust every single one of them. Have for years. But with what I have to say, it's always best, if at all possible, to have the fewest number of people hearing it. It's just easier that way. And so, I was hoping I could speak to you both privately."

"All right," the President said after getting the nod from Stubblefield. "Feel free to speak your mind."

Parker took a deep breath and then exhaled, like he needed to gear up for what was to come. If word of what he was about to say got out, he knew the wolves up on Capitol Hill would do everything in their power to make sure he never worked in Washington again. Or worse, make sure he spends a good chunk of his remaining life behind bars. And they might even use it as the first ground to impeach the President and Vice President.

"Mr. President, I have serious concerns with the stability of the Russian Government with President Volkov in charge."

The President nodded. "From what I heard in the Situation Room, most people share your concern."

"Yes, I think we're all on the same page with respect to the severity of the situation. As I said earlier, I think it's clear Volkov only has a short time left and he wants to put his mark on history like Lenin and Stalin. I have no doubt he wants to do something big, something that he thinks will cripple the United States and vault Russia into ultimate superpower status." Parker paused to look both men in the eye. "But with that in mind, I have a different take on how to deal with it. That's what I was hoping to talk to you about."

"And what does your take entail?"

Another breath and then an exhale. That was followed by a pause, like he was considering keeping his mouth shut and bolting from the room. "Sir, I think we have to consider taking out President Volkov."

The President leaned back in his chair, his eyes not leaving those of the CIA Director. The only sound in the room came from the humming of the air conditioning. *Take out the Russian President.* He rolled his neck, the long night and Parker's suggestion reminding him of the weighty matters of the job.

"You mean assassinate him?"

Parker winced, like he didn't want anyone to even utter the words out loud. He glanced out the Oval Office windows to his left, as if worried someone might be eavesdropping on them. But he then nodded that the President was correct and softly said, "Yes, sir."

Drumming his fingers on the desk, the President mulled over the idea. Assassinate the President of Russia? What would Americans think? What would the rest of the world leaders think about it? Would U.S. allies support the decision? Or would it put an even bigger target on America's back? His political enemies would have a field day and raise holy hell about it like never before. Heck, half of them acted as if they liked Volkov more than him. He shook his head, hardly believing he was even considering it.

"Bill, we don't assassinate world leaders. It's just something we don't do. I mean, I can't tell you the number of times I've thought about it. Trust me, I've wanted to. I can give you a dozen names right now. But it goes against the way America does things in this world. And if we did do it, we'd all be on our enemies' hit list more so than we already are. Everybody would be fair game."

Parker reached for his briefing binder. "You're not wrong, Mr. President. And I understand your way of thinking. The Executive Order outlawing political assassinations goes back to the days of President Ford." He flipped to the second page and read from a copy of Executive Order 11905. "'No employee of the United States Government shall engage in, or conspire to engage in, political assassination.'"

"That's always been in the back of my mind, Bill."

"The Executive Order was strengthened by President Carter in seventy-eight to ban indirect American involvement in assassinations. President Reagan continued the ban in his own Executive Order."

The President rocked in his chair, having heard the story before. "But then things began to change, didn't they?"

"Yes, sir, they did," Parker said, flipping to the next page. "In the late nineties, the ban on assassination was relaxed when it came to those foreigners connected to terrorist activities. After nine-eleven, the U.S. assassinated a large number of targets, many of them senior leaders of al-Qaeda. Most of those were conducted by drone strikes."

"Outside of that, the CIA hasn't always had the greatest success when it comes to the assassination of foreign leaders."

"That's true, Mr. President. We made attempts to kill Gaddafi and Saddam without success. They met their end in other ways."

"I know we've had other plans in the past. Castro comes to mind. We tried to take him out in the sixties but he remained in power for another forty or fifty years."

"That's true, too. We also had plans for the Prime Minister of Congo and the Presidents of the Dominican Republic and South Vietnam, but those plans didn't go anywhere. So it's not out of the question. And it's something that we have done in other situations. You yourself gave the go-ahead to take out Karl Bonhoff."

"He literally tried to have one of our operatives killed," Stubblefield snapped, referring to Duke Schiffer. The big man looked like he was ready to pounce if Parker somehow tried to suggest the President was in the wrong on that call.

Parker raised his hands in defense. "I understand. It was a different situation considering Bonhoff was not an elected world leader. And we were right to take out Bonhoff. He was causing great damage to the United States. He had to be stopped." He looked at the President. "I'm just saying that you've given the order before."

The President nodded, but Stubblefield kept his glare on the CIA Director.

Parker returned the binder to the chair next to him. It was time for him to make his case. "Sir, the crisis we are now facing is much larger than any one we faced with the Dominican Republic or South Vietnam. We're not talking about taking out someone because he's trying to spread communism to his little corner of the world. This is not simply regime change for the sake of regime change. We're talking about the survival of the United States. Imagine a nuclear missile detonating on the South Lawn or up on Capitol Hill."

"I've imagined that more than people might think."

"Volkov is bound and determined to strike the U.S. if it's the last thing he does. I think he's going to try and do it, Mr. President. I really do."

The President sighed. "You want to give me odds on it happening?"

Parker didn't hesitate. "One-hundred percent, sir."

"No doubt in your mind?"

"Without a doubt. From all the intelligence we've gathered, I believe it is inevitable . . . That's why I'm here to tell you we can't afford not to act. We have to go on the offensive or we might be unable to respond."

After opening his portfolio, he handed a sheet of paper to the President.

"I hope you don't mind, but I have written up a draft of a National Security Presidential Directive for you to look at. It has the same substantive legal effect as an executive order. It says the ban on political assassinations does not prevent the United States from taking action in self-defense of the country. Given what happened last night, I think Volkov's actions are sufficiently egregious to justify any action on our part as self-defense. Of course, as you know, the directive would be highly classified and would be known only by your National Security Council."

The President studied the directive, an elbow on the desk and his chin in his hand. The ramifications of signing off on it were huge. He needed time to think.

"Anybody else know about this?"

"Just the three of us, sir."

The President saw there was a place for his signature. That's all it would take to make it official and get the ball rolling. But he needed more time. "I'm going to study it further, Bill."

"I understand."

The President set aside the proposed directive and sat back. "What about the other two guys that were mentioned? The Defense Minister Balakin and Dernov the top general. Why not go after them? It might even be easier than taking out the President."

Parker shook his head, like he had already thought of that possibility. "Volkov would just replace them with like-minded friends. People who would like nothing more than to carry out the President's orders and strike the United States. It might buy us some time, but in the end it wouldn't make any difference."

"Do we have assets in Russia that can get to Volkov?"

Parker nodded once.

"We do?"

"Yes, sir," Parker said, preparing to give the options available to the President. "We have three operatives that could carry out the mission in a variety of ways. Poisoning, which would be ironic given that the Russians are so fond of that tactic, a sniper shot, and a car bomb. They can all be made to look like the assassination was an inside job by one of Volkov's enemies, of which there are many but they hide in the shadows in hopes of staying out of his crosshairs."

Obviously intrigued, the President gave the possibilities some thought. "Can poisoning be made to look like it has to do with his cancer, like the disease became super aggressive and caused a quick end?"

"It's definitely something I can look into, Mr. President."

Vice President Stubblefield chimed in. "What happens if we succeed? What happens then?"

"By making it look like an inside job, we keep the Russians off-balance. They won't know who to trust in their own government. We'll be sure to play it up like it was one of Volkov's own confidants. They'll be too focused on their own inner turmoil to continue their saber rattling abroad. If nothing else, it will give us more time."

The President fired off the next question. "Who would replace Volkov? Would we be looking at someone worse?"

"There are four or five men who have their sights on succeeding Volkov. My money would be on Balakin. He's been putting himself in all the right places for years now. He has the support of the military and is seen as acceptable to the Russian people."

"And he'd be more palatable than Volkov?"

"Yes, sir. Much more so. I think Volkov is close to becoming unhinged. Balakin could be tolerated."

The President leaned back in his chair and massaged his forehead with his left hand. Director Parker had given him everything he wanted—options to solve a problem. A big problem. One that wouldn't go away until Volkov was no longer in charge—whether by being forced out of power or meeting his end on this earth. And he provided him with legal justification for signing off on a plan. It was a lot to think about and not something that could be decided without more thought.

"You've obviously put a lot of time and effort into this, Bill."

"Yes, sir. That's what I'm here for."

"I appreciate it," the President said, gesturing toward Stubblefield. "Can you give us a minute?"

"Sure," Parker said, standing and grabbing his materials. "I'll be across the hall."

"Thanks." The President stood and waited for Parker to exit the Oval Office. Once the door closed, he walked to the windows looking out toward the Rose Garden. With all its greenery and colors, it was so calm and peaceful in the midst of all the turmoil in the world.

"It's always something," he mumbled under his breath. He turned to Stubblefield, who had joined him at the window. "How many times have I told you it's always something?"

Stubblefield smiled. "Too many to count, sir."

"Assassinate the Russian President," the President said, shaking his head. "My goodness. Can you believe that? How have we come to this?"

"It's a crazy mixed-up world we're living in."

"That it is."

"And you're in charge of dealing with it."

The President grunted. He put his hands behind his back and looked down at the floor, his mind trying to think of every possible pro and con of the current situation. Parker was adamant that Volkov was serious about striking the United States. The CIA Director always gave it to the President straight, and his directness struck a chord. A hundred percent chance of a Russian strike was more than enough to get his attention. The thought of the nation's capital becoming a nuclear wasteland flashed through his mind. There was no other choice. The President had to act.

"What do you think?" he asked Stubblefield.

"I've never seen Parker so certain about anything. I think we have every reason to worry that Volkov is going to launch nuclear weapons on the United States." He eyed the President. "We need to stop him from doing that."

The President nodded, having already made the same conclusion. *But how? What was the best way to make it happen? Were Parker's suggestions the only options? Or was there a better plan?*

"You think Duke would want in on this discussion?"

The makings of a smile crossed Stubblefield's face. "It's almost like you were reading my mind, Mr. President."

"Seems like something up his alley. He might have some ideas."
"I can sure find out. I'll get in contact with him if you want me to."
"Yeah, let's do that."

CHAPTER 6

Vancouver, British Columbia

"I'm going to kill you, you lying whore!"

The wild-eyed man with the knife was spitting blood with every hissing threat. The rage inside him had only increased after taking a hard fist to his mouth from the woman he was attempting to straddle into submission. He had been hiding in the darkened alley, lurking and waiting for his prey to walk by so he could pounce and rob her, assault her, or kill her just for the fun of it. It happened all the time in that part of town. The cops never did anything about it.

With hardly a sound, he had come up from behind, forcibly grabbed her with one arm, and used his other hand to stick a long-blade knife to her throat. She never saw it coming, and the look of fear in her eyes was as real as it could get. Gasping for any breath she could muster, she first tried to scream. But the gloved hand quickly covering her mouth prevented any calls for help.

Not like it mattered. The streets were deserted at that hour of the night, definitely not a place for a woman to be walking by herself. There was no one around, at least no one who would step forward and save her from the knife-wielding madman. She was on her own.

But the woman recovered quickly.

She had slammed her stiletto down on the man's shoe, sending a lightning bolt of shock through his foot before radiating up his leg. He grunted in pain, causing him to loosen his grip on her. She responded with a sharp elbow to the nose and then a fist square to his mouth, his teeth quickly covering with blood.

The attacker was able to regain his footing and took the woman hard down to the pavement. Now on top of her, he promised to kill her and used the knife to slice the skimpy half-shirt she was wearing. He ripped it off, exposing her black jogging bra restraining her ample breasts.

When he readied to plunge the knife into her throat, she managed to grab his wrist and deflected the blade. His momentum thrown off balance, the man fell toward her, allowing her to bash the bridge of his nose with her forehead, stunning him. She scratched at his face with her red fingernails before grabbing his hair, pushing his head back, and thrusting a fist into his exposed throat. Losing control of the knife, he choked for a breath.

With the upper hand, the look of fear vanished from her eyes, replaced with a white-hot vengeance. The man had picked on the wrong woman. Now she was in control, and she was going to make him pay for his sins. She jammed a thumb into his eye socket, and the man screamed in pain. When he moved to his left exposing his crotch, it took a direct hit from her knee, crushing his nuts. He howled in agony.

"Cut!"

When the woman smacked her attacker's temple with the palm of her left hand and rolled on top of him to deliver the knockout punch, the director yelled again.

"Katia! . . . I said cut!"

The whole set went quiet, everyone wondering whether the set medic was going to have to rush in to save the stuntman from the ass-kicking he was taking from Katia Balakina. Finally, she heard the call to end the scene and stopped, her fist balled and arm cocked in mid-air. Her chest was heaving, the sweat from the action sliding down her tanned cheeks and exposed cleavage. Her eyes were full of fury, her nostrils flaring, like a raging bull ready to charge. She looked like she could have pummeled the man to death.

"I thought you said you were going to kill me," she muttered under her breath.

Seeing stars, the stuntman held up his hands in surrender, hoping she wouldn't bust his nose or gouge his eyes out. Tasting blood, he reached up and touched his mouth. He could feel his lips starting to swell.

"Let's get a towel and some ice!" the director yelled.

Gary, the stuntman, struggled to sit up on the pavement. Feeling the blood pooling in his mouth, he spat on the sidewalk. He hurt all over—his head, his back, his nuts. "You kind of overdid it, didn't you, Katia?" he said with a healthy dose of frustration.

He stopped short of uttering an unscripted profanity at her. They had practiced every move before the scene—every kick, every punch, every thrust and jab. The initial assault and ensuing fight would have looked plenty realistic if Katia had followed the choreographed plan. But she went off script, and thus ol' Gary became the recipient of a first-class female beatdown.

"Sorry, Gary," she said, reaching out her hand to help him up. "It must have been the adrenaline. Sometimes I get in the heat of the moment and can't stop myself."

Someone handed him a tissue and he dabbed at the blood dripping from his mouth. "Thanks for the heads-up," he said to Katia. "I'll be sure not to sneak up behind you in real life." Thankful there was no need for a second take, he limped away, but not before mumbling something derogatory about Russian actresses under his breath.

After the director announced that they were going to take an hour to prep for the next scene, a production assistant handed Katia a towel to wipe the sweat off her face and a script with her lines for her upcoming dialogue.

"That was intense," the young woman said.

"Yeah," Katia said, her breathing returning to normal. She handed back the used towel. "I'm going back to my trailer."

The production of *Maximum Payback* starring Katia Balakina was well underway and it was on schedule to be released in time to be one of next year's summer blockbusters. Despite the location of filming, the movie was set on the streets of Los Angeles, where Katia played Abigail Johansson, an ex-cop who was forced out along with her partner after they uncovered their superiors' illegal kickback scheme with local gangbangers and drug lords. With Johansson intent on exposing the corruption and exacting revenge on those who wronged her, the higher-ups know they have no choice but to make multiple attempts to take her out and silence her once and for all—one of those attempts being Gary's ill-fated portrayal of the knife-wielding assassin that, of course, ended poorly for the bad guy.

As one of the hottest commodities in Hollywood, Katia had been the director's first choice for lead actress. Blonde-haired and blue-eyed, she was twenty-nine, sexy, athletic, and the type of actress that both men and women would gladly shell out fifteen bucks for a ticket to watch on the big screen. Russian to the core, she could turn off her accent at the call to action if the role so required, and anyone who didn't know her upbringing would think she was a hot Midwestern girl who could hold her own in the big city.

As she walked to her trailer, her co-star, Jason Dumond, sidled up next to her. "You were a little rough on Gary, weren't you?"

"I guess I got a little carried away."

"A little? I don't think I've seen that much real blood before."

She shrugged but didn't break stride. "It happens."

"All I can say is I'm glad that wasn't me you were kicking the crap out of."

Dumond kept pace with her. At six-foot-three, he had four inches on her, which gave him plenty of opportunity to glance down at her breasts. On a previous movie, back when they were two of Hollywood's freshest faces, they had fooled around a handful of times, as co-stars are known to do. Both thought little of it, enjoyed the moment, and then moved on. But now with Katia being recently dubbed one of the sexiest women alive by a host of supermarket tabloids, the tall, dark, and handsome hired hunk Dumond would be considered a fool not to take the chance to score with one of the hottest chicks on the planet.

The rumors were swirling that they were dating, and their agents and publicists were keen to remind them that being seen out in public together never hurt to keep their names in the headlines and the box-office receipts humming. So the paparazzi were notified that they'd be at a trendy club together or having lunch at a posh restaurant, and the photos would then find their way to the entertainment shows and Hollywood gossip sites, ensuring the two actors would remain on the A-list of stars and on the mind of studio executives who had the power and the money to greenlight seven-figure paydays for them.

Before she entered her trailer, Dumond reached out and touched her toned upper arm. "How about we get together tonight? Vancouver doesn't have much to offer in terms of nightlife. We could work on our lines for tomorrow." His fingers slid down her toned arm until he caressed her hand. "Or maybe we could forget the lines and make our own entertainment like we used to. We could practice our upcoming sex scene. Make sure it's nice and hot. You know what they say, 'practice makes perfect.'" He winked and gave her a smile that had helped him bed so many women over the years he'd lost count.

She looked at him, noticing that his eyes couldn't keep focused on hers as they were too busy looking down at her chest.

"Sure, give me a call later," she said. With the cameras off, the Russian accent returned and she too gave him a wink. "Maybe you can pretend to be Gary." She left him to ponder what she meant.

Being the lead in the film, Katia had all the trappings of the big stars. A hair and makeup team, a dedicated assistant that followed her everywhere, and her own trailer, which had been outfitted with a shower, toilet, and air conditioning.

She tossed the lines for the next scene on the small table and grabbed a bottle of Perrier from the mini-fridge. A bowl of fresh fruit sat on a counter along with a dozen of the latest entertainment and style magazines.

With time to kill, she changed into a pair of blue shorts and a white L.A. Dodgers T-shirt. Rumors that she was dating the Dodgers centerfielder had been bandied about, even mentioned to the delight of her agent on ESPN, but they were, for now, just rumors as the two were simply neighbors in the Holmby Hills neighborhood of Los Angeles.

She picked up one of her phones and scrolled through her social media feeds. Her publicist made sure to update the feeds each day, tweeting, sharing, and posting anything that would keep Katia in the minds of her followers. Katia would add a few photos of her own, and she snapped a quick selfie that she posted along with letting everyone know she just finished shooting another scene for her upcoming release and that it was "such a blast." She added a half dozen emojis to emphasize her feelings.

Once completed, she picked up her other phone—the one her father had given her and told her to only use to contact him. The phone was said to have all the latest Russian technology to prevent eavesdropping by foreign governments. "You can never be too careful," he constantly reminded her. "The Americans are always listening."

She powered up the phone and it showed a text from her father: *Call me.*

If anything could snap her out of her current life in Hollywood, it was her father. It was like she was living two different lives—celebrity actress on one hand and daughter of the Russian Defense Minister on the other. She never mentioned her father's position, fearing it would get her blacklisted by studio execs who didn't want the hassle of dealing with questions about their main character's loyalties. Her use of the Russian female spelling of her father's surname helped throw off the uninformed. And although a search of the Internet would reveal her ties with the Russian Government, there was so much other content about her career, dating life, and upcoming films that her family tree was hardly noticed.

But his request that she call him concerned her. Usually he would leave a message asking how she was doing and hoping they could talk sometime. But the two-word message felt more urgent, like there was something wrong.

She checked the time on her phone and figured, if her father was in Moscow, it would be early morning.

"Hello, Father, I just received your message."

"My darling, Katia. It is so wonderful to hear your voice."

"I hope this is not a bad time."

"No, of course not. I always have time for you."

She thought his voice sounded different, like something was amiss. She dismissed it, figuring it must be the early hour. "Where are you?"

"I'm in Moscow. I have a meeting with the President later this morning."

Katia waited in silence for her father to say more. He usually asked about her day, where she was, and what she was doing. But she heard nothing, like he didn't know what to say or was afraid to say it.

"You asked me to call you. Is everything okay?"

Taking a few seconds to find the right words, Balakin finally said, "You need to come home, Katia."

The cryptic tone sucked the breath out of her lungs. There were so many reasons why he would say that, some worse than others. Her mind sped through them all.

"Father, are you ill?"

"No, Katia, it's not me. I am in excellent health."

"Is it Mother? I talked to her yesterday. She sounded fine."

"It has nothing to do with your mother, Katia. I just feel like you should come back to Russia for a while."

If it wasn't related to her parents' health, Katia knew it could only mean one other thing.

"Father, is this about the United States? . . . Is something going to happen?"

Her father's grunt could be heard over the phone. "Katia, I cannot speak to such things over the phone." His voice was gruff and harsh. "I have told you that a thousand times."

"Father, you are worrying me. Something is obviously wrong. I have never heard you sound so serious."

Nothing but silence followed. Long enough that Katia wondered if the call had dropped. Finally, her dad's voice returned, almost in a whisper, and it did nothing to lessen her worries.

"You need to come home."

CHAPTER 7

Washington, D.C.

"Don't make any sudden movements unless absolutely necessary," Duke Schiffer said from the passenger seat of his Jeep. "Abrupt lane changes, head turning every direction. Those are dead giveaways that you're worried you're being followed."

The admonitions were directed at his wife, Alexandra Julian, who had a firm grip on the steering wheel as she traveled the streets of the nation's capital. Traffic was heavy, as it was most weekdays when the noon hour approached. It added to her anxiety. The radio was off and there was no small talk. Alexandra was intensely focused on the road and her surroundings. This was her training time, her husband the instructor giving her the directions for the test.

"Are we being followed?" Her voice was shaky, like she wondered if her examination had begun.

Schiffer scanned to his left and then his right. "You tell me."

She looked up at the rearview mirror.

"Don't move your head," he scolded.

"What? How can I see what's in the mirror if I don't move my head to look at it?"

"Keep your head straight and level like you're looking out the front windshield. Then move your eyes to look at the mirror. You don't want to let the bad guys know you're looking at them."

As she drove through an intersection, she did as she was told—keeping her head level and moving her eyes to the mirror. She had to catch herself from moving her head a couple times, but after a few seconds, her eyes saw something she thought was suspicious.

"Two cars back there is a blue sedan. It's been behind us for a while now."

"Don't just tell me it's a blue sedan. Is it light blue, dark blue? There are lots of blue sedans out there. Try to narrow it down as best you can. It will help you remember. Two door? Four door? Is it a Ford or a Chevy?"

She took her time—noticing the color and the gold bowtie emblem on the front grille. "Dark blue Chevy. Maybe an Impala or a Malibu. Four doors."

"Good. What else?"

"Two people in the front seats."

Schiffer gave a quick glance in the mirror. He saw what she saw. "Male or female?"

"Two males. Both wearing sunglasses."

"Color?"

"White males."

Alexandra took a breath, trying to focus on two things at once—the mirror and the traffic in front of her. Rear-ending a car would probably knock a few points off her score. She checked her speed and continued onward.

"Turn right at the next light and see if they follow. Nice and easy."

With the light red, Alexandra flipped on the turn signal and pulled up to the car stopped at the intersection.

Schiffer hadn't told her if and when she would be followed. And she didn't have any clue as to who would be the ones following her, not wanting her to be on the lookout for specific individuals. But the guys he got to volunteer were some of the best in the business at tracking and stalking. Hoping to throw her off, he thought he'd fill her mind with more instructions.

"Don't get too close," he said, pointing at the car out the front windshield. "Keep at least five feet behind the car in front of you. Far enough that you can see the rear wheels."

"But there's a car behind me."

"I don't care. What happens if the doors of the car in front of you open and guys with guns get out? If you're kissing his back bumper, you have nowhere to go. You're a sitting duck while he shoots you before you can reach your weapon. Stay back and keep your options open." Schiffer pointed to the open lane to their left. "If the driver gets out with a gun, you can hit the gas and go left. Head straight for him. If you're lucky, you'll crush him against his door and break his back before he can pull the trigger. Barrel through and keep going." He pointed to his right. "Or if the left lane is blocked, you can gun it and go right, jump the curb, and haul ass down that street. Don't stop and try to get low in your seat in case they start shooting."

Alexandra gripped the wheel, trying to keep it all straight and envision the scenarios in her mind. When the light turned green, she made a smooth right turn. Her eyes immediately went back to the mirror. "They're still there. Right behind us now."

"What's the license plate number?"

She almost moved her head but quickly kept it level. Her eyes moved toward the mirror. She could see the license plate and the numbers on it. But there was a problem.

"It's backwards in the mirror, Duke. I can't read it."

"Well, then figure it out, Alexandra. During their training, CIA officers are taken into a theater and shown photos of license plates—frontwards, backwards, night, day. Not only do they have to get the letters and numbers correct, they have to look at the plates and figure out which ones are shown more than once. Your life could depend on getting those numbers correct."

Alexandra swallowed and then licked her lips. Her eyes went to the mirror again. She squinted slightly but she rattled off the letters and numbers correctly.

"Where's the plate from?" Schiffer asked, adding one more question to the test.

She looked again. "Virginia plates."

"All right. Good job. Pull over here."

Alexandra pulled to a stop in an open space. The car that had been following them pulled in behind them. She peeled her hands off the leather wheel and exhaled the breath that had been pent up inside her.

From the car behind, the man in the passenger seat got out and walked to the passenger side of the Jeep. When Schiffer lowered the window, the white male removed his sunglasses.

"Well, did she pass?"

The question was asked by Ariel Segel, Deputy Director of Israel's Mossad Collections Department, which is responsible for its vaunted espionage program. In the driver's seat of the car behind was Noah Wolfson, also a member of Israel's Mossad, the Kidon to be exact, a group that Mossad claims doesn't exist but includes some of the world's most lethal assassins.

Schiffer had first met the men a few years back—the three of them brought together after Ambassador Julian and Segel's wife Ayala were kidnapped in Egypt. The rescue operation in Cairo forged a friendship that would never be broken, and Schiffer didn't hesitate in asking for their help when Karl Bonhoff needed to be taken out. The Israelis were two of the best in the world, and Schiffer knew he could trust them with his life.

In town on "business," the two men took Schiffer up on his offer to follow Alexandra around for the morning. Segel, the master strategist, had tracked thousands of suspected terrorists around the world. Wolfson, the master hunter, could blend in like a chameleon, and his passing understanding of Russian, Arabic, and Farsi enabled him to stay one step ahead of his prey in nearly every corner of the globe.

Schiffer knew there wouldn't be anyone better at clandestine operations than the two Israelis. Still, they took it easy on her. If they wanted to be ghosts, she never would have seen them.

"She passed," Schiffer said to Segel. "Even got the license plate exact."

Segel leaned down. "Nice job, Alexandra. Sounds like you're a natural."

Alexandra blushed. "Thank you, Ariel."

"She's getting the hang of things. Not too much longer and she'll be ready for field work."

"Good to hear. Maybe we could use her someday."

"Thanks for your help. And thank Noah for me, too."

"You got it. Anytime."

"How much longer are you two going to be in the U.S.?"

"About a week."

"That's good. I'll give you guys a call some time."

Once he raised the window, Schiffer looked at his wife. He could tell what she was thinking. The flattery was going to her head. She had the look of someone who couldn't wait to conduct secret operations on behalf of the United States of America.

But contrary to what he was telling her, her husband had no intention of turning her into a spy or a covert operative. He'd pretend to teach her all the skills necessary to infiltrate the enemy and escape without a trace. But the last thing he wanted to do was put her life in danger. He still didn't think she was capable of clandestine operations. Sure, she was highly intelligent, quick thinking, and a world-class charmer. Those were great attributes for a woman on the diplomatic stage during her days as U.S. Ambassador to Egypt. But it took time to take those same attributes and mold them into something useful for spying on the enemy.

The real reason why he was taking the time to train her was to keep her safe. As much as he hoped to put his past behind him and move onto the next phase of his life, he knew as long as President Schumacher and Vice President Stubblefield were in charge, he'd be on call for their special assignments. And he could never put out of his mind the fact that he had ticked off his fair share of people in his life, and they would like nothing more than to exact revenge on the man who had thwarted whatever devious plot they had devised.

So he would forever have a target on his back. And as much as he regretted it, his past also put a target on his wife's back. Their kids, too, once they had some, which Schiffer hoped was soon. He thought it best to have Alexandra home nurturing a growing family. He hoped to be there too, spending his working days serving his country by training the next generation of warriors and home at night taking care of his wife and children.

In the meantime, he felt it best to train Alexandra on how to keep herself and, hopefully someday, her kids safe. If she was under the mistaken impression that he was teaching her how to be a spy, that would be Schiffer's little white lie. Harmless, he thought . . . as long as she didn't find out.

They had spent hours on the gun range, and she had become proficient with the rifle, shotgun, and pistol. She kept a fully loaded Glock 43x in her purse at all times and had a pistol mount installed in her car. They had practiced getting to the safe room in the house in case someone broke in, and she had memorized a dozen safe places around Washington and rural Virginia where she could seek shelter if an emergency arose. What they had done that afternoon was simply learning how to be observant, to free herself from the distractions of driving and focus on her surroundings. All in the hopes of staying safe.

He prayed she would never have to use what he taught her.

CHAPTER 8

Moscow, Russia

With the early evening traffic heavy in Moscow, Oleg Roznak saw none of it. Seated in the back of a delivery van, Roznak bounced around with the boxes of fruits and vegetables destined for Novo-Ogaryovo, the official government residence of President Volkov west of Moscow. He could have taken an armored SUV to see Volkov or he could have driven his Aurus Senat, one of Russia's most luxurious cars and fancied by the super-rich and Volkov himself. Roznak had stolen his from a disgraced Russian oligarch.

But he kept them both in the garage. There was no need to highlight his meeting with Volkov. In fact, the meeting was not on the schedule, completely off the books. That was normally the case when Volkov met with the leader of his private mercenaries.

Once the gates to the grounds were closed and the van backed to the loading dock, Roznak exited and headed to the President's private dining room. A table setting had been laid for Roznak.

"Sit," Volkov said as Roznak approached the table.

Roznak pulled out a chair and sat, an arm's length from the table. He stretched his legs out before resting his ankle on his right knee.

He offered no pleasantries, no bowing or genuflecting, none of the usual fawning that occurred when Russians greeted their President. Roznak felt no need. He had no reason to kneel to Volkov or kiss his ring. That was for the politicians and sycophants looking to move up the ladder.

Killers like Roznak didn't worry about climbing the ladder. They were more focused on cutting the legs off the ladder if Volkov didn't like who was trying to climb up.

He had ditched his normal green fatigues and gone with all black. The combat boots were scuffed and dirty, the product of a month's worth of hard work and violent action. His chin showed two days of growth, some gray hairs starting to sprout. The stubble helped cover the lower half of his face, pockmarked with the remnants of acne from his youth and fistfights from adulthood.

"You look like hell," Roznak said.

Volkov nodded like he couldn't disagree, but then he gave it right back. "Pretty soon, I'll be as ugly as you."

Roznak smiled. He picked at a piece of mud on his boot. It flaked off and fell to the floor.

The two men had known each other for years. When Volkov was with the KGB, the then Russian President had tasked him with finding someone who could set up a private "security firm," one that would carry out the President's bidding while giving him plausible deniability for any "unfortunate accidents" that might befall the President's political opponents and personal enemies. It would be claimed that the Russian Government had no control over a private security company, and thus it could plead innocence toward the bloodshed that it had secretly ordered.

In Roznak, Volkov found the right man for the job—he was ruthless, cold-blooded, and had no qualms about taking someone's life. In fact, he lived for it.

He had killed at a young age, first when he was ten years old. A classmate had tried to fondle his sister. Roznak waited until the boy was on his way home and pummeled him to death with a baseball bat. Roznak's parents were so horrified by their son's violent streak that they abandoned him, sending him to an orphanage in hopes of washing their hands of the monster they had created. Housed with a hundred other teenage animals, he found the only way to survive was with his fists and the occasional shank.

As a grown man, he bribed his way to becoming a police officer, wanting to exact vengeance on anyone he thought deserved it. Beating confessions out of criminals or torturing them to death were some of his tactics. He enjoyed making others suffer, and anyone who knew his capabilities prayed he never showed up at their door in the dark of night.

Volkov caught wind of him, and the only thing he wanted was to make sure Roznak was on his team. Upon establishing the private security firm of mercenaries, it was Roznak's idea to hire Russian prisoners to do his bidding in exchange for pardons for their crimes. The men of violence jumped at the chance at freedom and the hope of killing again. As his power and influence grew, Roznak sent them, along with hundreds of other operatives and contractors, all over the world, some going straight into the fight and others hiding themselves in foreign lands until they got the call.

With Roznak's help, Volkov was able to push Russian President Vitaly Yaroslavsky out of power. And when Yaroslavsky started flexing his muscles and angling for a return to power, Roznak showed up in the man's bedroom where a needle to the neck resulted in death from "natural causes," according to Russian authorities, and "suspicious circumstances" by everyone else.

There were hundreds of others. Most never saw it coming—the needle while sleeping or the bullet to the back of the head. But for those who did see Roznak show up on their doorstep, there was no negotiation, no point in begging. It was best to let the man do what he came to do and be done with it. Prolonging the inevitable risked the promise of sadistic torture—first for the victim and then the victim's family.

Now Volkov intended to use Roznak's skills to ensure his dreams of destroying the United States came true.

"How much longer?" Roznak asked, bypassing the salad in front of him for a glass of vodka.

"Until we launch?"

"Yes."

"It will be soon, Oleg. With the *Belgorod*'s launch, it will be within two weeks."

Roznak nodded, calculating what he had to do and how long he had to do it. "That's good."

"You can get all your men in place within that time period?"

"Yes, I believe so."

"Good."

"I have been planning for this moment for years."

"So have I."

"You have everyone else on board?"

Volkov looked away, as if thinking about all the boxes he had to check. "They will all be on board when the time comes. If I need to convince anyone at the last minute, I will let you know."

Roznak smiled. "Please do. You know how persuasive I can be."

Volkov put down his spoon and used a napkin to wipe his mouth. "I can't emphasize enough, Oleg, that your men have to be ready to act. When we're ready to launch, all the pieces must be in place and everything has to go as planned. I need you to make sure that everyone in the chain of command is following my orders. Whatever it takes to make that happen, you have my authorization to do it."

Roznak felt a tingle up his leg. He had been given the green light to do whatever it takes—beatings, torturing, killing. Anything he wanted. It was like Volkov had injected him with a drug, and the euphoria of what was on the horizon gave him a high that would fuel him for weeks.

"We will be ready."

"I need your people to be stationed throughout the world so they can react to the changing situations. I can't wait for them to get to Europe or the U.S. to carry out their activities. I need them there now."

"It'll be done, Yuri. You know you can count on me. This is what I live for. I want nothing more than to execute your orders in the bloodiest way possible."

Volkov raised his glass of vodka. "I figured you'd say that."

CHAPTER 9

Near Mineral, Virginia

"Duke, there's someone following us."

Schiffer glanced toward Alexandra. Her head was level, like she was looking out the front windshield. But her eyes were intently focused on the rearview mirror.

After a morning of training, the two had a long lunch before taking a walk along the National Mall. After working their way through the workday traffic jam around the Beltway, they took a leisurely drive home hoping to enjoy a nice dinner. That was until Alexandra sensed something.

"What?"

"For the last five miles I've seen that black vehicle behind us," she said, her voice beginning to shake. Her eyes moved from looking out the front windshield to the mirror again. "I wasn't sure if I should say anything but it's three cars back. Black Ford. Maybe an Explorer or an Expedition."

Schiffer looked straight ahead, but his eyes moved down and to the right at the passenger-side mirror. He saw the black SUV that she was talking about. In the disappearing light of the day, he couldn't make out the occupants. "License plate?"

Alexandra squinted slightly, trying the rearview mirror first before moving to the one on the driver's side. The skill of reading license plates in a mirror was a work in progress, but she could see the front of the vehicle clearly enough to say, "There isn't one."

"Keep going," Schiffer said. His mind was quickly calculating their current location and where they could lose the tail. They weren't that far from home, which would give them home-field advantage if one was needed.

"Is this another one of your tests, Duke?" Her hands had a death grip on the steering wheel, the tension making her body rigid. "Because if it is, I've kind of had enough for the day. I'm sorry."

Schiffer reached forward and grabbed the Glock 19 from the pistol mount below the dash. He wished it was part of her training. But the racking of the slide putting a bullet in the chamber gave Alexandra the answer to her question. "No. I don't know who it is."

"Are you serious?"

"Yes. I haven't planned this."

"What do I do?"

Schiffer cursed to himself. He had a reason for letting Alexandra drive earlier. It was part of her training, but on the drive back, he should have been behind the wheel. His wife's defensive driving sessions were still in their infancy, and all those were in her car, not his Jeep. He glanced in the mirror again. The SUV was still there keeping a steady pace. Whoever it was, they were professional. They weren't making moves that would draw attention to themselves. Only a trained eye would notice them. At least Alexandra had that going for her.

"Duke, what do I do?"

"Pick up the pace a little bit. Don't gun it, just ease into it. Get around the car in front of us and we'll see if the people behind keep pace."

Alexandra took a breath and did as she was told. She made a quick glance over her left shoulder and then gave a flick of the turn signal. She eased into the left lane and gave the accelerator a push to pull even with and then pass the car in front of them.

"Stay in this lane," Schiffer said. A check of the side mirror showed the black vehicle making a move into the left lane, mirroring Alexandra's pace. There was a car between them, but it was clear the vehicle was intent on following theirs.

"You don't want me to move back to the right lane?"

"No. Stay in this lane and keep ahead of that car we just passed. Don't give enough space for the car behind us to go right. I want to keep it in between."

Alexandra's eyes focused again on the rearview mirror. "Duke, is that another vehicle behind them? Are there two of them following us?"

Schiffer's glance to the mirror revealed two SUVs with at least four individuals. *What the hell?*

After returning his pistol to the mount, he leaned back to reach behind his seat and grab his go-bag. In it contained his Sig Sauer Rattler rifle and three thirty-round magazines, much more firepower than his Glock and capable of going fully automatic with a flip of the selector. He could use it to blow out the back window and lay down suppression fire across both lanes. Or he could pick off the drivers to disable their vehicles. He had options.

He jammed a magazine into the rifle and racked the slide, then kept it down between his legs.

"What do I do?

"Get ready. Stay in front of the car on the right." He pointed toward the coming exit. "As soon as we get to that on-ramp, I want you to jerk the wheel to the right and take the ramp. Let's hope the people behind us don't have time to react. Then gun it and go."

Alexandra gripped the wheel, her palms sweating. She tried to breathe. Her eyes went to the right-side mirror, the car in the right lane still there.

"Get ready," Schiffer said. As soon as the on-ramp opened, he yelled, "Now!"

Alexandra jerked the wheel to the right, crossing in front of the now honking car in the right lane, and hit the ramp.

"Go! Go! Go!"

The Jeep accelerated as Alexandra pushed the pedal to the floor.

"Don't stop!"

"Duke, there's a stop sign!"

"Blow through it! There's no one coming!"

She took a wide right turn, the tires on the Jeep squealing in pain as the rubber struggled to grip the asphalt.

"Keep going!"

"Duke, there's one still behind us!"

"I see them." He reclined his seat as far as it would go and looked out the back window. The black SUV was gaining on them.

"What do I do, Duke?"

"Go faster. We're almost home. Let's get to the house. If I start shooting, don't stop."

Alexandra took a right and then gunned the engine. They were almost to the road that led to their driveway.

Schiffer turned around, the SUV still behind them and closing the gap fast.

He didn't see what was ahead of him, but Alexandra did.

"Duke! That guy has a gun!"

Schiffer spun in his seat. Seeing the man on the right side of the road, he flinched and used every bit of his thousands of hours of training to keep from raising his Sig Rattler and letting the bullets fly at the target.

In that split second, he had recognized the man, knew him well. Hell, he had trained the guy. It was Curt from the United States Secret Service.

"Son of a . . ." He let out a breath. "Slow down."

"What? What's going on?"

He reached out to grab her arm, which was rigid with tension. "Slow down."

He then pointed toward the right out the window.

In the field to the west of their house sat the familiar green VH-3D helicopter with the white top, an American flag painted over the door and *United States of America* stenciled in white letters near the tail. Its call sign was Marine Two when the Vice President was on board.

"Looks like we've got company."

* * *

"Evening, Duke . . . Alexandra," Vice President Stubblefield said as the two stepped out of the house onto the back deck. With his suit coat off and tie removed, he was sitting comfortably in a rocking chair like he owned the place. His ever-present pistol was safely tucked away in his shoulder holster.

"Evening, sir," Schiffer said.

"How's it going? I've just been out here enjoying the view. Sure is nice and quiet out here at this time of the day. So peaceful and relaxing." He grabbed a glass of iced tea from the end table, took a sip, and then held it up. "Can I get you two something to drink?"

To the left of the Vice President, Schiffer sat down on the bench in front of the deck's railing. "You could have called and let us know you were coming. I could have warned the neighbors that they weren't under attack from all the heavily armed security swarming the place."

Stubblefield shrugged. "I was in the area and thought I'd stop by. Hope you don't mind."

"You just happened to be flying around in your chopper and thought you'd stop by."

Stubblefield smiled. "That's right."

Alexandra took a seat next to her husband on the bench. "How did you get in the house?"

Stubblefield shot Schiffer a look that said *Really?*

"Don't ask," Schiffer said to her. It wasn't the first time that the Vice President had showed up unannounced and made himself at home. The last time was when Schiffer, Wolfson, and Segel were using the lake to train for the insertion into Bonhoff's Swiss mansion. Schiffer almost shot the Vice President on that night, thinking he was an intruder. Stubblefield hadn't flinched an inch. Schiffer returned his focus to his old boss. "Maybe you should look into buying property in the neighborhood. Then you'd have your own house to come home to."

Stubblefield leaned back in the chair, rocking back and forth as he pondered the thought. "Not a bad idea. I'll run it by Tina. She might like it out here on the lake. Speaking of wives, how's your new protégé coming along?"

Schiffer looked at Alexandra. She was beginning to get some color back in her face after everything that had gone on—the vehicles following them on the interstate, the harried driving episode, and the guy with the automatic weapon at the end of the driveway. Oh, and then it was finding the man next in line to the presidency sitting on their back deck. Schiffer reached out and patted her on the knee.

"She's getting the hang of things. She spotted a couple of your boys when we were out on the interstate. Kept it cool under pressure. Had to take some evasive action, though. Lucky for them I didn't start shooting."

"That's good to hear. And you know how the guys are, always taking every last precaution. They knew you were on the way. So they wanted to secure the perimeter and make sure you were the only ones coming onto the property. I'll be sure to pass along the warning for next time."

"How did they know we were on our way?" Alexandra asked. She looked at the Vice President and then Duke before raising her hands in defeat. "I know, I know. Don't ask." She shook her head in disbelief at the situation.

"Really, you should have called," Schiffer said. "We just came from D.C. We could have met you up there. Saved you a trip."

Stubblefield shook his head, like he didn't want to be meeting with Schiffer with the prying eyes of the D.C. press corps on the constant lookout for breaking news. He leaned forward, the time for relaxing over. "I've got some things to discuss."

Schiffer chuckled. "I kind of figured that."

"Can we talk inside?"

Schiffer nodded. "Of course." He stood and then gestured toward his wife. "Her, too?"

The big man stood. "Yeah, her too."

The trio went inside and then headed down to the basement, where Schiffer had created his own SCIF, a sensitive compartmented information facility, that kept any and all electronic signals from getting in or getting out. In other words, a place that people like the Vice President could feel safe speaking freely. They took seats around the small table in the middle of the room.

"We've got some problems that we need to take care of," Stubblefield said, laying a tablet and the expandable folder he brought with him on the table.

"By we, you mean . . ."

"Me, the President, the United States of America, the whole world for that matter."

"Well that doesn't sound good. What kind of problems?"

The Vice President grabbed the tablet and punched the screen with his finger. After entering his security code and a few finger swipes, a video appeared and he turned the tablet so they could see the screen.

"The SecDef and Joint Chiefs briefed the President about this yesterday." The video began to play and Stubblefield narrated. "This video was taken recently in Severodvinsk, Russia. It's on the White Sea in northwest Russia east of Finland and farther north than Helsinki. It's where the Russians build and repair their nuclear submarine fleet. President Volkov was there to launch Russia's newest nuclear submarine, the *Belgorod*."

"I remember seeing that on the news," Schiffer said.

The screen showed a belligerent Volkov, pounding the podium to the delight of the Navy men in attendance. The giant black *Belgorod* loomed ominously behind him.

"He looks like he's lost weight," Alexandra said. "His hair looks like it's thinning."

"You're not the only one who has noticed that. I'll get to that." He pointed to the screen and continued. "In the background, you can see the submarine. It left port in the Barents Sea, north of Severodvinsk."

"I have a feeling," Schiffer said, "you're going to tell us something about that submarine that's going to keep you and the President awake at night."

"Yeah, big time. The *Belgorod* is the largest submarine in the world. It has been dubbed the 'Doomsday' submarine. It is well equipped to conduct seabed warfare, whether that be cutting cables or destroying oil pipelines. And, based on all the intelligence the CIA has been able to gather, it is believed it contains four Poseidon drones. The drones contain their own nuclear reactors and are capable of launching conventional and nuclear warheads. The problem is their ability for deep diving. Something smaller than a typical submarine that can slip underneath our defenses and prevent us from responding in time.

There's also concern that its one-hundred megaton nukes could cause radioactive tsunamis. So just imagine what that could do to places like Manhattan, Boston, or Miami. All in all, it would not only provide Russia an opportunity to launch a first strike, but also a second strike after we have retaliated."

"You think Russia is going to use this . . . this *Belgorod* submarine against us?" Alexandra asked.

"Our intelligence says President Volkov doesn't have long to live—lung cancer, stage four—and he's intent on striking the United States before his time is up. Bill Parker thinks he's serious. From everything we have been able to uncover, we believe Volkov is unstable and might want to go down in a blaze of glory. He'd be the man in the history books that destroyed the United States. And with what went on the other night with the Russian bombers, all signs are indicating it's going to happen."

"Unless you can stop it," Schiffer said.

Stubblefield gave each of them a hard look. "Unless we can stop it."

"We?" Alexandra asked. "What do you mean by 'we'?"

Stubblefield didn't answer. Instead, he grabbed the folder and pulled out three red files. He turned them around and laid them in front of Duke and Alexandra. Each of the files corresponded with the three nuclear decision makers in the Russian Government—Volkov, Balakin, and Dernov. The folder on Volkov was the thickest, the one on Dernov the thinnest.

"These are the guys we're looking at," Stubblefield told them. "We need to make sure they don't give the orders to start launching nukes. All three of them have to be involved. The CIA is currently planning operations to present to the President for his authorization." He stopped and eyed them both. "Nothing is off the table."

"Nothing?" Schiffer asked, knowing the more options, the better.

"Nothing."

Alexandra caught the Vice President's tone and glanced at Duke before returning her focus on Stubblefield. "Does that include assassination? . . . We don't assassinate world leaders."

"It includes everything, Alexandra."

Schiffer noticed that the Vice President did not say "Yes." Even in the SCIF and even among trusted friends, the big man chose his words carefully when it came to the ultimate option.

"Like I said, this is the most serious nuclear threat since the Cuban Missile Crisis. And serious threats require serious decisions."

"And the President has signed off on this?" Alexandra asked, not believing what she was hearing.

"The President has asked that plans be developed and put into place so that, if the time comes, he can give the order. Like I said, the CIA is developing plans . . . and that's why I'm here."

Alexandra looked at Duke, like she expected him to say something. Maybe offer a protest. Nothing. He sat staring at the three folders in front of him, his eyes going back and forth between the three names labeled on each one.

Schiffer opened the one closest to him—the one on President Volkov. "I take it they're all ex-communists," he said, flipping through the thick stack of intelligence.

"Yes," Stubblefield said. "If there ever is such a thing as an 'ex' communist."

"In other words, they can't be trusted."

"The only communist I'd trust is a dead one, Duke. And even then I'd check for a pulse every half hour."

"So they'd be susceptible to bribes, beautiful women, promises of power and riches."

"That's right."

Schiffer moved on to the next folder—the one on Balakin. He noticed the picture included with the dossier the CIA had on him. It was an official government photo, the one every minister, legislator, and bureaucrat sat for, but his included the standard of the Minister of Defense behind him. Tanned with his hair combed to the side, his appearance was known to turn heads. It was obvious he was someone who cared about his looks and knew how to present himself. Not one who spent his days drinking vodka, smoking cigarettes, and enduring the harsh winters of Russia. A few pages later showed Balakin with his daughter as well as multiple photos of him with different women.

"A bit of a playboy," Stubblefield said, noticing Schiffer's interest in the pictures. "Divorced now, he's been known to sleep around. Might be something that can be exploited."

Schiffer's head stayed down, but his eyes moved to the left to see if his wife picked up on Stubblefield's idea. He hoped not, and he hurried to move on.

The first page of the third folder showed a picture of General Dernov that portrayed the man as he truly was—stodgy, puffy faced, a mean and nasty prick. The man's military records filled three pages, and it was easy to see that his life had been devoted to the Russian war machine.

After his cursory glance through Dernov's file, Schiffer shoved it away, his mind already thinking of what could be done. He had conducted operations around the world—Paris, London, Rome, Monaco, Munich, Cairo, Switzerland, but never Moscow. The Russians were suspicious people, always on the lookout for Americans acting as spies. Working in Russia could be done, but it would be a huge challenge for an outsider.

Needing to say something, Alexandra asked, "What do you want us to do?"

"Look over the files," Stubblefield said. "Give me your thoughts on plans to deal with these men. I wanted both of you here because I think you two have different areas of expertise that can help us develop an operation or operations. Alexandra, you've dealt with a lot of foreign leaders and diplomats in different parts of the world. Take what you've learned over the years and see what you both can come up with. See if something can be exploited."

Schiffer sat still, his eyes focused on the folders, deep in thought. For a second, he wondered if he would ever be able to get out of this line of business. He had been trying to retire for years now, only to be dragged back into the fray by the President and Vice President. He didn't dwell on the thought long, not with the Russian madman with nuclear weapons threatening to destroy the United States. That was enough to put off retirement a little while longer.

He looked up at Stubblefield "Can the plans include me putting a team together?"

"Absolutely. Whatever you need."

"And the President is okay with doing this?"

"Duke, the President is the one who sent me here."

Schiffer considered it and then shot Alexandra a look, giving her a chance to be in on the decision making like it was a family matter. She nodded without hesitation.

"All right, sir, we're in. I take it this is on the fast track."

"Yes. This is priority one." His job done, Stubblefield stood and put on his suit coat. "Let me know what you think."

After shaking hands with the Vice President, Schiffer said he would walk him to the chopper. With darkness having set in, the headlights of two Secret Service SUVs helped illuminate Marine Two in the distance.

The two men walked across the lawn. Before the big man got on board, Schiffer had one last thing to add to their earlier discussion. "Sir, I didn't want to say this in front of Alexandra, but I don't want her getting involved in any operations."

Stubblefield stopped walking but didn't respond.

"We're trying to start a family, and it's too dangerous for her. I don't want her getting into something she has no business getting into. We've already had too many close calls and I don't want to lose her."

Stubblefield nodded like he understood. "Even with you teaching her the tricks of the trade?"

"I'm not teaching her the trade, Mr. Vice President. I'm teaching her how to be observant so she doesn't fall victim to someone trying to come after me. I know I can't protect her every minute of the day. What I'm doing is little more than teaching her self-defense skills."

"She has talent, Duke. She's smart and quick on her feet. She might be useful out in the field."

Schiffer shook his head adamantly. "No. It's too much risk. Any plan I come up with will not include her in it. I want her safe. I want our future children to be safe. I don't want them to have targets on their backs."

"She can help make the world safer, Duke. Just like you are doing."

"No," Schiffer said gruffly, hoping to end any thought of putting her in harm's way. "I hope I can count on you not to ask her to do anything that will put her in danger. I think you at least owe me that."

The big man took in a deep breath, his eyes focused on the American flag atop the door of Marine Two. Duke had certainly earned it, what with everything Stubblefield asked of him over the years. He exhaled and said, "I won't ask her to do anything that will put her in danger, Duke. You have my word."

Schiffer seemed appeased by the response. "Thank you, sir."

The two men shook hands again.

Stubblefield took a step toward the stairs of the chopper before stopping and saying, "Let me know what you two come up with ASAP."

CHAPTER 10

Near Mineral, Virginia

Alexandra woke first the morning after the Vice President's visit to the house. She was seated at the kitchen table when her husband walked in for breakfast.

"You're not eating?" he said.

She shook her head, her eyes looking at the contents of the red folders in front of her. "Cereal didn't sound good so I had some orange juice." She waved her hand across the table. "I guess I'm too busy thinking about all this to be hungry."

Schiffer poured himself a bowl of corn flakes, chopped up a banana on top of it, and filled the bowl with skim milk. He took it to the table and sat down next to her.

"Any ideas?" he asked. "What's your initial impression?"

Alexandra leaned closer and covered her mouth with her hand. "I can't believe the President is thinking about assassination," she whispered, as if someone was on the other side of the glass doors leading to the deck. "It's almost unbelievable. It's something that never would have been discussed in the past."

Schiffer finished a bite. "Tells you how serious he thinks it is. Desperate times . . ."

"I know, but still . . . the ramifications it will cause across the globe if he goes through with it." She shook her head at the unknown.

"It might keep those leaders with questionable loyalty to the United States in line. They might think twice about trying to screw with us."

Alexandra sat back in her chair. "Could you take Volkov out?"

Schiffer put down his spoon and looked out the window across the lake and into the trees. He had worked as a sniper with the FBI for twenty years and now trained rookie sharpshooters for a dozen federal law-enforcement agencies. With his Remington .308, he could hit a ten-inch target at a distance of a thousand yards. If need be, he could put a second bullet in the same spot within two seconds. His record included shots that saved the lives of the President and the Vice President and took the lives of terrorists across the globe.

He picked up his spoon and scooped up another bite. A sniper shot was usually his first option. He had dreamed about just such a scenario last night. He knew he could do it. Before he put the spoon in his mouth, he said, "Yeah . . . I could take him out."

"You think that's an option?"

He finished chewing and gave a quick shake of his head. "It'd be tough. I could get into Russia—either the easy way or the hard way. And a sniper rifle wouldn't be difficult to acquire. But getting a decent shot would be the issue. When is Volkov going to be somewhere out in the open where a shot could be taken? You've seen his recent itinerary. Other than that submarine launch, he doesn't get out much and, if he does, it's in a controlled environment. It would almost have to be a Russian traitor to make it happen. Someone on the inside. Maybe a security guard or personal assistant. Whatever, it would probably take too much time to get it all set up, and time is not on our side."

"Yeah, that's what it sounds like."

Curious, he looked at his wife. "What about you? What's your best plan to get him?"

Alexandra frowned before chuckling. "It was to have you take the shot."

Schiffer laughed. "Thanks for the vote of confidence, babe."

He finished his cereal, gave her a kiss on the forehead, and took his bowl to the sink. For the rest of the day, the two studied the intel and threw out ideas. They quickly moved on from Volkov, deciding it was too difficult for an American operative to get to him. It would have to be an inside job.

Their take on Dernov was much the same. The military man had little outside interests. Single and unattached, the intelligence didn't show he used his position of power to sleep around. He rarely left Moscow. From all accounts, the man lived and breathed the Russian military. If he had an Achilles' heel, it was bribery. He liked to live well, and his bank account had grown much faster than most military men in Russia. Money wasn't his only desire either. He had been known to shake down local businesses for their finest booze, cigars, and food.

It all offered possibilities. If, of course, someone could get to the man. Easier said than done. Duke and Alexandra agreed they'd pass their thoughts along to the Vice President.

For the rest of the day, their focus was on Dmitri Balakin. After having left the KGB, Balakin moved up the ranks, swindling and sweet-talking his way to money and power. The man was a world traveler who slept around and made decisions that could best move him up the ladder of life—lust and greed being his favorite sins. The intelligence indicated he was known to frequent the beds of women in Paris, London, Brussels,

Beijing, and New York City.

"Typical horndog" was Schiffer's description of the man.

He flipped through the pictures in Balakin's dossier. Most of them showed a new woman on his arm, all of them looking like they just stepped off the modeling runway. Blonde, brunette, red—didn't matter. It appeared he was partial to long legs and big chests, all of them displayed by women who weren't afraid to show them off. An operation to seduce the man was a definite possibility. While still difficult, a beautiful woman in a skimpy dress was known to find her way past many a security perimeter.

Bribery was also an option. Balakin was known to collect high-end sports cars and he had an impressive liquor collection, everything from French champagne to Italian wines to American bourbon. There were only two ways he could have gotten the cash to buy all of it on the salary of a KGB agent turned government bureaucrat and then Defense Minister—by stealing it or accepting bribes for special favors. Par for the course in Russia.

Schiffer made a mental note and then went back to the first set of pictures—the family section. There was a picture of Balakin with another blonde bombshell. Schiffer flipped through the pictures to see if he saw the woman again, but the rest were different. He read the small print under the photo. The woman was Balakin's daughter and it noted she was an actress.

Schiffer tapped on the name of Katia Balakina next to the picture. "Does she look familiar? The name seems to ring a bell."

Alexandra looked at the photo and the name and knew instantly. "Yeah, she's the actress. Big-time Hollywood star. She's supposedly dating the centerfielder for the Dodgers . . . Or is it the shortstop? I can't remember. Anyway, I told you about that movie she was in."

"You did?"

"Yes, last week. Geez, sometimes I think you never listen to me."

"I do. I just don't remember the movie."

"We haven't watched it yet, but I'd bet you'd like it. It's supposed to have a lot of action in it."

He looked at the picture of Katia again and it gave him an idea. "Maybe we should watch it tonight."

* * *

That evening, after a long day of studying intelligence and a light dinner, Duke and Alexandra settled into bed early and turned off the lights so they could watch *Extreme Revenge* starring Katia Balakina.

The movie started out with plenty of gunplay between the bad guys and federal law enforcement. Schiffer did his best to keep from saying "that wouldn't happen" or "that's not how it works" every five seconds but, for the most part, it was watchable.

Then Katia showed up, clad in skimpy enough clothing to clearly show off her athletic body. She quickly took charge of the movie and proceeded to take out a dozen bad guys with her prowess with a handgun and her martial arts moves. Schiffer watched in appreciation. He knew those moves. He was sure a good actor or actress could learn them, but even that would take a lot of time and determination. From what he could tell, unless she had a stunt double, she knew what she was doing and she was good at it.

Alexandra reclined close to her husband, engrossed in the movie and putting a kernel of popcorn into her mouth one at a time. "I told you you'd like this movie," she said during a lull.

"It's okay."

The next scene showed Katia wrapped in a white bath towel, having just stepped out of a hot, steaming shower after a long day of crime fighting. Her wet hair was slicked back, and the camera caught sight of her ice-blue eyes and seductive red lips. When the towel hit the floor as she got dressed, the camera, much to the chagrin of male viewers, only caught sight of her naked back side. Still, it was long enough to let them have a good look at her curves.

"Do you think she's cute?" Alexandra asked. Her fingers held a kernel of popcorn, ready to be eaten. But she held it midway between her mouth and the bowl, wanting and waiting to hear her husband's answer. When he said nothing, she said, "Huh?"

Schiffer shook his head before looking at his wife. "I'm smart enough to know that I'm not supposed to answer that."

Not happy with the response, Alexandra dropped the popcorn back in the bowl and then grabbed the remote. She hit the pause button, just in time to show Katia sliding a pair of skin-tight blue jeans up her toned legs. Her red thong that provided little cover to her buttocks was staring them straight in the face.

"Come on, Duke. You can tell me if you think she's cute or not."

"No thank you."

"I promise I won't get mad. Just tell me if you think she's cute."

"I don't think so."

Alexandra pointed at the screen. "You don't think she has a hot body?"

"I'm not going down that road, Alexandra," he said, laughing. He knew the rules. Rule number one: When your wife asks you if another woman is hot, don't answer it and change the subject as fast as you can. "That's a no-win question for any man. If I say yes, you get mad. If I say no, you won't believe me. Nothing good ever comes from answering it. Any sane man will tell you that."

"You don't think she's cute?"

Schiffer leaned down and kissed her on the forehead. "She's not as cute as you."

Alexandra scooched back, her voice raising. "So I'm . . . cute."

"What?" he asked, struck by the verbal blowback.

"Just cute? That's all I am? Cute?"

"Cute is good."

"Cute is how you describe little girls or puppies, Duke."

Schiffer threw his hands up and yelled at the ceiling. "Aaagh! I can't win."

"I can't believe you."

"Oh, babe." Schiffer said, trying to pull her back to him. "You're way hotter than she is. And if it came down to it, I bet you could take her in a fight, too."

"Oh, you're just saying that."

"Babe, how many times did I tell you how hot you were last night? Right here in this bed. If I remember correctly, you seemed to find it agreeable."

"Whatever," she snapped, tossing the remote at his chest. "Why don't you go ahead and dream about *her* tonight."

She scooted away and turned her back on him, acting like she was ready for bed. Schiffer rolled his eyes. She had been a little testy lately, more so than usual. But he always liked her feistiness. He found it sexy. In the end, he didn't think it went as bad as it could have. She could have thrown her drink in his face. He figured she'd forgive him by morning. He put the bowl of popcorn on the floor and grabbed the remote to turn off the TV.

But he didn't.

He sat there looking at the screen, still frozen with the luscious Katia seductively bent over as she put on her jeans. He had a thought. He remembered the picture of Dmitri Balakin with her on his arm, their faces lit up by the bright camera flashes as they walked a red carpet. The smile on the man's face was genuine—the look of a loving father proud of his one and only daughter. His flesh and blood had become a superstar known the world over. Schiffer would bet good money that the man would do anything for her—anything. That included keeping her safe at all costs. It might just give the President and Vice President the plan they needed to prevent the start of World War III.

In the silence of the bedroom and with her back still to him, Alexandra's voice emanated from the pillows. "If you're going to stare at her ass all night long, would you at least do it in the other room."

Schiffer smiled. For more than one reason. The idea was taking shape. "I think she's the one, Alexandra."

After a second of silent thought, Alexandra raised her head and turned to the left, pausing as if trying to understand what he said. "She's what?"

"I think she's the one."

She rolled over, now fully intrigued. "She's the one what?"

"I think she's the one we need to go after . . . We need to go after Dmitri Balakin's daughter."

Sitting up, she reached for the lamp on the nightstand and switched it on. Then she grabbed the remote and shut off the still shot of Katia's nearly bare butt. The screen went black, and Alexandra's focus went to her husband.

"Are you serious?"

"Yes. Think about it. It would be incredibly difficult to get to those three men. Balakin maybe, in the right scenario, but the others are almost impossible, especially inside of Russia. Too much security and too little opportunity. But the daughter . . ." He stopped to think some more, his mind working in overdrive. "If we grab the daughter, that changes the whole ballgame. The decisions Balakin would have to make become much more difficult for him. He may hesitate. He may change his mind. It might be what we need to stop Volkov from launching his nukes." He paused to let it all sink in. "What do you think?"

"It's plausible. Do you think the President will go for it?"

Throwing off the covers, Schiffer sidestepped the bowl of popcorn on the floor and stood. "There's only one way to find out."

CHAPTER 11

Moscow, Russia

Emerging out of the elevator in the underground parking garage, Dmitri Balakin patted the pocket of his suit coat. His card for one of Russia's three nuclear briefcases was tucked safely inside. His hands were sweaty, knowing the day might soon come that he would have to take out the card and do his duty in taking part in Russia's deployment of nuclear weapons on its enemies. A shudder rippled through his body. That day was approaching. He could sense it.

He got into the back of his armored Range Rover and, within seconds, the security convoy was on the move. The drive from the Ministry of Defense complex to the Kremlin would take less than five minutes, even less if his driver wanted to push it. Balakin wondered if sometime in the near future he would be driven, not to the Kremlin, but to some secure undisclosed location outside of the capital to escape the missiles falling on Moscow, a top-secret place where he, the President, and the Chief of the General Staff could respond in kind to the American aggressors and their onslaught of nukes.

The thought had kept Balakin awake at night. What would happen to him? What would happen to his countrymen? His capital? His country? His future? His daughter's future? The call from Katia haunted him. Would he ever see her again? If so, what would the world look like then?

He had a thought that Volkov might back down. Like that North Korean dictator, Volkov enjoyed rattling Russia's sabers every once in a while, just to remind the world that he had a nuclear stockpile that could destroy any major city any time he wanted.

But Balakin's thought was usually outweighed by fear—fear that his friend's physical and mental well-being would cause Volkov to decide to make a decision that he wouldn't have time to regret. Balakin and his fellow Russians would then be left to suffer the consequences as they attempted to pick up the pieces of a once proud empire.

Sighing, Balakin looked out the tinted windows, the Moskva River flowing on his right. A handful of his fellow Muscovites were walking the sidewalks—on their way to work or taking in the warm sunshine. There were roughly twelve million residents of Moscow—*twelve million*, Balakin thought to himself. He wondered how many would be left after the bombs stopped falling. Would the flowing water on his right become a river of fire? Or would it be reduced to a trickle amongst a sea of poisoned ash?

The driver of the Range Rover watched as the lead vehicle prepared to turn left at the southwest corner of the Kremlin. A follow-up vehicle full of Russian security agents closed in from behind.

Balakin decided to change plans and leaned forward from the back seat. "I would like to walk this morning."

Both the driver and the security agent in the front passenger seat turned their heads but did not look at Balakin. "Sir?" the man in the passenger seat asked.

"It is a nice day. Let's take a walk through Red Square. We should enjoy it while we have the chance."

The security agent made a passing attempt at reminding Balakin of the security concerns, but only because it was his job. He had been trained to follow orders, especially from those who are friends of the President. The man radioed to the front and lead vehicles, and the three sped along the Kremlin Embankment until they made a hard left at the Beklemishevskaya Tower.

The convoy stopped near the edge of Red Square and, after surveying the area, Balakin's lead security agent opened his door. Balakin stepped out and breathed in the air, his eyes drawn to St. Basil's Cathedral. Its iconic nine domes, as colorful as children's lollipops, basked in the morning sunshine. The eyes of those in Red Square were focused on the cathedral, not the Defense Minister exiting his vehicle behind them.

He handed his briefcase to a security agent. A military aide stayed close by with the nuclear *Cheget*. The entourage walked along the sidewalk near the Kremlin walls and away from the crowds, mostly Asian tourists, all of them with camera phones that were being put to good use. A stiff breeze blew from the south, and the tri-color flag of the Russian Federation blew stiffly atop the Senate Palace. Balakin saw a plastic bag being blown across the cobbles of Red Square. It stopped briefly near the spot where Reagan and Gorbachev once met, a meeting between Presidents that would most likely never occur again, *glasnost* and *perestroika* having been replaced in favor of destruction and domination.

The group of ten men continued at a brisk pace, the looks on the faces of the security agents indicating they were ready to whisk the Defense Minister inside. Nothing good could come of Minister Balakin being recognized.

They made their way on the sidewalk behind Lenin's Mausoleum. Balakin noticed only a handful of people were in line to see the remains of the former Soviet leader. He figured most of them were foreigners, his fellow Muscovites too busy to spend time reminiscing about the glory days of Soviet power.

Balakin knew that on the other side of the Kremlin wall, his old friend was in his ornate office inside the Senate Palace. One current Russian leader and a dead one—their bodies probably only a couple hundred yards from each other. One had been dead for nearly a hundred years. The other would be dead soon.

As they passed the mausoleum, a few tourists pointed in their direction. Some cameras and phones were raised and pointed at them. Balakin's fine tailored suit and perfectly coiffed hair stuck out like a sore thumb amongst the thick-necked Russian linebackers surrounding him. Someone called out his name, and Balakin raised a hand without a look. His hand found its way to his jacket and he gave his pocket a quick pat.

"Sir, perhaps it's best that we make our way inside," Balakin's lead security man said.

Balakin reluctantly nodded. Delaying the inevitable, he knew he would have to make his way to President Volkov's office at some point. He was expected, and he was at risk of catching the President's ire for keeping him waiting. The entourage entered the Kremlin through a nondescript door and headed to the Senate Palace, home to President Volkov and his administration.

He could hear Volkov coughing before he even made it into the office.

"You are late," President Volkov said without looking up.

The President was standing, his palms on the desk. Balakin didn't know whether Volkov was bracing himself to keep from falling after another coughing spell or if it was something else. When he approached, he realized it was the latter. The desk was strewn with maps littered with red markers that dotted the entire globe. Fresh from Russian intelligence, the dots indicated Russian military assets around the world—all of them poised to strike whenever Volkov and his command authority gave the order to unleash their hell on the enemies of the Russian Federation.

Under the bright lights of the crystal chandelier, Balakin noticed his friend looked smaller than the time he saw him in Severodvinsk for the launch of the *Belgorod*. The President's hair appeared thinner, his skin paler, the white dress shirt looking a size too big on him. The man was wasting away a little more each day.

Volkov took his eyes off the maps to look at Balakin. "I said you are late." His voice was firm, unhappy.

"My apologies, Mr. President. It is such a nice day that I decided a walk through Red Square was in order."

Volkov grunted. He didn't have time for leisurely strolls, no time to stop and smell the roses. His time on this earth was short and he knew it. He went back to studying his maps. His finger tapped a red dot currently in the North Atlantic. The *Belgorod*. It had become Volkov's pride and joy. The most lethal submarine on earth was, at that moment, prowling the seas and getting into attack position. The sub's might was all his—and he intended to use it to its maximum effect.

"Did you bring the plans?" Volkov asked, still looking at the chess pieces of war on his maps.

"Yes, sir." Balakin set his briefcase on a chair, unsnapped the clasps, and opened it. "Just as you ordered." He took out a folder and removed three sheets of paper. He handed them to Volkov, who promptly put them over his maps so he could study them.

The plans gave President Volkov three options—a small-scale attack on U.S. military installations in Eastern Europe, a mid-scale attack on U.S. submarines in the Atlantic and Pacific, and a full-scale attack on the U.S. mainland, with the focus on Washington, D.C. and New York City.

After a quick study, Volkov started nodding his head, as if he liked what he was seeing. It gave him what he wanted—a chance to stick it to the Americans once and for all. He stood up straight and looked at Balakin, a smile on his face.

Balakin didn't return the smile. He had to ask. "Are you sure you want to do this, Mr. President?"

Volkov's smile vanished. His eyes narrowed slightly, a flash of his legendary temper crossing his face. "I've never been more sure of something in my life, Dmitri."

Balakin held out his hands, hoping to ward off any fire from his old friend. "I'm just saying. Once you give the order, there's no going back."

Volkov took a step out from behind his desk to look Balakin directly in the eye. They were both the same height, and even though Volkov looked weak physically, it would be risky to think he could not use the fighting skills he had learned from his days in the back alleys with the KGB. "You mean when 'we' give the order, don't you, Dmitri?"

With only words, Balakin could feel a punch to the chest, a threat that had been conveyed for years to generals, mercenaries, and underlings to do what they were told or find themselves out of a job or, for some, on their way to a life of hard labor in some squalid Russian prison camp.

Volkov didn't let up. "I hope you aren't going soft on me, Dmitri. That would be a serious miscalculation on your part. I wouldn't want the people of Russia to think that you don't have their best interests at heart."

Balakin swallowed. *Was nuclear war in the Russian people's best interests?* "Mr. President, I'm saying that once the strike occurs, it will change Russia and the world forever. I hope you realize that."

"Well, of course it will change the world, Dmitri, that's the point." Volkov flicked his hand toward the window, his voice rising. "I shouldn't have to tell you, Dmitri, but Russia is not the superpower it once was. The Americans are selling their own oil and the price of ours has plummeted. We are losing a billion dollars a day." He kicked the side of his desk. "A billion! The Americans are ruining us! They are trying to destroy our country. It is an act of war! We must respond with force! It is the only way we will survive!"

Balakin could do nothing more than nod like he understood and agreed with the President's assessment.

The overexertion was causing Volkov to wear down. He took a few shallow breaths to calm himself and then lowered his voice. "You know, Dmitri, you are the one who will replace me when I'm gone. You have spent years plotting and playing the game to get where you are. You are this close to becoming President." Volkov put his bony thumb and index finger together. "This close."

Balakin swallowed but remained silent.

"I hope I can count on you, Dmitri, when the time comes." When Balakin didn't respond immediately, he added, "Or I guess I could find someone else to do your job. Of course, that would mean the end of your hopes of becoming President. Or it might mean the end of you." The look in Volkov's eyes said it all. "I hope I don't have to do that to an old friend."

Balakin absorbed the threats to his career and to his life. They were not unexpected. Volkov knew how to push his friend's buttons. He had the power to take everything Balakin loved and desired and make it go away, if Balakin didn't carry out Volkov's orders. Volkov held all the cards, and Balakin, who desperately wanted the billions of dollars and the ultimate power that came with the presidency, knew it all too well. If he wanted to become President of Russia, he had no other choice but to carry out Volkov's orders.

"You can count on me, Mr. President. We have known each other far too long for you to think otherwise."

Volkov's cheeks rose. "That's what I like to hear, Dmitri. Loyalty can be a fleeting thing, but it is good to know that I have a friend to count on." He moved back behind his desk. He shoved the war plans off to the side and returned to looking at his maps.

Balakin walked to a spot where he could see the maps, the red dots looking like pieces on a game board. He contemplated his next question, wondering if asking it was wise. It might cause Volkov to make a decision, one that hadn't been finalized yet. He thought it was worth the risk.

"When do you want to strike?"

Volkov didn't respond immediately. He put his finger on a red dot and traced its path toward the United States.

"Where is President Schumacher?" he asked.

"He is currently in Washington. According to press reports, he will be heading to his home in Indiana in the next couple days."

Even with his head down looking at the maps, Balakin could see a smile forming on Volkov's face. He could almost read the man's mind. The President of the United States would be out of the capital. He would be far away from his bunkers and his military commanders. It would give Volkov an advantage.

He could send Russian bombers off the coast of Alaska to rattle the Americans' cage. Or he could launch a missile from any number of subs in the Atlantic or Pacific to show off Russia's military might. Maybe a cyberattack on the Pentagon or one of the big banks in New York City. So many options. The American President would be forced to hurry back to D.C. to deal with Russia once again. Maybe this time he wouldn't make it.

"Get ready. Things are about to get interesting."

CHAPTER 12

Camp David

Defense Secretary Russ Javits was the first to arrive at Camp David. The military chopper had whisked him from the Pentagon to the presidential retreat high in the Catoctin Mountains northwest of Washington, D.C. Once he landed, he exited the chopper with two black briefcases, both stuffed full of classified intelligence and secret plans on how to deal with the growing Russian threat.

The Chairman of the Joint Chiefs of Staff Hugh Cummins and CIA Director Bill Parker were the next to arrive—Cummins by helicopter and Parker by armored SUV. Each of them carried a briefcase that held their laptop containing everything they needed to brief the President on top-secret plans and military readiness. Had there been any news reporters around, the cameras would have shown the serious looks on the faces of the men given the reasons for their visit.

Marine Two was the last to arrive. Along with the three Marines on board and the four Secret Service agents, the only other occupants were Vice President Stubblefield, Duke Schiffer, and Alexandra Julian. Late the night before, Schiffer had called Stubblefield to pass along his idea about Dmitri Balakin's daughter. Stubblefield said the President wanted a meeting at Camp David the next day, and the Vice President wanted Schiffer to come up with the makings of a plan to present to the Commander-in-Chief. Stubblefield cautioned Schiffer that he wasn't sure the President would go along with it.

"So come prepared with your best argument," Stubblefield told him.

With five of the six attendees situated in the conference room of Laurel Lodge, the President walked in wearing a Camp David windbreaker and blue jeans. He had a silver can of Diet Coke in one hand and an expandable file folder in the other.

After the usual greetings, the President looked around the table and, seeing one chair unoccupied, asked, "Did Alexandra make the trip?"

"She's a little under the weather, Mr. President," Schiffer said. "I think it's a stomach bug. The chopper ride was a little bumpier than usual so that might not have helped. I told her to rest a bit, so maybe she'll be able to join us later."

"Well I hope she feels better," the President said, situating his folder in front of him. "All right. Let's get started. Again, thank you all for coming. Normally a meeting like this would include a lot more chairs around the table, but I wanted to keep it small so we can focus on what we discussed last time. The White House will put out a statement later on this evening that I met with the Vice President, Secretary Javits, and General Cummins." He paused to look at Parker. "Sorry, Bill, but we thought it might be best to keep your presence a secret."

Parker grinned. "It's the way I prefer, sir. And totally understandable given the situation."

"It'll keep the Russians guessing at what you're up to. The official statement will say that I am being kept up to speed on any Russian developments and discussing options on how to respond, whether economically, diplomatically, or militarily. It will also note we are speaking with our allies across the globe."

The President looked at Secretary Javits. "Russ, what's that Russian sub up to?"

With two stacks of papers and folders bookending his laptop, Javits made a quick click on the keyboard and a map of the world popped up on the flat screen on the wall of the conference room. The map showed land masses in green and the earth's oceans in blue. A red dashed line began from Severodvinsk, Russia, and charted a course through the White Sea, around the west coast of Norway in the Norwegian Sea, and then south into the open waters of the Atlantic Ocean.

"The *Belgorod* is currently in the North Atlantic, Mr. President. South of Iceland and northwest of Ireland. As you can see from its present course, it could be heading in a number of directions—most likely either staying close to Europe or heading for the United States."

The President rocked in his leather office chair. "So do we know its exact location or is that our best guess?"

"At this moment, we know where it is. We have a sub tracking it."

"Do we know if the Russians know that we're on to them?"

Javits shook his head. "We don't know that. Maybe they know we're there or maybe they don't."

"Tell me again about the *Belgorod*. What type of weaponry are we talking about?"

Without notes, Javits ran through the list of weapons possessed by the Russian sub. "It's a nuclear submarine, one of the longest and largest that's ever been constructed. It is equipped with a weapons system codenamed by the Russians as Status-Six or Poseidon. NATO refers to the system as Kanyon. Whatever you call it, the *Belgorod* can utilize stealth drones that can reach speeds of a hundred twenty miles per hour. They are unmanned and are capable of evading our missile defense systems. They can act as a second-strike mechanism and can launch nuclear warheads against the U.S. mainland or one of our carrier groups. We believe the warheads could carry cobalt bombs, which would increase the amount of radioactive fallout and could decimate the affected area to the point that no one will be safe to live there for at least a hundred years."

Hearing such gloom, the President could only offer a resigned sigh. "Thank you, Russ. Are we seeing any other Russian movements anywhere else in the world? Any more bombers in Cuba?"

"Sir, we have satellite footage over Venezuela that shows the two Russian bombers that invaded U.S. airspace. They've been joined by two more. Our people down at Guantanamo Bay have seen three other bombers land in Havana over the last twenty-four hours."

The President drummed his fingers on the table. "So it looks like Volkov is getting his pieces in place."

"Yes, sir. Unfortunately, it doesn't appear that he is intent on backing down."

"All right. Well, I guess that's why we're all here. Something is going to have to be done, and we need ways to deal with it."

Chairman Cummins raised a finger to signal he had something to say.

"Yeah, go ahead, General," the President said.

"I would add the Russians tested one of their Sarmat ICBMs this morning. The launch was in western Russia and landed in the Kamchatka Peninsula near the Pacific. It was just a test, but obviously it could be seen as provocative."

"Did they provide any advance warning?"

"No, but that's not surprising. Since Volkov suspended participation in the New START Treaty, Russia said it wasn't obligated to notify the rest of the world about the test."

Javits then had something to add. "This might be a good time to have the Missile Defense Agency conduct a weapons test, sir. Show the Russians that we can intercept ballistic missiles."

Chairman Cummins nodded.

"Okay, let's do it ASAP," the President said.

"Sir, if I might add something before we talk further about options," Javits said. Getting the nod from the President, he said, "Thank you. Because of the seriousness of the threat, I hope you will be open to taking precautions for your safety. I know when we had that hijacked train that you wanted to stay in D.C. to monitor the situation, and we all admire you for that. But the Russians could bring a much greater degree of destruction to the capital. You won't be doing the country any good if you're trying to run the government from a bombed-out bunker underneath the East Wing of the White House. I just wanted to throw that out there. I think it's important."

The President gave it a thought. He didn't want to look like he was running away in fear. "I will consider it, Russ. Thank you for bringing it up." He opened his folder and pulled out his materials. "Now, let's start with Volkov. Bill, what have you come up with?"

"Mr. President, we have several possibilities that could take him out," Parker said. He pointed across the table. "I had a conversation with Mr. Schiffer before the meeting to discuss his ideas on a sniper shot, and we both agreed that it would probably have the least likelihood of success."

Schiffer nodded and said, "I agree. The odds of even getting the opportunity to take the shot are extremely low."

"Okay," the President said. "What else, Bill?"

"A car bomb. Volkov travels to his office inside the Kremlin almost every day. We also have intel that he is seeing his doctor at a military hospital just outside the city on a regular basis. Obviously, given the armored vehicles he travels in, it would need to be a sizable device. Probably something the size of a moving van."

Stubblefield stuck his hand out to stop Parker and then chimed in. "You'd still need to get the van near Volkov's vehicle and that's no guarantee. Neither the President's motorcade nor mine would ever pass by a van that the Secret Service didn't know what was in it."

"I agree, Mr. Vice President. The van could be parked alongside the road or, even better, ram Volkov's vehicle, but like you say, it's questionable whether it could be done. He has also been known to chopper into the Kremlin from his residence, so we'd really have to get lucky to take him out on the road. I'd put a sniper as option three and a car bomb as option two."

"So what's option one?" the President asked.

"Option one is poisoning. As I said in our last meeting, chemical assassination is one of the Russians' favorite tactics. They've been developing poisons since Lenin's day with Lab X—everything from ricin, dioxin, polonium two-ten, and Novichok. And they've been known to use them all over the world, quite often on their own countrymen. Polonium two-ten was said to have been used against the Russian defector in London. He was ex-KGB and the KGB is the one that carried it out. The Russians make it in their nuclear reactor facility in Ozersk so we can make it look like an inside job—like the former head of the KGB was killed by one of his own. That's what the CIA's official line would be."

"And the Russians are no strangers to backstabbing one another if it suits their needs."

"That's right."

"Novichok is another possibility. It's a nerve agent that is even more potent than VX."

The President grunted. "Don't get me started on VX."

"Yes, sir. Novichok was developed in Uzbekistan and we got some of it from the Germans for scientific testing. The Russians were suspected of using it against a double agent in Salisbury, England. It can be administered as a liquid or aerosol."

The President twirled a pen in his right hand. "How would the polonium or Novichok be administered? And what are the odds?"

"They can be carried in a vial of water and placed in a drink. Easy enough to do if the right person is on the inside. In the end, it would cause acute radiation or nerve agent poisoning and the chances of recovery are nil, especially someone in Volkov's current state of health."

The President's pen stopped twirling and he offered a slight smile. "Did you give me the odds?"

The CIA Director grimaced. He wasn't one to put odds of success or failure on an operation. In his line of work, success can have varying degrees. But everyone around the table knew the President liked numbers in making his decision. "I'd say there's a forty percent chance of success. We have two people on the inside who might be persuaded to do the job. Once done, they would want immediate evacuation from Russia and be granted asylum in the United States."

The President looked at Stubblefield. "You have any questions?"

The big man leaned back in his chair. "Let's say one of the poisons is administered. How long before it incapacitates Volkov to the point that he can't make the decision to launch? I think the Russian defector exposed to polonium lasted three weeks. What if Volkov is poisoned but has the capacity to blame the United States and order a launch? It'd be like us kicking a hornet's nest."

Everyone's eyes focused on the CIA Director.

Parker removed his glasses and set them on the table. "It's possible that he could continue to function for days or weeks. The Novichok is faster acting. Whether the uncertainty that follows either poisoning would be enough to stop the others from executing his orders is unknown. The CIA would, of course, ramp up the rumors that it was an inside job and try to throw the Russians off."

"Which one do you favor—the polonium or the Novichok?" the President asked.

"I would go with the Novichok. It can lead to immediate cardiac arrest and heart failure."

"What about General Dernov?" the President asked, placing his hands behind his head. "What type of plans do we have for him?"

Parker gave a summation of the scenarios the CIA had considered, but he concluded there was only one option—bribery. Dernov was rarely seen out in public and only kept a small cadre of staff around him. But money was known to open doors, and if the CIA was able to provide someone with a large enough amount to make Dernov think twice about agreeing to launch nuclear weapons on the United States, it would be money well spent.

"And Balakin?"

"Balakin is intriguing, Mr. President. There are several avenues of attack against him. He likes women, and he's been known to enjoy the services of high-end Russian prostitutes. I think that is the way to get to him. From there, he can be bribed. And given the fact that he has his sights set on becoming the next President of Russia, I think he can be persuaded to not go along with Volkov's decision to launch. Otherwise, if it comes down to nuclear war, he's either going to be dead or Russia isn't going to be worth being president of."

"Can we get to him?"

"He offers our best chance. He likes to travel the world where, I might add, he likes to have prostitutes brought to his hotel suite." Parker looked around the table to make sure he had everyone's attention. "He's scheduled to be in New York City next week to attend the U.N. Security Council meeting."

"He's coming to the U.S.?" the President asked.

"Yes. He's supposed to be a part of the Russian delegation along with Foreign Minister Sokolov."

"What happens if we get to him?" Stubblefield asked. "What's to say Volkov won't replace Balakin and use that new Defense Minister to execute the launch order?"

Parker nodded like he had thought of that. "We would need to get to Balakin and keep him occupied long enough that we can convince him to not go along with the launch. Someone will have to do a great sales job to make him realize that it's not only in Russia's best interests but his own not to get Russia into a nuclear war. In the end, we'll have to convince him to be the driving force behind a coup attempt."

The President nodded more than once. "I like this plan, Bill." He then turned his eyes to the other side of the table. "Duke . . . Ty tells me you've got another idea as to Balakin."

"Yes, sir." Schiffer leaned forward and placed his forearms on the conference table. He took a breath and then looked the President in the eye. "I think we need to go after the daughter."

Those in the room sat silent, wondering whether they heard correctly and, if they did, what Schiffer meant by it. The President was one of them.

"What do you mean 'go after the daughter'?"

"I think we need to grab her, sir."

"You mean kidnap her?"

"Yes, sir."

"Kidnap the Russian Defense Minister's daughter?"

"Yes. Grab her, kidnap her, take her into protective custody. Whatever you want to call it, it's the same thing."

The President looked at Stubblefield, wondering if he had heard Schiffer's idea before the meeting and took the time to consider the ramifications of it. The thought of his three kids flashed through his mind. His two girls—Ashley and Anna—were both adults, but, in the President's eyes, he still saw them as the little blonde girls he used to push on the swing set in the backyard. Ashley now had two little girls. He shook at the image of someone kidnapping any one of them.

He ran a hand over the top of his head and down his face. There was a quick but noticeable shake of his head before he said, "A guy's family, Duke? You know we don't do that."

Schiffer raised his hands. "We don't assassinate world leaders either, Mr. President, but here we are discussing it."

"This is different. These guys are all in on it. They're the ones threatening nuclear war."

"That's why grabbing the daughter makes it different." When the President didn't offer a retort, Schiffer continued. "Balakin's daughter is an actress. Alexandra says she's very popular. But she's here in the United States. I don't know what type of security she has, but I can bet it's less than any of the three men we talked about here. We might be able to get to her and use her to our advantage."

"What type of advantage? You think her dad is going to refuse to launch nukes if his daughter is in the crosshairs?"

After a moment of silence, Schiffer said, "What would you do, Mr. President?"

The President squirmed in his seat. As much as he didn't like the idea of assassination, he could easily make the decision to take out someone trying to kill tens of thousands of Americans with nuclear weapons. But going after the man's family? Kidnapping his only daughter? He couldn't get the images of his daughters vacationing in a foreign country, being grabbed off the street, and taken hostage until the President gave in to the kidnappers' demands.

Feeling sick at the thought, he needed more time to think.

"Let me hear your final thoughts," the President said to those assembled. "What's the best option?"

Javits and Cummins thought Parker's plan for Dernov was the best choice. Parker thought going after Volkov was best, "cutting the head off the snake," as he called it. The Vice President thought there might be a chance to get to Balakin.

"And you, Duke?"

Schiffer didn't hesitate. "Balakin's daughter."

* * *

The meeting broke up for an hour, so the President could have an opportunity to walk the trails and be alone in his thoughts. He stopped at a bench in the middle of the woods, the only others in sight were the Secret Service agents trailing him at a distance and giving him a chance to think. The decision would be the most momentous of his presidency, and it could change world history forever.

Several thoughts kept coming to the forefront of his mind. Parker's complete belief that Volkov was going to strike the United States was number one. The other was Volkov's recent actions—the launch of the *Belgorod*, the bomber run on the U.S. mainland, and the ICBM test in Russia. The signs were all there. It would be a dereliction of duty as President to ignore them.

With all that in mind, the people he relied on had given him options. Now it was time to act. Still, he didn't want to use American nukes. He didn't want it to become the norm. If he could take out one man or all three men who make the decisions for Russia, it could save the lives of millions of Americans, Russians, and countless others across the globe.

After reconvening the meeting, those seated around the table all had their eyes focused on the President.

"I've made my decision. I want to go ahead with option one with respect to Volkov. I think we can use his cancer to our advantage." He took a folded sheet of paper out of his portfolio. It had been signed in blue ink with the President's distinctive flare. "This is a presidential directive authorizing the United States to take any and all action to remove Volkov from office in defense of the country." He looked around the table. "Only those of you in here are being made aware of it."

He passed it over to Director Parker.

"I know the plan is risky and not what we normally do, but everyone here agrees these are not normal times. The survival of freedom-loving people is at stake. Doing nothing is not an option. I'll leave the avenue of attack up to you, Bill. Whatever you think is best.

We'll try the bribery plan with Dernov, although I know it doesn't sound promising. Now, with respect to Balakin. I think the option to go after Balakin in New York City is our best plan. Let's see what we can do with him. Maybe we can convince him that it's in his best interests to not follow Volkov's orders."

He looked at Schiffer and held out his hand. "Duke, I can't sign off on kidnapping Balakin's daughter. Not right now. There's so much risk involved that I need more time to think about it."

Schiffer nodded. "I understand," he said in deference.

"I appreciate you coming here and bringing me options."

When the President said no more, Schiffer hurried to add, "Would you at least allow me to put a tail on her? That way we can see what we're dealing with in case you need to make the call. Just a couple guys seeing where she lives and what she has in terms of security."

The President's gaze met that of the Vice President, who gave an almost imperceptible nod that could only be caught by Stubblefield's wife or the friend of thirty years who sat next to him.

The President grimaced, still not happy with the thought of kidnapping another man's daughter. He sighed and rubbed his tired eyes. When he opened them, he had made the decision. "Surveillance only. Come up with a plan. You don't grab her unless I give you the direct order."

Schiffer's eyes widened slightly, like he was surprised the President was even open to the idea. He nodded once and said, "Yes, sir."

CHAPTER 13

Moscow, Russia

Like she did five days a week, Mila Kalashnika stepped off the bus on the south side of the Moskva River across from the Kremlin complex. The wind was out of the south, bringing warm temperatures to Moscow. She straightened her black skirt and then fingered the dragonfly brooch clipped on the left side of her black jacket.

Looking to the north and then the south, she contemplated which direction to go. North was the direction of her work—part of the secretarial staff for President Volkov inside his Kremlin office. South was the direction of her favorite little bakery where she bought a small cup of coffee every morning.

She ran her fingers lightly over the brooch again. She was fond of wearing brooches and favored dragonflies, butterflies, bees, and ladybugs. Given her paltry salary, the brooches were inexpensive, encrusted with fake diamonds and imitation jewels. But they added a splash of color to her otherwise bland work attire and none of her superiors had ever objected to them adorning her jacket.

Given that she was not late, she decided to go south. She was told it was important that she follow her exact routine because anything else would raise suspicion. Still, she couldn't help but look over her shoulder. There were security cameras at every corner, and most buildings in that area had cameras pointing in every direction. She knew she was being filmed and recorded—every person walking on the sidewalk and driving in their car was being filmed and recorded. It was a way of life there and every other capital city in the world. But she didn't know whether she was being followed. Were the Russian authorities on to her? She tried to look at the faces of those passing by. Did they look familiar? Was someone out of place? Were they going to spring into action and arrest her?

"Good morning, Mila."

Upon entering the bakery, the greeting came from the barrel-chested man behind the counter. Constantin Laskin owned Connie's Bakery and had been serving baked goods and coffee in that location for the last thirty years. With his shiny bald head and familiar red apron dusted with flour and powdered sugar, he had become a regular fixture in the lives of those working in the Kremlin and he had the knack for remembering their names.

Mila had come to like the man, a grandfatherly type who took interest in her work and told her she would go far in life. She would miss his warm smile and genuine kindness.

"Your usual?"

"Yes," she said. When she saw him reach for a cup, she blurted out, "No!"

Constantin paused, a cup in his hand and surprise on his face.

"I'm sorry. I've changed my mind. I would like a decaf today."

"Oh, decaf. Changing things up a bit, are we?"

Mila stifled a gasp. On her first stop, she had broken the rule not to change her routine. She smiled and quickly added, "I have been having trouble sleeping lately." It wasn't a lie, especially the last few nights. "I thought a little less caffeine might do me some good." But there was another reason for her change in order. She was nervous enough and didn't need the jolt of caffeine to make her more jittery. She handed over her money and took the cup.

"See you tomorrow?" Constantin asked.

She eyed him, as if burning the memory of his warm smile into her brain. It would be the last time she would ever see him. She had to suck in a breath to not choke up at the thought. "Like always," she said softly.

She gave him a wave, the last one she would ever give him. She wouldn't return the next day. In fact, she would never return to her favorite little bakery. She would never return to Moscow. Or Russia for that matter. Tomorrow would be the start of her new life.

The CIA had found her the year before.

With plenty of young men and women working in the Kremlin, the Agency had no shortage of targets to try and convince to turn on their own country and spy for America. A special push had been made to recruit the young women, especially those who worked for President Volkov. They were paid poorly and treated worse. The men in power took advantage of them on a regular basis, threatening them to do their bidding. Most of the women took it, believing they had no other choice if they wanted to keep their job. But every once in a while, the CIA would find a dreamer—someone who longed to live a life in a place where dreams could come true. Russia wasn't that place.

There were half a dozen women like Mila working in Volkov's vast office. They were all in their late twenties and attentive to duty. All of them were attractive, but not the model type that Volkov was partial to and known to bed. It was well known that the help was just the appetizer for the main course. Still, Volkov did not want unattractive women around him, and Mila and her cohorts passed that test while adhering to the uniform requirements of tight blouses and short skirts.

A CIA operative named Andrew made his first contact with her at a Moscow dance club. It was the end of the workweek and Mila had joined her colleagues for a night of drinks and dancing. The handsome Andrew caught her eye, and soon the flirting began. They danced, had a few drinks, and then found a booth in the back where they talked late into the night. After they hit it off, they made plans to have coffee the next day. Over time, coffee turned into lunch and then to dinner. Mila thought Andrew might turn into a long-term relationship. That was until he popped a different question—would she be willing to provide him with inside information about her boss? Along with it, he promised to pay her handsomely.

Initially, she was scared she was being set up. Trust was in short supply in Moscow, and especially those who worked in government. Every bureaucrat knew to watch their back and to be wary of strangers. But once she realized it wasn't a Russian trick to test her loyalty, her fear turned to anger that Andrew was only trying to use her. But, over time, she began to warm to the idea. It was her way out.

With the amount of money she could receive, far more than she would ever make as a secretary, Mila agreed to the proposition. The chances of success were so good that the CIA rented the apartment next door to hers. It made making contact with her much easier.

The Agency started her off easy, hiding a miniature camera in a ladybug brooch. By simply going about her business, Mila filmed the interior of Volkov's inner sanctum and was even able to catch video of valuable intelligence on Volkov's desk when she was serving him coffee. She also documented everyone Volkov met with on a daily basis.

As she became more confident, the CIA had her swipe a pen on Volkov's desk. A listening device was placed inside the pen and Mila was able to return it to Volkov's desk the next day. The CIA heard every meeting Volkov had in his office for three months until the ink ran dry and he threw the pen in the trash.

But the job for Mila that morning went well beyond anything she had ever done before. Getting caught taking a video or planting listening devices would be bad enough. She'd probably end up spending the rest of her life in some harsh, dank prison with the other Russian traitors. But if she got caught that day. If they found out what she was doing—they would torture her without mercy before slowly killing her. Then they would probably drag her naked dead body through the streets as a warning to anyone thinking about committing treason against Mother Russia.

Walking north toward the river, every step felt like she was getting closer and closer to the lion's den. Andrew had convinced her that drastic measures had to be taken. Through a panel cutout in her closet, he had laid it all out for her. He told her she was smart enough to think for herself, and she had to know by what was going on in Volkov's office that the man was dangerously close to starting nuclear Armageddon. If war started, Moscow would soon be in ruins, and Mila's life and the lives of her fellow Muscovites would be worse than ever, if they weren't ended in a mushroom cloud flattening the entire city. She could prevent it from happening.

She initially balked at the plan, saying it couldn't be done. The problem was that she didn't think she had what it took to make it happen. But Andrew praised the work she had done in the past and knew that she could pull it off.

"Russia is counting on you," he said before upping the drama. "The whole world is counting on you."

After a night of sleeping on it, she agreed to do it. She knew she could back out of it. She could go to work like usual and no one inside Volkov's office would know what she had planned. Then she could tell the CIA that she couldn't go through with it. It was too much to ask of her.

But there was something else that convinced her to do it beyond preventing Russia from starting World War III. She wanted a new life. The deep yearning to live in a place like the United States burned inside her. She wanted to live in freedom, where she could open her own bakery like Connie's, work hard, and enjoy life as a successful businesswoman. Russia didn't provide that kind of opportunity. It was backsliding into the old ironfisted Soviet days. Success was all about who you knew or who you bribed. Even working for Volkov wouldn't give her a leg up. Those in charge would simply treat her and demean her like the low-level servant she was.

That morning, Andrew handed the dragonfly brooch to her through the hidden panel in the closet. While normally pinned to her jacket, this one had a clasp that clipped to her lapel making removal easy.

"Don't drink or smell what's inside. Don't spill any on you." As she clipped it to her jacket, he smiled and offered her a simple, "Good luck."

The CIA told her that if she succeeded in her mission, she was to immediately make contact with Andrew, give him the signal, and then head directly to the airport. He would meet her there and provide her with a fake passport and a plane ticket to Amsterdam. Once in the Netherlands, the CIA would help make her disappear and start a new life in the United States.

Mila passed through the first security station upon entering the Kremlin. Walking through the magnetometers didn't set off any alarms. She was told the brooch wouldn't get a second look since it looked like her others. But she knew getting through the first checkpoint was only the first hurdle.

Not wanting to see anyone on the elevator, she took the stairs up to Volkov's office in the Senate Palace. Her heart was racing, and she had to stop at one of the landings to catch her breath. She thought she might be having a panic attack. Her teeth chattering, she felt the chill of the air conditioning on her bare legs.

She thought about calling it off. It was too dangerous in her mind. She closed her eyes and took deep breaths. With her coffee in one hand, her other hand reached up and fingered the brooch. She knew she had to go through with it.

Once she came to the top of the stairs, her stomach dropped.

The second security checkpoint outside of Volkov's office suite was empty of her fellow secretaries. She had hoped they would be there to offer a distraction to the guards as they wanded, frisked, and groped the women before being allowed to enter. But there was no line to pass through the metal detector. There were just three thick-necked men waiting to violate her like they did on a daily basis.

Ivan the Ape, as he was called in whispers amongst the secretaries, was eyeing her as she walked closer, her heels clicking on the polished marble floor. She could see his coffee-stained teeth as he smirked at her.

"Where's my coffee?" he barked. Bald headed and barrel chested, he had been on Volkov's security team for as long as Mila had been there. Each of the three guards had their favorite secretaries, two apiece, and the other two let Ivan take the lead.

Mila sucked in a breath. She was told to act natural—like it was an ordinary workday. Easy for the CIA to say. If found out, she would immediately be taken into custody and questioned. Then the torture would begin. She licked her lips as she approached.

"Huh? Where's my coffee?"

She lowered her eyes and shook her head. "I'm sorry. I only bought one for me."

Ivan grunted like he was offended. Another perverted smirk crossed his face, his eyes widening with the anticipation of what was to come. "I guess I'll have to enjoy something else then." He motioned to the conveyor belt to the X-ray machine. "Jacket, coffee, purse, and shoes on the belt."

Mila did as she was told. It was like that every day. She put her purse and coffee on the belt first. As she was taking off her shoes and removing her jacket, she noticed Ivan taking his sick pleasure in watching her disrobe. She had the wherewithal to fold the jacket so the brooch was covered, although she had no idea if that would do any good.

"Arms out," Ivan said. When she complied, he waved the wand around her arms, chest, back, and down her legs. Nothing beeped. Then he put the wand down. "Turn around."

Once her back was to him, Mila stiffened. She steeled herself as best she could, knowing what was coming next. She told herself to remain calm. It would all be over shortly.

Ivan came up from behind and leaned closer to her. He took a deep breath near her neck. "Oh, yeah," he whispered in her ear. "Someone smells like Connie's."

Mila licked her lips. She kept telling herself this was the last time she would ever have to endure this humiliation. The sicko Ivan ran his hands down her hips and cupped her buttocks, giving them a good squeeze, before making his way back up to her breasts and fondling them. The two other guards laughed, enjoying the show and knowing they would get their chance when "their" secretaries arrived.

The only thing that ended the groping was the elevator bell announcing its arrival on the floor. Ivan leaned closer, smelled her again, and smacked her on the butt.

"Bring me coffee next time!"

Mila let out a rush of breath, her heart pounding against the wall of her chest. She quickly turned and went through the magnetometer. She put on her jacket and shoes, straightened the brooch, and grabbed her purse and coffee. Then she headed to Volkov's secretarial suite down the hall from the President's office.

It was time to go to work.

"Good morning, Mila."

The greeting came from Ursula Antonova, Volkov's head secretary. At fifty years of age, she had been with Volkov for twenty years as he worked himself up the ladder of power. She had been hired for more than her secretarial skills back then, but, despite her age and graying hair, she had convinced Volkov that his office couldn't function without her, even if he wanted someone younger and prettier. So she stayed and acted as the sorority mother to the young women who Volkov handpicked to be his office maidens.

"Good morning, ma'am."

"Did Ivan the Ape get his morning feel in?" She looked at Mila over the top of her reading glasses, her eyes providing a moment of female bonding.

"Yes," Mila said, a resigned smile on her face. It was all they could do.

"The President is in early today," Ursula said before whispering. "He is in a bad mood."

"Thank you for the warning. What do I need to do first?"

"Get the coffee ready." Ursula looked at the clock on the wall. "He has a meeting in ten minutes. Put out some Danishes and croissants, too."

"Yes, ma'am. How many in the meeting?"

"Three. Minister Balakin and General Dernov will be joining the President this morning."

Hearing the men's names, Mila froze. The blood rushing through her brain made her feel faint. Volkov, Balakin, and Dernov—in the same place? She cleared her throat.

"All three of them will be in the office?"

"Yes. The President said it is a very important meeting. Now hurry along and get the cart ready."

Mila headed for the kitchenette, her legs shaking all the way. Her mind was working in overdrive. Andrew had told her that the three most important decision makers in Russia were Volkov, Balakin, and Dernov. They had to be stopped before they could unleash nuclear hell on earth. The plan called for her to go after Volkov. Nothing else was said. There was no Plan B or Plan C involving the others. It was just Volkov.

But now the situation had changed. Mila was presented with an opportunity that the CIA might not have imagined. Mila knew what she had to do. It would throw Russia into chaos, but it might just save the world. She made the decision.

She would take out all three of them.

CHAPTER 14

Moscow, Russia

The change in plans was actually a godsend for Mila. With the clock ticking, she was so focused on what she had to do that it pushed the nervousness to the back of her brain. She went to work getting water into the pot and putting the coffee into the filter. She had done it a thousand times before.

But this would be the first time it was to poison the leadership of the Russian military.

Once the coffee had brewed, she transferred it into a stainless-steel gooseneck coffee pot with the presidential seal stenciled on its belly. She rolled the cart over to the counter and placed the pot on it, along with a tray of blueberry croissants, lemon Danishes, serving plates, and cloth napkins. She positioned three coffee cups on their own saucer and then, as she always did, stacked three extra cups and saucers on the cart in case there were others in the meeting.

She looked at the empty cups—the receptacles of certain death for anyone who drank from them. Andrew didn't give her any specific instructions beyond "pour the liquid in the cup." She didn't know whether she should pour it into the cup first or after she had poured in the coffee. She stared at the cups, frozen, not knowing what to do.

The phone ringing in the outer office snapped her out of her trance. She quickly decided to put the coffee in first. She held the top of the pot, grabbed the handle, and tipped the gooseneck, filling each of the three cups well below the rim. Once she placed the pot on the cart, there was only one more thing to do.

She reached up and grabbed the brooch off her lapel, her stomach dropping at feeling the deadly dragonfly in her hand. Every ounce of her being shook.

She heard Ursula end the call. She needed to hurry.

After looking to her left and right, Mila turned the dragonfly upside down and unscrewed the tip of its tail. She had no idea how much liquid was inside, but Andrew told her a single drop of Novichok was deadly.

She turned the dragonfly over and watched a single drop of the clear liquid fall into a cup. She went to the next and then the next, a drop in each one. Figuring she got something in each cup, she poured generously on the second round. As she did so, an eagle-eyed observer would have seen the dragonfly's dark blue wings turn a lighter shade as the poison drained from its framework of veins.

Once the liquid stopped flowing, she screwed the tail back on.

"Morning, Mila."

Mila jumped at hearing the voice. She spun around to find Anna, her best friend in the office. "Oh, Anna, you scared me." She put her hand to her throbbing chest, her face the color of an apple. "I didn't hear you."

"I'm sorry, Mila, I thought you heard me." She cocked her head to the right. "Are you okay? Your face is all red."

Mila shook her head, trying to catch her breath. "No, I'm fine. I was a little frazzled by Ivan this morning. And then I had to rush to get the coffee ready. I'm a little behind."

Anna eyed her and Mila saw the look, like her friend knew something wasn't right. Whether she thought Mila was lying or hiding something, Mila couldn't tell. But even the secretaries didn't fully trust one another.

"Mila, where's your brooch? I don't think I've ever seen you without one."

Mila's body seized. She felt like she had the breath sucked out of her lungs.

The brooch.

Her friend had zeroed in on the very object that would enable Mila to carry out her plot. It felt like the interrogation had begun. Anna would tell the authorities about Mila's strange behavior and missing brooch. The case was already building against her. She would surely die in prison now.

Mila struggled to find an excuse before finally holding up the dragonfly in her shaking hand. "It's a clip-on instead of a pin so I have to keep repositioning it. I shouldn't have bought something so cheap."

After getting a nod of belief from Anna, Mila clipped the brooch to her lapel. Wanting to take the focus off it, she quickly turned toward the cart and straightened the contents.

"I had better get in there before President Volkov bites my head off."

* * *

Behind the desk in his ornate office with its high ceilings and brilliant chandelier, President Volkov sat in the black leather chair that dwarfed him as his weight continued to decline. He seemed to get smaller and smaller each day.

He coughed roughly, each bout louder than the last and more painful on his dying lungs. He had brought a bottled water with him on the helicopter ride from his residence west of the city. His caddy full of pills awaited, and he washed them down one by one in hopes of keeping himself alive long enough to strike a deadly blow to the United States.

Nothing would make him feel better.

General Dernov and Minister Balakin entered the office doors at the same time, both men pausing their march toward the President's desk as Volkov suffered through another coughing fit. The two men winced at the sights and sounds, both thankful they weren't in Volkov's shoes. Once the hacking spell had ended and seeing them standing and staring at him, Volkov motioned them forward.

"Are you okay, Mr. President?" Balakin asked with the sincere concern of an old friend.

Volkov offered a mild grunt, clearly worn out by the episode. "Actually I'm getting used to it." He pointed to the chairs. "Sit. They will be bringing coffee shortly."

The two men situated themselves in front of Volkov's desk—Balakin on the left and Dernov on the right.

"How are we doing on the strike plans?" Volkov asked, getting down to business and focusing on Dernov.

"We're getting the pieces in place, sir. We need a little more time."

Volkov frowned. "We don't have more time, General." He paused before adding, "I don't have more time. We must increase the pace."

"I understand, Mr. President. I can assure you that we are moving as quickly as possible. But if you want the strike to be at maximum strength, we must get all the pieces in place before we launch."

"How much longer until the *Belgorod* gets into position?"

"By the end of next week."

Balakin made the calculation in his mind. Only nine days away. Nine days before Volkov's nuclear war would start.

Volkov turned his attention to his right. Balakin caught the look from the President, a look that reminded him that his future depended on him executing Volkov's orders.

"And Dmitri, are you ready?"

Balakin shifted in his chair, his right hand reflexively touching the pocket of his suit coat that contained his nuclear authentication card.

"We are getting ready, Mr. President. As General Dernov said, we need a few more days to get our subs and bombers in position. As you can imagine, it is an immense operation that takes time. But we will get there."

Volkov nodded, like he knew he couldn't get them to move any faster than they already were. "What else?"

"Sir, the Americans successfully tested their missile defense system yesterday," Balakin said. "One of their Navy destroyers intercepted the missile over the Pacific. They are making preparations to defend themselves."

Volkov waved off any concern. "I saw that. Don't believe everything you see, Dmitri. Next thing they'll say is their Star Wars laser system is functional. They are lying. They didn't do anything other than shoot a target out of the sky that they were expecting. It's like shooting a tin can off a post with a BB gun. It will be different when we surprise them with our hypersonic missiles."

The discussion ended and he moved on. "What about New York?"

With its two-day meeting at the end of the week, the United Nations was set to play host to the member countries of the Security Council. The President of the Security Council had called the meeting in hopes of tamping down the rhetoric from Russia and lowering the volume on the war drums. Leonid Sokolov, as Russia's Foreign Minister, and Balakin, as its Defense Minister, were scheduled to attend and show everyone that Russia meant business. The eyes of the world would be focused on the Big Apple.

"New York is a go, sir," Balakin said. "I will see how scared the United States and its allies are."

Volkov nodded. He had other things in mind.

"Try to get the Americans to lower their guard. Make them think we're not going to attack. It will give us an advantage when we do."

"I can do that. Anything else?"

Volkov waved a finger at him. "Be on alert, Dmitri. You will be going into enemy territory. Don't say anything that will compromise our plans. The Americans are devious. They are always listening and trying to infiltrate our own. You know that as well as I do. Be careful who you talk to." He lowered his head and raised his eyebrows. "And be careful who you sleep with."

Balakin gave a single nod in reply.

Volkov fell victim to another coughing fit, bracing himself with one hand on his desk as he shook in his chair. He reached for his bottled water but it was empty. When the coughing subsided, he yanked the phone out of the cradle and pounded the yellow button with his finger. When Ursula answered, he struggled to yell, "Where's the coffee!?"

CHAPTER 15

Moscow, Russia

Mila had a death grip on the bar to push the cart out of the kitchenette. The time had come. Everything was being rolled into position. Volkov, Balakin, and Dernov were all there. All she had to do was take the coffee into Volkov's office, hand a cup to each of the three men inside, and then leave. After that, she knew the next few hours would be unlike any she had ever experienced.

She would be on the way to America by that evening, and the men threatening to start nuclear war would be well on their way to certain death. How long that would take, she didn't know. But that wasn't her immediate concern. She just needed to get to the office.

She opened the door to the secretarial suite and pulled the cart through. She could barely believe it. It was going to happen. She took shallow breaths as the cart's wheels began to roll across the marble floor. She took her right hand off the push bar and wiped her sweaty palm on her skirt. She did the same with her left. It was only fifty steps to the door of Volkov's office. She noticed the coffee sloshing in the cups so she slowed her pace, trying to calm herself and not spill any over the rims.

"Hey!" the voice came from behind her. "Stop!"

Mila instantly froze. She knew the voice. It had terrorized her to no end. Instead of ignoring the man and heading directly to Volkov's door, she made the mistake of turning around.

Ivan the Ape was barreling in her direction. The two other guards were following close behind. The looks on the three men's faces made her tremble. *Did they see me in the kitchenette? Did they see me pour something out of my brooch? Had Anna ratted me out?*

Mila waited for Ivan to approach, waited for him to turn her around and roughly put the handcuffs on her and take her away to some dungeon where she would never taste freedom again.

He stopped and glared at her, his yellow-stained teeth providing an even more menacing smirk.

"Where's my coffee!?" he spat out.

The force of the verbal blow almost sent her tumbling backwards.

When she hesitated, she couldn't stop what happened next.

Ivan reached out his muscular hand, grabbed the cup from the saucer, and brought it to his lips.

"No! That is for the President!"

"Shut up," Ivan hissed. "You've got more cups, don't you?"

With her eyes filling with horror, she watched as Ivan gulped down the coffee like it was a cold cup of water on a hot day. His two comrades did the same. Mila could do nothing but watch as the three men drank down the poison that would soon kill them.

"This stuff is awful," Ivan said, making a face. "I don't know how he can drink this crap."

The others concurred, and Mila had to think fast to explain the unexpected taste. "This is the way he likes it now. I think the medicine has dulled his senses."

Ursula opened the suite door behind them and snapped, "Mila! Take the coffee to the office. Now!" Seeing what was happening, she added, "You three! Leave her alone! She has work to do!"

The three guards snapped to attention and stalked back to the checkpoint, their coffee cups still in their hands.

Mila turned around and looked at the cart. All she had was three empty cups and the pot of coffee. Her mission had failed. She would still have to leave Russia immediately. The guards would be hospitalized, and the investigation would point to her. What's worse, the world would be that much closer to nuclear war because she was a failure.

Or was she?

Her eye caught the dragonfly on her lapel. *Is there any left?* She turned to see the guards with their backs to her. Ursula had returned to her desk inside the suite. Mila hurried to put three new cups on the saucers and filled them with coffee.

With her back to the guards and knowing there were no security cameras looking down on her, she grabbed the brooch and unscrewed the dragonfly's tail. She turned it over one cup.

But nothing came out.

She did the next best thing. She dipped the dragonfly's tail in the coffee and hoped any residue inside would make its way to the cup. Whether it would be enough to take down Volkov, there was only one way to find out. Without screwing on the end, she put the brooch in her pocket and moved the cart forward toward Volkov's door.

Once inside, she saw the three men, their attention focused on her.

Before Volkov could yell at her, she stammered, "I'm sorry for being late, Mr. President."

Volkov grunted and waved her forward. She rolled the cart to a stop and eyed the cup that she had singled out for Volkov. She had to use both hands, both of which were trembling, causing the cup to rattle on the saucer and the coffee to ripple in the cup.

She set it down in front of Volkov. Then she walked around the desk and handed cups to Balakin and Dernov.

Positioning the tray of edibles near the desk, she returned her focus to Volkov. "Can I get you anything else, sir?"

Volkov said nothing, but his eyes zeroed in on her. Squinting, he gave her a look like he thought something was out of place. Did he notice she was trembling? Did he see the sweat beginning to slide down the side of her face? A former KGB agent would notice those tells in a heartbeat.

"Is everything all right?" Volkov asked.

Her knees shook. Volkov never asked her questions, never cared if she was okay. She felt like she was going to start crying and collapse in a heap. She struggled to say, "Yes, sir. I am sorry again for being late."

Volkov's eyes widened like he saw what was wrong. Mila saw the look. He had detected something. But what was it? *What is he going to do to me?*

He motioned for her to step closer and said, "Come here."

Mila gulped, her heart beating so hard it felt like it was going to explode. There was nowhere to run, nowhere to hide. She feared she would lose control of her bladder. The frightening thought of being hung by her wrists while sadistic thugs like Ivan the Ape whipped her mercilessly filled her mind. Fearing this was her last moment of freedom, she inched forward to the corner of the desk, waiting for him to grab her and call her a traitor.

She noticed his eyes looking at her chest.

"You're not wearing a brooch today."

Mila wondered if it would ever end. Had Russian security services discovered the plot? Had she been found out? Did Volkov know? She swallowed and pulled the dragonfly out of her pocket, dragging the open end of the tail on the inside of the pocket to dry any liquid that might have remained. She held it up and showed it to him.

"It broke, sir, and I'm having trouble keeping it attached to my jacket. I'll have to try and fix it later."

Volkov reached out his hand. "Let me see it."

Mila hesitated, her hand holding the brooch feeling like it weighed a thousand pounds. She felt like she was giving Volkov the gun or the knife that the assassin would have smuggled in to carry out the mission. She squeezed it hard to keep her hand from shaking and handed it to him with the open tail away from him.

Volkov fingered it, looking at the clasp and then running his thumb over the jewels. "Are they real?"

"No, sir. They are fake . . . but I like it."

He nodded and handed it back to her.

After clipping it to her lapel, she bowed slightly and said, "Enjoy your coffee, sir."

As he reached for the cup, Volkov dismissed her with a wave of the hand.

It was the last time they would ever see each other.

CHAPTER 16

Los Angeles, California

The Vine Street pizzeria sat a block and a half south of Hollywood Boulevard and a block north of Sunset Boulevard. By eight o'clock, the place would be packed with tourists, film students, and aspiring actors and actresses having a bite before they hit the clubs hoping to party with the celebrities. At five o'clock, though, the dinner crowd was light.

Duke Schiffer sat alone at a table for four in the corner of the pizzeria. His back was to the wall and he had a clear view out the front window as he kept his eyes on the cars passing by and the bank parking lot across Vine Street. He had been there for fifteen minutes, waiting and watching, thinking about his reason for being there and getting the lay of the land.

Ever since President Schumacher gave him the go ahead to start surveillance—"surveillance only" being his exact words—Schiffer went to work. Two days before, his first call was to the National Security Agency, where he nearly scared the wits out of his old friend Dustin, the hacker turned NSA tech expert, who thought, maybe even hoped, he would never hear from that "intimidating guy" named Schiffer ever again.

The first time they met, Schiffer was a little put off by the man—a twenty-something tech geek with a ponytail and timid nature. Hesitant to make eye contact, the guy acted like a frightened dog, afraid of being hit again and wanting to run away with his tail between his legs to cower in the corner. But Schiffer quickly came to appreciate Dustin's talents, and the young man had done great work for him when he needed to find the target Bonhoff in Switzerland and Monaco. Schiffer was so impressed he told him he might utilize his services in the future. "I need you to find somebody for me," Schiffer had told him. "I'm going to need her number or numbers and whatever else you can get on her."

"Okay."

"And I need it ASAP. This is a priority one matter."

"Yes, sir. What's the name?"

"Katia Balakina." Hearing nothing in response, Schiffer looked at the screen to see if the call had dropped. "Dustin, are you still there?"

"Yes, I'm still here. Did you say Katia Balakina?"

"Yeah. She's Russian. You need me to spell it?"

"Katia Balakina? The actress?"

"Yes. Have you heard of her?"

"Oh, yes!" Dustin gushed. In an instant, it was like the man took on a different personality. "I've seen all of her movies. She is a huge star. Very popular. My friends and I think she's one of the best actresses out there right now."

Schiffer grinned. *Dustin has friends?* He had envisioned Dustin living in his mother's basement, heavy into online gaming, and watching movies by himself late into the night. Hearing the guy going on about Katia and her acting, he thought he might have gotten at least part of it right. He wondered if Dustin had a poster of Katia on his bedroom wall.

"Yeah, I need info on her. Just like last time. I want to know where she is every minute of the day."

"So you're giving me authorization to surveil Katia Balakina?"

"Yes."

Still on his high, Dustin asked, "Can I ask why?"

"No," Schiffer snapped, probably a bit too harshly. He softened and said, "If I'm asking, Dustin, you know I can't tell you why."

"Yes, sir."

"And I want to be able to track her on my phone. Can you make that happen?"

"Yes, sir. I can do that."

"Good. You're the best."

Within twelve hours, Dustin had provided Schiffer with Katia's home address and the numbers to two of her cell phones. If she had them on her, the phones indicated she was in Los Angeles. Dustin was also able to give him access to one of her phones, and he spent half a day reading her emails and going through her calendar. Having everything he needed, Schiffer took a jet on loan from the CIA and headed to L.A., telling Alexandra he was going to see what type of plan he could come up with.

Besides having Dustin on call twenty-four-seven, the plan Schiffer had in mind included two other men. He needed them. He knew he could trust them, and he knew they were some of the best in the business. He had worked with them before, and with a snatch-and-grab operation a real possibility in this instance, he knew they had the experience to get the job done.

He didn't need to raise a hand when the two men entered the pizzeria. They had already spotted him from their vantage point in the bank parking lot.

"Evening," Duke said as Noah Wolfson and Ariel Segel sat to his left and right. Neither one of them sat across from him, instead positioning their chairs where they could keep an eye on the front window and door. Old habit in their line of work. "Glad you two could make it. This your first time in L.A.?"

Segel shook his head and answered for both of him. "No. We've been here before."

Not feeling the need to answer, Wolfson busied himself by scanning the place, memorizing faces, noting the two exits, and deciding who he'd shoot first if, for some reason, guns were drawn. Of course, there were other weapons within reach—the napkin dispenser, the candle jar, and the open chair at the table.

He had a long slim face with dark eyes that flashed with constant intensity. By his look, he was either hungry or ticked about something. Schiffer knew the man well enough that he thought it was the latter. The guy was always on. Had been since the day Schiffer first met him. It's why Wolfson was the best out there.

"I was wondering why you picked this place," said Segel before pointing out the front window. "Walking in, now I know why."

Schiffer looked outside. It was just a pizzeria he found near the target location for the evening. "I thought you guys liked pizza. We had it in Monaco."

"Oh, we do," Segel said, again pointing outside. "But the star of John Wayne on the sidewalk? 'The Duke' himself?"

"You know who John Wayne is?"

"Of course. He's a big star everywhere, even in Israel. We like old cowboy movies where the good guys win. I guess it was just a coincidence that you asked us here, huh . . . Duke?"

Schiffer shrugged, a sly grin on his face. "Yeah, a happy coincidence. I always liked his movies." He turned to Wolfson. "So, Wolf, you want to do some sightseeing later? I can take your picture with the Hollywood sign in the background."

Wolfson glared at him for a second before returning to scan for threats.

"Maybe I can help you find a nice California girl while you're out here."

Gritting his teeth, Wolfson said, "I don't need your help. I could pick up a half dozen women by the end of the block."

"Oh, I don't doubt that. Just be careful where you spend your money. You never know what you're going to get in this day and age. Could be a surprise when the clothes come off."

Wolfson let out a low growl like he was bored with the ribbing. The guy was definitely always on. He snatched a menu next to the napkin dispenser in front of him.

"You guys just get in?" Schiffer asked Segel.

"I got in yesterday from Seattle. Wolf came in this morning from Dallas. Probably overkill but we always take precautions when an operation is being planned." Segel grabbed a menu. "Will Alexandra be joining us?"

"No, she's back home helping the Vice President with another possible plan."

"Is she operational?"

"Hell no. I hope I put an end to that once and for all. It's too dangerous for her to get involved like that. But with the U.N. Security Council meeting in New York, the V.P. thought she could offer her expertise. I'm all for that. Whatever it takes to keep her out of harm's way."

The three men ordered—individual pizzas for each of them. Once the waiter brought their food and drinks, the focus of their meeting began.

Schiffer had told the two Israelis that there was a chance they could grab the daughter of the Russian Defense Minister and use her as a bargaining chip if the order to launch nukes was imminent. With the chance to stop World War III and save the world, the Israelis jumped at the chance to get in on it. They knew that if the United States was target number one, Israel wouldn't be far behind if the bombs started dropping.

Schiffer mentioned the President said the operation was only in its surveillance phase, but he wanted to be ready in case he got the green light. If that meant following Katia Balakina across L.A., the U.S., and Canada, he was prepared to do it.

Knowing Segel and Wolfson would do their own intelligence gathering, there was little need to send emails or texts back and forth on who the target was.

"Here's her most recent picture," Schiffer said, sliding his phone over to Wolfson and then to Segel.

Once Segel got a good look of the selfie Katia took in her Dodgers T-shirt, he said, "She's pretty good looking, isn't she?"

"Yeah," Schiffer said, taking back his phone. "But don't tell my wife I said that."

According to the tracking app on his phone, Schiffer said Katia was at her mansion in the Holmby Hills neighborhood of Los Angeles, a little more than seven miles from their current location. Schiffer had scouted the place earlier in the day and noted the tall trees, ficus hedges, and privacy bushes surrounding the grounds on each of the four sides save for the single vehicle entrance. He hoped Segel and Wolfson would take a look later to see what they thought.

Segel wiped his mouth with a napkin. "What kind of security does she have?"

"Unclear. That's why I invited you down here. She's supposed to be in the area within the next thirty minutes."

Wolfson's head snapped toward Schiffer. "She's coming here?"

"No, down the street a bit at what used to be known as Grauman's Chinese Theatre. One of her former co-stars is having his hand and footprints put in concrete. They make a big deal out of it, lots of press, and Katia is supposed to be there to celebrate with the guy. I thought it'd give us a chance to see her out in public. Find out what kind of people she has around her."

Once the meal ended, the waiter brought the bill and Schiffer paid. They lingered a little while longer until Schiffer's phone vibrated.

"The target's on the move. We better walk."

The three headed north on Vine, the palm trees swaying in the light breeze. Under clear skies, the Capitol Records building loomed up ahead. They turned left on Hollywood Boulevard and headed west, the sun still visible over the horizon but not for long.

The sidewalks were bustling. Wolfson, wearing a hat and sunglasses walked alone, as was his custom, on the southside. On the north side, Segel, also with a hat and sunglasses, kept three steps ahead of Schiffer, who went with his dark shades. Although there were plenty of people around, Schiffer wasn't worried about being remembered. Those walking paid no attention to the three men, too busy gazing at the stars on the Hollywood Walk of Fame at their feet.

Being the seedier part of town, the men passed the bars, strip clubs, and tattoo parlors. Schiffer looked across the street in time to see Wolfson eyeing the window of a psychic. The further west they went, the more touristy it became—the souvenir shops, the Hollywood Wax Museum, the Disney store, all of them offering a little more class to the area.

Eyeing the giant guitar sign on the side of the Hard Rock Café approaching, Schiffer knew they were getting close.

The foot traffic began to get heavier as the three neared Highland Avenue, and the cops had blocked off Hollywood Boulevard to the west with the exception of a single lane for VIPs. Spotlights shone their beams into the heavens, beckoning one and all to come to the old Grauman's Chinese Theatre for the main event of the evening—the concrete ceremony for legendary actor Michael Hawthorne.

Schiffer looked at his phone. According to his tracker, Katia was on the move and heading east on Sunset Boulevard. He figured she would have to pass the theatre, turn north, and then return west so she could make a big show on the red carpet that extended out to the street.

Look alive. It's showtime. Schiffer texted to Segel and Wolfson.

Wolfson hurried across the street and stood behind the two men. Acting like a tourist, Segel snapped a few pictures on his phone.

A black Lincoln Navigator, currently the preferred luxury ride of the rich and famous, crept past the police barricade and made its way west. The crowd buzzed, wondering who was inside. The vehicle stopped.

A lone male exited the front passenger seat. The muscular man nearly bulged out of his black suit. Bald head, thick neck, large hands, a radio earpiece.

A seemingly eager Wolfson leaned forward between Schiffer and Segel, his phone raised like everyone else in the crowd, and said loud enough for only the two men to hear, "Russian?"

Schiffer nodded. On the opposite side of their position, they could see a pair of black shoes drop down from the vehicle and walk around to the rear. He looked like the bodyguard's twin brother. Two Russians. Maybe another one behind the wheel. All of them employed by someone who could pay top dollar for bodyguards who knew what they were doing. These guys were not rent-a-bodyguard-for-the-night-to-look-famous types.

The Russian at the rear held his hands near his stomach, his fingers touching, ready to execute one of three moves—grab the protectee, pull his gun, or snap the neck of anyone who tried to attack. His eyes scanned the crowd, the bright lights shining back at him making it more difficult to see any threats. He radioed to his comrade.

The Russian at the rear passenger side door nodded. He looked left and then right, as if building the drama that his protectee was a prime target for something nefarious.

If he only knew, Schiffer thought.

The man opened the door, and the crowd breathlessly waited. Soon, the long, tanned legs of Katia Balakina appeared and she elegantly stepped out in her short red dress. She looked stunning and glamorous, a true Hollywood starlet. The crowd erupted in cheers, the camera flashes erupting and brightening Katia's face, her diamond earrings twinkling in the flashing lights. Taking her steps on the red carpet, she waved to her adoring fans.

Segel took a picture, not of Katia but of the Russian bodyguards that trailed two steps behind her. The bulge under the back of their suit coats at the beltline was a dead giveaway to a trained eye. The two Israelis and Schiffer both noticed them. Schiffer watched Katia's Navigator proceed slowly onward and then make a right at the next light.

An overexuberant female fan managed to scale the metal barriers holding back the crowd and dashed toward Katia, a phone in her hand and a selfie, no doubt, on her mind. The Russian bodyguard on the right spotted the woman and made a beeline to intercept her, strongarming the woman without manhandling her and keeping her at a safe distance. The bodyguard on the left took a step closer to Katia, his head on a swivel, but his calmness kept everyone's focus on Katia.

Schiffer was impressed. It was the work of trained security agents. Recognize the threat, which was nonexistent, and remove it without causing a scene. These guys were professionals. Formidable opponents if it came to violence.

Katia caught the attention of her man and said it was okay. The woman was brought over, a quick selfie full of smiles was taken, and Katia, appearing like a woman of the people, had a fan for life. Theatre security then ushered the woman away, while Katia and her guards proceeded to the theatre entrance.

The guest of honor was next to arrive, and Michael Hawthorne's appearance drew even louder applause. He walked the red carpet to the theatre where Katia was waiting to give him a hug.

With all of the attendees assembling, the crowd waited for the ceremony to begin. Schiffer wasn't one of them. He had seen all he needed. The target had two bodyguards, maybe three, who were most likely armed and not afraid to use their weapons in defense of their protectee. His quiet snatch-and-grab plan was going to take more thought. He needed time to think.

But the clock was ticking. He needed to come up with something fast.

He tapped Wolfson on the back and Segel on the arm.

"Let's go guys. We're done here. We need to get to her house."

CHAPTER 17

Los Angeles, California

Schiffer took the wheel of the Ford Explorer that the FBI's Los Angeles Field Office had provided him to use while he was in town. Segel sat in the front passenger seat and Wolfson sat in the back by himself. Schiffer turned left on La Brea and then made a right on Santa Monica Boulevard where the traffic was thick but moving.

"I'm going to send the pictures of the Russian bodyguards to Tel Aviv," Segel said, thumbing a message on his phone. "We'll see if we have anything on them. My guess is they're former Russian special ops. She could probably pay for that level of protection, but I'd bet her dad had some pull to make it happen."

"Yeah," Schiffer said. "Let's hope there aren't any more at the house."

The traffic lightened near the end of West Hollywood as the majority of vehicles headed for the Sunset Strip. Schiffer veered left on Santa Monica toward Beverly Hills. He made a right on Rodeo Drive and drove past the high-end shops on both sides of the street—Louis Vuitton, Giorgio Armani, Hermes, Vera Wang. It reminded the three men of their time in Monaco.

Schiffer looked in the rearview mirror. "Wolf, you want me to stop so you can pick something up? Maybe a nice twenty-thousand-dollar handbag for your lady friend?"

"No."

As they continued, Segel looked at the businesses, Ferragamo on one side and Rolex on the other. "I bet you ten bucks that Katia Balakina spends some time in these shops. With her distracted and with her guard down, it might be a place to get her."

Schiffer leaned forward toward the steering wheel and looked out the front windshield. "Lots of security cameras around. I'd be afraid of civilians getting caught in the crossfire if it comes to that. Maybe if we knew what store she was going to and could wait for her inside. Get her out the back door and into a vehicle."

"You have access to her phone?" Segel asked Schiffer.

"Yeah."

"Have you been looking at who's she calling or getting calls from?"

"She gets a lot of calls from a guy named Dumond. He's an actor. I think they're filming a movie together right now. He leaves messages wanting to hook up. It sounds like he's got a big-time crush on her and wants to get her in the sack. She usually only responds with a text. There's another guy that calls. Name's Sam Rothstein. He's the head of one of the top movie studios. He's obviously important enough that she takes his calls or returns them quickly."

"She sleeping with him?" Segel asked.

"It's unclear. But what is clear is that there's a big difference between Dumond and Rothstein."

"How much of a difference?"

"About five-hundred-million dollars."

"That'll do it."

"He's invited her out to his place in Palm Springs. We might have to take a road trip if she takes him up on it. There would be a lot less people around to have to worry about."

"What about her dad?"

"If she talks to him, it's not on the phone I've been listening to. She has a second phone, but my guy at the NSA hasn't been able to crack it. He's working on it."

Schiffer followed Rodeo Drive until it ended at Sunset Boulevard, which took them into the Holmby Hills neighborhood. As they rounded the bend on Sunset, he pointed to the tree line out the right-side window.

"This is it."

Wolfson scooted over to the right side to get a good look. With no sidewalk along the street, the grass berm above the curb rose until it met a forest of thick shrubs and trees. Whether the foliage covered a fence was unknown because of the thickness of the greenery.

"The tree line would provide some cover in the dark," Wolfson said. "Might need to do some landscape removal to get in, though."

With no traffic behind, Schiffer took it slow and made a right at the next street. The trees continued, but a few gaps revealed a six-foot-tall brick wall.

Segel pointed above it. "It's hard to tell, but I think there are bars that extend above the wall. I can't see how high it goes."

Schiffer acted like the local real estate agent. "Beyond the trees, we have an eighteen-thousand square foot estate in the French-chateau style. Seven bedrooms, a dozen baths, pool and guest house, all on one-and-a-quarter acres. She's renting it now, but the last time it was up for sale it went for twenty-three million."

With the stop sign approaching, Schiffer slowed to a crawl in front of the mansion's only vehicle entrance. The iron gates were closed shut. Along with the expected signs from the home security company planted in the dirt, two more were affixed to the stone pillars framing the gates. One read: *No Trespassing. This property is protected by video surveillance. Trespassers will be prosecuted.* The other: *Warning: Attack Dogs on the Premises. No Trespassing.*

"Dogs," Schiffer said. "Plural."

"Yeah," Segel said. "Could be a ruse, though. Only one way to find out."

Schiffer turned right at the intersection, and the north side of the property had a similar tree line. But as the road descended down the hill, the high shrubbery ended and showed a wall topped with three-foot-high stone pillars.

"We might be able to rope our way over that wall," Segel said. "It would be easier than the south side but without the cover."

Schiffer slowed at the neighbor's driveway on the backside of the mansion. A car could pull fully into the drive before it had to stop at the gate.

"Right here's a good spot," Schiffer said pointing to the right of the driveway. "You run up the drive, up the neighbor's hill, and you'll have easier access to get over the wall. All under the cover of the trees."

With darkness having descended over southern California, the three men all agreed it was a good time to take a walk around the property. On-foot reconnaissance was always better than trying to imagine the terrain by looking at pictures or videos or making a quick drive-by.

Schiffer backed out of the drive and, seeing other cars parked along the street, he pulled to a stop at the curb. He checked his tracker app.

"Her phone's still at the theatre. It might not be for long, though, so let's make it quick."

The three men exited, pausing at the vehicle to scan and listen. There was no traffic on the street, although they could faintly hear through the trees a steady flow of cars on Sunset Boulevard. With the warm evening, it wouldn't be out of the ordinary to see a jogger pass by, but they saw and heard no one.

With the tall trees and heavy shrubs covering the high walls surrounding the homes in the neighborhood, there was little chance any of the residents could see them snooping around. The security cameras were mainly focused on the entrance points, but security sensors lining the property were a concern.

"All clear," Schiffer said, pointing to the house of Katia's next-door neighbor. "Let's go."

Schiffer took the lead. He didn't waste any time lingering in the driveway, hustling up the path, hopping up the three-foot-high wall, and then scrambling up the small hill leading to the back wall of Katia's property line.

Shrouded by the neighbor's shrubs and trees, Schiffer moved left to allow Segel and Wolfson to take cover. Now able to see into Katia's backyard, the rear of the house was lit up with lights, which filtered their way through the foliage giving Schiffer the ability to see the two men with him.

He made eye contact with Segel and pointed at the wire that ran across the top of the wall. "Probably a pressure monitor to set off the alarm," he whispered.

Wolfson leaned over the wall without touching the wire. He used a red penlight to scan the bushes. The light stopped when he saw something.

"Alarm sensors," he said.

Taking stock of what they had learned so far, Segel leaned toward Schiffer. "We're going to need night vision. And it would probably be best if you can get your tech guys to switch off the security system and the lights. It would make things a lot easier."

"Yeah. I'll add it to the list. My guy at the NSA can probably hack into the power company and cut the electricity if we give him enough heads-up. Let's move down and see if we can get a better vantage point. Keep your hands off the top of the wall."

Schiffer took two steps and winced when his boot snapped a twig on the ground. He continued on, ducking under the bushes until he found a spot where the shrubs opened and revealed a clear view of Katia's backyard.

Segel and Wolfson soon joined him. All three of them eyed the mansion, stylishly lit up even with no one home. The small pool house sat in front of the wall. Beyond that, the water in the rectangular pool sparkled with night lights as it drew one's eyes toward the mansion. An impressive spread. An oasis in the sprawling metropolis of L.A.

"Trees on both sides," Segel said softly, pointing to the area beyond the pool deck area. "Might provide a good run up to the house."

Once beyond the pool, a stone walkway led to the stairs leading to the main rear door of the mansion.

Wolfson gestured to the second floor of the mansion. The right quarter of the place had an upper deck area off the master bedroom. "Those are good firing positions up there and to the left. If someone was up there and paying attention, we could be sitting ducks on approach."

"I agree," Schiffer said. "We might need someone to hang back for overwatch."

"You got a layout of the interior?" Segel whispered.

"Yeah," Schiffer said. "It's all online. But I'll see if I can get anything more detailed."

Schiffer's phone vibrated in his pocket. He fished it out and then looked at the screen.

"Look alive, guys. She's on her way back."

The three men crouched in silence, using the time waiting for Katia to listen and think. Each of them envisioned running up one of the tree lines beside the pool, taking the steps two at a time, and then entering the back door. All of their thoughts ended with Katia being taken.

Segel reached out to Schiffer, a touch that indicated he was going to try something. He looked out over the backyard and whistled like he was calling a dog. They listened, waiting for the appearance of the snarling dogs patrolling the grounds. Unless Cujo and his buddies were locked up in the house, the men saw and heard nothing. Not even from the neighbor's yard.

"That's a good sign," Segel whispered.

Schiffer checked his phone again. "Turning in now."

The three men heard a faint noise coming from the west side of the house, opposite their position. With all the lights already on, it was difficult to see where Katia and her guards entered. Then they saw movement. On the second floor, they could see a figure walking in front of the windows from the left to the right. It was Katia—still in her short red dress and still looking glamorous, even from their distant vantage point. She stopped in the master bedroom, grabbed a remote off the dresser, and pointed it at the window. On command, the drapes slowly came together to block the view.

Schiffer pointed to the rear door, where the three Russian bodyguards had congregated. While still on duty, they were out of the public eye, so they all lit up cigarettes, the orange glow from their drags visible to the men hiding in the trees. With the west wind off the Pacific, Schiffer could smell the tobacco. Still no sign of any dogs.

"I think we've done all we can, guys," Schiffer whispered to the men on his right. "Let's get out of here."

After finding their way back through the bushes and trees, they got in their vehicle and headed back east to the Israelis' car on Vine Street.

"What are we going to do with the bodyguards?" Wolfson asked from the back seat.

Schiffer took a breath and then exhaled, his mind thinking. He didn't like the idea of killing the guards. Sure they were Russian and were probably prepared to join Volkov's war. But a part of Schiffer couldn't help but think that the guys were just doing a job with the talents they were given. He respected that. Maybe Segel's intel would change his mind.

"I'll have to think about it some more."

"What do you think of the plan in general?" Segel asked.

"It's doable," Schiffer said, thinking about the grounds one more time. It was plenty doable. Grab the girl, get her to a secure location, and don't let her leave until her dad puts a stop to Volkov's madness. Easy—as long as everything went as planned.

"I'll let the President know."

CHAPTER 18

The Midwestern White House – Silver Creek, Indiana

  Nearing noon, the President sat alone on the covered back deck of his family home looking west. Down the steep hill, the Wabash River flowed gently by, a solitary piece of driftwood slowly making its way south toward Terre Haute. The evidence of a late summer drought showed itself on the opposite bank, the foliage having changed colors where the water line used to be.

  Across the way through the thick stand of maple and sycamore trees, he could make out a field full of corn reaching high toward the sun. Three years prior, the President and the First Lady had bought the property across the Wabash, in part to keep the Secret Service happy so the agents could fence it off, patrol the grounds, and prevent any assassins across the river from taking a shot at the President in his current position. It was either that or be forced to look at the bullet-resistant glass panels the Secret Service said it would have to install on the deck. It all allowed the President to sit out back, enjoy the view, and think in peace and quiet.

  And that's what he needed right then—time to think.

  The President had not received word from Director Parker on the success of the plot against Volkov. Parker said Novichok poisoning could take a day or two to show its effects, depending on the amount of exposure. He didn't give specifics on the operation but said he would call as soon as he heard anything from his people on the ground.

  The First Lady was in the kitchen, helping to set up lunch for the President. Their oldest daughter Ashley and her two twin daughters—Emma and Sarah—were set to join them.

  The President took a drink from his can of Diet Coke. He heard a woodpecker in the distance, its distinctive rat-tat-tat echoing through the trees. He wondered if this was what retirement would be like. His watching of a hawk in flight was interrupted by the secure phone ringing on the side table next to him.

  Back to work, he thought. He picked up the receiver. "Yes."

  "Mr. President, Prime Minister Martin is now on the line."

  "Thank you," the President said. He had been waiting for Philip

Martin, Prime Minister of Great Britain, to call. He checked his watch to judge the time difference and then pushed the blinking button on the phone.

"Mr. Prime Minister, this is Anthony Schumacher, how are you?"

"I am well, Mr. President. It's always good to talk to you. Where are you currently?"

"I am at my home on the banks of the Wabash in Silver Creek, Indiana. I thought I needed to get out of D.C. and get some fresh Midwestern air. It always helps me recharge the batteries."

"I understand, Mr. President. The Scottish Highlands are my go-to place for rest and relaxation when I need to get out of London. It helps."

"I appreciate you taking the time to call. With everything that's been going on in the world, I thought we should talk."

"Absolutely."

The President and Prime Minister discussed various hotspots around the globe, including China, Iran, and North Korea. There were concerns with all of them, but both leaders felt they had a strong united coalition that could hold back any aggressive moves. But there was one other foe that the President really wanted to talk about.

"Russia," the President said, moving on. "President Volkov has been yanking our chain recently. We had a bit of an issue with Russian bombers invading our airspace the other night. We were a couple seconds away from shooting them down."

"I saw that, Mr. President. A bold move on Volkov's part. Reckless, too."

"I agree. I almost couldn't believe it."

"Are you as concerned with Volkov's stability as we are?"

The President watched as a cardinal landed on a feeder in the backyard. He reminded himself he needed to choose his words carefully. The United States had not told its closest ally that it had initiated multiple plots against Russia's nuclear decision makers, including an attempt on Volkov's life. He didn't like keeping secrets from the Brits, especially if allied force was needed if the plans turned sour. Still, there were some things best left unsaid for the time being.

"Extremely concerned. I have had multiple intelligence reports tell me that Volkov is on his last legs and wants to strike a decisive blow against the United States before he dies. I'm not sure I've seen my intel guys so worried, so I think there is a lot of truth to those reports."

"We have heard similar rumblings, Mr. President. I think Volkov is unstable and he's willing to risk his country's future to be the one who destroys the United States. It is so worrisome that I have had some plans drawn up for a preemptive strike . . . just in case we hear he has put London in his crosshairs."

The statement made the President smile. At least he and the Prime Minister were on the same page. "We have done the same. I can tell you that we are getting all our pieces arranged so that if it comes down to it, we can act quickly and decisively."

"That's reassuring to hear."

The President gave a hint of what might be ahead. "All options are on the table."

"Good," Martin said. "That's reassuring to hear on our end."

"I've sent Vice President Stubblefield and Secretary Arnold to New York City for the U.N. meeting. I'm hopeful something positive will come of it."

"The Foreign Secretary is on his way, too. I'll be sure to tell him to get in touch with your delegation before the meeting starts." He paused and then said, "I hope I can speak frankly, Mr. President."

"Of course."

"I know you have a lot of important decisions to make, as do I. But I hope you will not hesitate to make the decision—one that might end up saving the Western world. I know you don't want to do something drastic, but it might take a drastic decision to keep Volkov from doing something that will take decades to recover from, if recovery is even achievable."

"Understood." The President did understand. The Prime Minister was telling him that it was the President's responsibility to make the toughest decision he would ever have to make—launch nuclear weapons in a preemptive strike. Not wanting to divulge the current plot, but wanting to keep the Prime Minister on alert, the President said, "It might come sooner rather than later, and I just wanted you to be aware so that you can prepare and be ready."

Prime Minister Martin considered the statement before saying, "I read you loud and clear, Mr. President. Thank you for letting me know. And please know that Great Britain will be at America's side in full support."

"Thank you. That means a lot. I'll keep you updated on any new developments."

The call ended, but not before the two men agreed to meet soon. Once the President returned the receiver to the cradle, he felt better about the situation. The Prime Minister knew him well enough to realize something might be afoot and the Brits should be on their guard in case a response was needed. The President also knew the Prime Minister would relay the warning to the Canadians and the Australians. They would all be ready, which put his mind slightly at ease.

Not completely though. Because he knew the current plan might not work. If it didn't and Volkov remained in power, he could be emboldened to the point of wanting to exact maximum revenge—complete annihilation of the United States. And he might be able to get China, Iran, and North Korea to join him in his final mission of ultimate destruction.

"Grandpa!"

The shriek from the two girls rushing out the back sliding door shook the President from his thoughts. His granddaughters had arrived. He rose from his chair and swooped them into his arms.

"Oh, it is so good to see you."

He took them to the porch swing and sat one on each side of him. As they swayed back and forth, he listened to them babble on and on—something about bubbles and puppies. His mind went back and forth between the evils of Russia and the sweet innocence of the two girls, both of whom were oblivious to the dangers of the real world.

The thought of something happening to them or the country they called home struck him with fear. The sense of relief felt after the Prime Minister's phone call vanished. What if the Russians attacked the United States with nuclear weapons? Where would the girls be? Would they be safe? What would their future look like?

But what if something other than a nuclear blast happened? The President had multiple plans at his disposal regarding the Russian nuclear trio. One of them was Duke Schiffer's idea to kidnap Dmitri Balakin's daughter. With his granddaughters next to him, his stomach dropped at the thought of giving the green light for such an operation. What if the Russians tried to kidnap Ashley and the girls? The thought shook him to his core.

"Lunch is ready," Ashley said, stepping onto the back deck.

The President stood and suggested the girls go help their grandma in the kitchen. With just father and daughter on the deck, he motioned for Ashley to come closer for a private moment.

"You look tired," she said before he could speak.

The President blinked a couple times and nodded. "There have been a lot of things keeping me up at night lately."

"I can imagine. Mom told me all about the other night with the Russians."

He nodded and then lowered his voice. "Speaking of that, I need to tell you something. With everything that's going on in the world, I want you to be extra careful. I'm going to tell your brother and sister the same thing. Be careful out there."

"We are. We take precautions. It's been drilled into us for a while now."

"Well, that's good. But don't let your guard down. And if the Secret Service says it's time to go, you go. Do what they tell you. It's their job to keep you, and Stephen, and the girls safe."

Ashley reached out and touched her dad's arm. "Is everything okay?

You make it sound like something's going on that I should be worried about."

"There's nothing specific right now," the President said, giving her a hug. "I just want you and the girls to be safe. Be careful and be on alert."

Air Force Two
"I'm glad you could come along, Alexandra," Vice President Stubblefield said.

Alexandra Julian had walked into the Vice President's office aboard Air Force Two once the jumbo jet took off on its way to New York City for the U.N. Security Council meeting. She took a seat across from his desk.

While the Vice President was not planning on playing a public role—Secretary of State Mike Arnold and U.N. Ambassador Ben Lawton would be the main players—the President wanted the big man in the background to talk to allies and get a sense of their support for preemptive strikes. Stubblefield said he would do it, and he brought Alexandra along to assist.

"I appreciate the opportunity," she said.

As Alexandra sat back in her tan leather chair, she appreciated the chance more than Stubblefield knew. With her husband in California conducting surveillance on Katia Balakina, Alexandra was on her own. He wouldn't be hovering over her and telling her what she could and couldn't do because something was too dangerous.

She knew she could handle herself, and she was ready. The last few years had given her more experience than most—the abduction and rescue in Egypt, the operation against Bonhoff in Monaco, and the nuclear scare on the Amtrak train. And the last few weeks had seen her undergo a crash course in surveillance, evasion, espionage, and spy craft. She could do it. She knew she was ready.

And now it was time to put what she had learned into practice. The United States was counting on her. That's what she kept telling herself. Plus, if she had to endure any more training it might cause her to lose the ability to act normally—and that would be a dead giveaway that she was up to something. No, she had what it took and it was time to get in the game.

A smile crossed her lips. All she needed was to figure out a way to help.

"You know, Alexandra, Duke told me I'm supposed to keep an eye on you," Stubblefield said.

Alexandra's smile vanished. She glared at him, her nostrils slightly flaring. "He said what?"

"He said I'm supposed to make sure you don't do anything crazy. It's a dangerous world out there and he doesn't want you getting involved in anything that might get you in trouble. He was pretty adamant about it. Made me promise him."

She crossed her arms across her chest. "I can take care of myself, Mr. Vice President."

"Hey, I don't doubt that. I even told him you might be useful out in the field." He nodded like it was true. "I told him you're smart and quick on your feet. Your talents could be of value to the country."

"That's what I keep telling him!" she snapped. "I want to be more involved. I want to be of service. But all he wants me to do is stay at home and bake cookies."

"Oh, I don't think he wants that." He leaned back in his chair, the fingers on his right hand tapping the desk. "Try to cut him some slack, Alexandra. The guy's seen the worst the human race has to offer. He knows what the bad guys are capable of."

"I know a thing about that too, Mr. Vice President. I've seen it firsthand."

"I know. He's just worried about your safety. Worried about your future family. He only wants what's best for you two."

"He wants what's best for *him*."

"Some might say he wants what's best for the country."

Alexandra squirmed in her seat, not happy that he was siding with her husband. Having enough, she stood and started pacing the office as the jet cruised at thirty-eight-thousand feet. She stopped and pointed a finger at Stubblefield. "I don't need my husband holding my hand every minute of the day. I'm a grown woman."

"Easy now," the Vice President said, holding up his hands like he was preparing to fend off an attack. "I'm only telling you what he told me. He means well, Alexandra. He's an alpha male who wants to protect those around him. That's not a bad trait for a husband to have."

Alexandra rolled her eyes. *Men. They're all alike.* She returned to pacing, in part to keep from saying something out of line. As she got her breathing under control, her mind started replaying what Stubblefield had said. There was something hidden in the Vice President's words. Something about the way he said it. He told her he thought she had talent and that she could be of service to the country. He said she was smart and quick on her feet. She appreciated the compliments. Finally, someone saw something in her, she thought.

Then it hit her. The big man wasn't telling her to drop any thoughts of conducting an operation to help thwart a Russian attack. Far from it. He was egging her on. If he wanted to keep her safe, he wouldn't have invited her along for the trip. He would have granted her husband's wish and kept her safe and sound at home. But he didn't do that, and he didn't say it either. All he was doing was telling her what Duke told him. That way he could tell Duke that he tried to keep her out of harm's way but she was so stubborn she wouldn't listen.

She turned to him and she noticed him looking at her. There was a twinkle in his eye before he winked. "Just be careful, okay?"

The smile was back. *He's going to let me do it!* "Yes, sir. I will."

There was a knock on the door, and Secretary Arnold looked in. CIA Director Parker stood behind him. "Is now a good time?" he asked the Vice President.

"Yes, come on in, guys. Let's all make sure we're on the same page."

Arnold, Parker, and Alexandra took seats surrounding the Vice President's desk. The focus of New York City was centered on Dmitri Balakin. The Russian Defense Minister was scheduled to attend, and it was rumored he was going to speak to the General Assembly on behalf of President Volkov. The world waited breathlessly to see if Russia would tamp down its rhetoric or escalate the tensions with the United States.

"What are you hearing?" Stubblefield asked Arnold.

"Balakin is supposed to stay two nights in New York City. There are suites booked at the Plaza and the Ritz-Carlton. We're not sure which one he will stay at. I would imagine Foreign Minister Sokolov will stay at the other hotel. It could be a last-minute decision based on what the Russian security team wants. It is always possible that he could stay at the Russian Embassy as well."

"I'd really like to talk to that guy," Stubblefield said. He leaned back and put his hands behind his head, the move opening his suit coat and exposing his holstered pistol. "If I could get a few minutes with him, I might be able to help him see the light that Russia doesn't want to enter a war it won't win. If I could play to his desire to become President of Russia, it might lower the volume of the rhetoric. Maybe you can use your backchannels to see if that can be arranged."

"I'll see what I can do," Arnold said. "I'm sure the French will help get the word to him."

"It could be at the U.N. or a secret location. Whatever he wants."

"I could help," Alexandra told the Secretary. She tried not to sound too eager, but the wheels were already spinning in her mind. "If you need anything."

Arnold nodded. "I'll keep that in mind."

Stubblefield eyed Alexandra before setting his focus on Director Parker. "Bill, a while back you told me and the President that Balakin likes his women. Is that something that we can look at? Something that can be exploited?"

"It's always a possibility, Mr. Vice President. Things like that don't go away just because there are other things going on. Some men will make time."

"What are the odds that Balakin would even take the time to be with a woman?"

"A guy like that, with all his power, he will figure out a way to make it happen. He's not going to pass on that opportunity. Even with everything going on, he'll think he'd better satisfy his desires while he can."

Alexandra caught a quick glance from Stubblefield before he looked away and nodded at Parker's thoughts.

As the meeting ended, Arnold, Parker, and Alexandra all stood and began to walk out. Alexandra knew it was time to take the initiative.

With Arnold in the lead, she tapped him on the arm when they got to the door and said, "Mr. Secretary, do you have a minute?"

"Sure." He stopped in the passageway and waited for Alexandra to shut the door to Stubblefield's office. "What's up?"

"I need a favor."

"A favor? What kind of favor?"

When Alexandra told him what she needed, Secretary Arnold said, "That's it? That's all you need?"

"Yes."

"I can do that. No problem." Before leaving, Arnold stopped and said, "Is there a reason why you're asking me? Just curious, but the Vice President or CIA Director could make it happen, too. Why me?"

"No, there's no reason," Alexandra said, shaking her head. She was surprised how easy the lie came to her. "I just thought you would have the best contacts in the embassies to make it happen without much effort." The last thing she wanted was to let the VP know what she was doing. It would inevitably get back to her husband and he would read her the riot act. It was much easier to butter up the Secretary of State.

Arnold smiled. A smile that showed Alexandra he bought her reasoning.

"I'll get right on it."

CHAPTER 19

Borough of Manhattan, New York City
"She's so beautiful."

The dark-haired woman who made the statement had her head near Dmitri Balakin's shoulder, her red-painted fingernails tracing a path down his bare chest. The TV was on at the end of the bed, and images of Katia Balakina had just flashed across the screen. One of the nightly entertainment shows had run a clip of her on the set of *Maximum Payback*, fighting off bad guys and looking sexy while doing it. The action shot cut to her recent outing at Grauman's Chinese Theatre, camera flashes lighting up her tanned face as she strode the red carpet in her body-hugging red dress, and the host mentioning that Katia was one of Hollywood's hottest stars.

"I hear that a lot," Balakin said to the woman. He ran his left hand down her naked hip, caressing her skin like it was the only care in his world.

Balakin had arrived in New York City earlier that evening. The news cameras were everywhere, all of the reporters breathlessly reporting on the arrival of the Russian delegation. There was talk of war, serious talk, and the red ribbons across the bottom of the screens running with breaking-news alerts wondered if Russia would escalate or the U.S. would capitulate. Still pictures of Volkov and Schumacher were interspersed with video of Russian and U.S. leaders making their way off the planes and in front of the microphones.

With the U.N. Security Council meeting designated a national special security event, the air in Manhattan was thick with tension, the constant sound of sirens and police choppers adding to the worry. And with many world leaders on the ground and more arriving every hour, traffic was a nightmare. Heavily armed agents and officers from the NYPD, the Secret Service, the Diplomatic Security Service, Homeland Security, the FBI, the Coast Guard, and a half dozen other agencies visually scanned anything that moved and checked anything that didn't.

From two-thousand feet, helicopters crisscrossed the airspace over Manhattan looking for suspicious vehicles and radiation signatures. Security checkpoints went up near the United Nations on the east side, and bomb-sniffing dogs were working overtime. Access to the Holland and Lincoln

Tunnels was severely restricted, and the locals knew better than to venture anywhere near the area if they wanted to get somewhere in a hurry.

After meeting with the Russian delegation at the Consulate General of Russia on 91st Street, Balakin had dinner with the Russian Ambassador and the Foreign Minister. His security entourage then took him to his suite at the Ritz-Carlton, where he enjoyed a bottle of scotch and the company of Eva, a Russian prostitute who was known to provide her services only to Russian oligarchs and political leaders who were in the Big Apple.

Balakin had been with her before, and he specifically asked for her again. There was a time for experimenting with different women, but not then. Not that night. He needed a clear head for tomorrow, and sharing a bed with Eva gave him the familiarity he needed to focus on the task at hand.

"She gets her looks from you," Eva said.

Balakin chuckled, his body shaking with the laugh. "She gets her looks from her *mother*," he corrected.

As she looked in his eyes, Eva ran a finger down the side of his cheek. "What did she get from you?"

"The ability to make people think she's someone she's not when the cameras are on."

"So you are good at acting?"

"No," he said, giving her a wink. "I'm good at lying."

When the entertainment show ended, Balakin grabbed the remote and pointed it at the TV. He thumbed through the channels until he came to CNN. For the next half hour, a parade of guests offered their expertise on the current U.S./Russian situation and pontificated on what President Schumacher should do to ease the tension.

With his polished white smile and giant ego, General T.D. Graham, who had been the vice-presidential candidate for President Schumacher's opponent in the last election and on the losing end of a historic landslide defeat, offered his two cents' worth, saying the President should bow to any of President Volkov's wishes, offer billions of dollars in aid, and promise to dismantle the U.S. nuclear weapons program, all in the hopes of averting war.

Rumors were swirling that General Graham was itching to take on the President in the next election, and thus he sought out any camera he could find to stay relevant in the minds of voters. The President's foes in the media were always willing to thrust a microphone in the General's face to let him spout off.

"He would be such a pushover," Balakin said to himself, dreaming of being President if the buffoon Graham occupied the Oval Office.

The secure phone installed by his security team rang on the nightstand. Balakin reached over and grabbed it. "Yes?"

"Dmitri," President Volkov said.

"Yes, Mr. President." Balakin gave a couple pats on the butt to Eva and motioned for her to give him some privacy.

"Is it safe to talk?"

Once Eva entered the bathroom and Balakin heard the shower come on, he said, "Yes, sir. It is safe. I am on a secure line."

"Are you alone?"

"Yes."

"What is the mood?"

"Tense, sir. You have scared the Americans. They fear you and what you might do. They are taking it very seriously."

"That is good." The President coughed and then grunted in pain. He coughed again to clear his throat. "I want you to do something tomorrow."

"Yes, sir. What is it?"

"I want you to tell the U.N., and make sure the Americans are aware of it, that I want two billion dollars in aid."

"Two billion dollars?"

"That's right. I just saw that idiot General Graham on TV saying President Schumacher should give us billions in aid."

"I saw that, too, Mr. President."

"He ought to be working for us, the fool."

"So you want me to tell them that you want two billion dollars? Two billion dollars in exchange for not starting World War Three?"

Volkov cleared his throat again. "Oh, I'm going to start the war, Dmitri. There's no doubt about that. I'm going to unleash everything Russia has in its arsenal against the United States. But before we go to war, we're going to take their money. Then we're going to lull them to sleep and strike when they're least expecting it. Plus, when we go to war, we're going to need money to keep the fight going. We're going to use their very own money to destroy them."

"Yes, sir."

"I want you to take a cut, Dmitri. Ten percent of what you get will be yours. If you can steal more from them, it will be more money for you." When Volkov heard nothing in response, he said, "How does that sound?"

Balakin had been lost in thought, the prospect of hundreds of millions of dollars filling his offshore accounts. Volkov had been robbing and looting from the Russian economy for half a decade, and the money had started to trickle down to Balakin. The balance had been steadily on the rise over the last several years. There was still a long way to go, but he knew that if he played his cards right, he could join Volkov as one of the richest men in the world. Not only would he be in charge of Russia, he could have anything he wanted. It was all within his grasp.

"I hope you're not having second thoughts, Dmitri," Volkov said, his tone ominous.

Balakin shook himself from his daydreams. "No, sir."

"It would be a shame for you to come this far and lose it all, my friend. I have given you much," Volkov said before pausing and saying, "but I can take it back. All of it. I can make your life a living hell."

The thoughts of grand estates, flashy cars, and private jets vanished. Those dreams were replaced by a vision of Balakin emaciated in a Siberian prison, penniless and hopeless, praying for a death that wouldn't come because Volkov wanted him to endure a long life of suffering for his disloyalty. It could happen.

"Of course, I don't want to do that. It's just one of the many options I have at my disposal. Are we on the same page, Dmitri?"

Balakin licked his lips. He had no other choice. If he wanted the money and the power, he had to follow Volkov's orders. It was the only way.

"Of course, Mr. President. I want what you want."

"And that includes the destruction of the United States?"

Balakin envisioned the city in which he was currently located being decimated by nuclear weapons, the island of Manhattan reduced to nothing more than twisted steel and smoldering remains. His mind thought of the Statue of Liberty lying face down in the toxic mud. He knew if he wanted his dreams to come true, he had to make sure he was on Volkov's side.

And if that meant doing whatever it took to ensure the destruction of the United States, he had no other choice but to go along with it.

"Dmitri, are you still there?"

Balakin made his decision. He was all in. "Yes, sir. I stand ready to execute your orders."

"That is what I wanted to hear, Dmitri. Get all the money you can out of our enemies tomorrow. Then get back to Moscow. We need to prepare for war."

The call went dead.

Balakin sat on the bed in silence, the phone in his hand. He could hear the water in the shower running, the thought of a naked Eva flashed through his mind. But it quickly left him. He needed to get his mind right. Volkov's threats struck him hard, his stomach beginning to ache at the thought of the decisions he would soon have to make. He knew he would have to do it. He knew he would have to go along with Volkov's commands. He had no other choice. Otherwise he'd be a dead man.

"Care to join me?" Eva asked. She had stepped out of the running shower, poked her head around the corner, and wrapped a wet naked leg around the wall, raising it up seductively, tantalizing Balakin with what else she had to offer.

Balakin caught the wink she gave him. He told himself he could do this. He could make the decisions he needed to make. When he did, the money and power would soon be his.

But there was one other thing he had to take care of first.

"I'll be right in," he said to her. "I just have to make one more phone call."

When Eva left and shut the door behind him, Balakin hung up the phone and grabbed his cell from the nightstand. He checked the time on the screen and made the calculations to Pacific Time. It was only eight in L.A. He hoped his daughter would take his call. He tapped the screen and hit the number for Katia. She answered on the third ring.

"Hello, Father."

"Hello, my darling. I'm glad I caught you. I hope you're not busy."

"No, it's a quiet night at home. I just saw you on TV getting off the plane in New York. Welcome to America."

Balakin grunted. What the country would look like in another week made him shudder. "Katia, I would like to get together. Can you make a quick trip to New York?"

"A quick trip? Father, I can't drop everything right now. I have to be on set tomorrow. We're back to filming in L.A. Can you come here?"

"No, that won't be possible. But it is very important that I see you." He lowered his voice, not wanting Eva or any listening devices to hear him. "Things are happening, Katia. They are happening very fast. It is important that you go back to Russia until things calm down."

"I cannot leave now, Father. I'm sorry, but I have so much going on. We don't have much filming left so maybe I can take some time in the next month to make a visit back home."

"Katia," Balakin said, his voice strained. "I cannot tell you how important it is that you return to Russia. It is not safe here in the United States."

The silence that followed told him she understood his concern and was thinking it over.

"Please, Katia. I don't want to see you harmed."

"I'm safe as long as you're here in the United States, Father."

"Katia, I won't be here more than a day or two. Don't be stubborn."

"It's my life, Father. This is what I want to do. If things change, I will come home when I can."

"Katia," he growled. "You are not understanding the seriousness of the situation. I would not joke around about such things. You must reconsider."

"I've made my decision, Father. Is that all you need from me tonight?"

Her tone hurt him—defiant and ignorant of his warnings. But there was nothing he could do about it that night. He would have to try again. "No, that is all. Please don't be mad, Katia. I love you very much and I only want you to be safe."

"I love you, too, Father. I will be fine. I'll talk to you soon."

CHAPTER 20

Borough of Manhattan, New York City

"Balakin was with a prostitute last night," Stubblefield said to Alexandra.

"Special White House Advisor" Alexandra Julian took a seat at the breakfast table in the Vice President's suite at the Marriott Marquis Hotel near Times Square about eight blocks west of United Nations Headquarters.

"Really? Wow."

The Vice President was halfway through his plate of scrambled eggs and hash browns, a toasted English muffin still to be eaten. He was fully dressed, minus his suit coat, and his ever-present Glock 19 pistol sat snugly in its leather shoulder holster.

Secretary of State Mike Arnold was on his way up for the last-minute get-together with the two before the high-level meetings early that afternoon.

"I guess he really can't help himself," Alexandra said. She set a fruit plate in front of her along with a glass of orange juice. "You'd think he might have other things on his mind. Must be an addiction."

"According to Bill Parker, the prostitute is well known for offering her services to Russian officials. We should have made a run at her to see if she'd be willing to flip on her countrymen."

Secretary Arnold arrived with briefcase in hand. He declined Stubblefield's offer of something to eat and took a seat at the table. The Vice President caught him up on the discussion.

"Yeah, I've heard he's that type," Arnold said of Balakin's desires. "It still might be something that can be exploited. If he's willing to risk it when the stakes are this high, we might be able to use it against him."

"Did we get anything else?" Alexandra asked. "Phone calls?"

Stubblefield finished a bite and then wiped his mouth with a napkin. "We haven't been able to get a tap on his phones. Unfortunately, the Russians are good with their phone security. We do know he made a call to his daughter."

"The actress?"

"Yes. The call went to L.A. and they spoke for about five minutes.

Like I said, though, we don't know what they talked about."

"The daughter might be something to bring up with him," Alexandra said, reaching for her glass of juice.

"I know Duke likes her. He's pretty high on her."

Alexandra stopped the glass from reaching her lips, her eyes looking at Stubblefield like he said something he shouldn't have.

He grinned, knowing the look. "I just mean he thinks she might be a way to get us out of this mess. That's all."

Alexandra frowned and set the glass back down.

"Have you heard from him today?" Stubblefield asked her.

"He's still in California conducting surveillance. He thought he might be following her to Palm Springs. He said he wanted me to tell you that he thinks he can grab her. He wants you to work on the President so he'll give the order. She only has three security guards."

Stubblefield rubbed his hands together and then pushed his plate away. "I'll pass it along to the President. Grabbing the daughter is the absolute last resort to him. He doesn't like the idea of using the kids as bargaining chips. I get it. I don't particularly like it either, but if it comes to it, we might not have any other choice. Let's see if we can make some progress today so we don't put him in that position."

"So what's the game plan?" Arnold asked the Vice President. "Beyond my prepared remarks to the Security Council, you still want me to take the lead?"

"I think that's best. I think it's important that you meet with Balakin and Sokolov in private. I know we've put some inquiries out there and they haven't responded yet, but I think it's important that we get them behind closed doors. That way you can feel them out without the prying eyes of the media watching over you. If you think you need me, call me in and I'll see what I can do."

"Call in the big guns if I need to," Parker said, smiling.

Stubblefield patted the pistol on his left side. "If it will help."

"What do you want me to do?" Alexandra asked the both of them.

Stubblefield looked at Parker before offering his suggestion. "I think she should be in on the meetings, Mike. It will be another set of eyes and ears on the situation."

Arnold nodded. "I agree." He then looked at Alexandra. "That okay with you?"

"Absolutely."

United Nations Headquarters, New York City

The sirens that echoed off the skyscrapers told the reporters at their fixed camera positions that another set of dignitaries was heading east on

46th Street to U.N. Headquarters next to the East River. A handful of protesters congregated on a far corner, well away from those set to attend the meeting, but loud enough that they could be heard above the din of sirens and choppers.

The U.S. Secret Service and the Diplomatic Security Service provided security for Stubblefield and Arnold, respectively, and their armored limousines and SUVs made their way to an underground parking garage. Stubblefield, Secretary Arnold, and the White House Special Advisor made their way into the building and their holding room.

The U.N. General Assembly includes representatives from over 190 countries. During the yearly meeting, leaders of every stripe—freedom lovers, communists, terrorist sympathizers, socialists, dictators and everything in between—fill the General Assembly Hall, dozens of languages being overheard by the trained ear.

But that day, only the fifteen member nations of the Security Council would be present. The five permanent member countries—the United States, the United Kingdom, Russia, China, and France—were joined by the ten non-permanent member countries that remain on the Council for two-year terms. The President of the Security Council rotates on a monthly basis between the member states, and, by the luck of the schedule, the French Ambassador to the U.N., Francois Bertrand, was currently in charge and the one who called the meeting.

With Stubblefield and Alexandra staying in the shadows, Secretary Arnold and U.S. Ambassador Lawton walked into the Security Council Chamber. Both of them noticed that the Russian delegation was speaking with the Chinese Ambassador—never a good sign when one communist was speaking with "former" communists. The pool photographer got his shots of the attendees before he was ushered out of the room.

The U.S. representatives, stone-faced and unsmiling, took their seats at the horseshoe-shaped table. The Chinese sat to their left in between the Russians, and Balakin and Foreign Minister Sokolov glared in the Americans' direction.

Bertrand opened the meeting. He welcomed all in peace and hoped that all would leave with peace in their hearts. He expressed concern with the rising tensions in the world, specifically mentioning the Russian bomber flights and the missile tests from Russia and North Korea. Those around the table had their eyes on the Russians, both of whom were shaking their heads in disgust, like neither thought they should be called on the carpet for anything their country did.

After three hours, it was clear that no progress was being made. The U.S., Britain, and France were all on the same page. None of them wanted war and were prepared to vote on a resolution condemning Russia's recent belligerent actions and calling on it to stand down. But, as each of the five permanent members of the Security Council has veto power over any resolution, the Russians and Chinese took a great deal of pleasure in shooting down any calls for peace. A frustrated Bertrand finally threw up his hands and called for a break.

Secretary Arnold saw the opportunity and made his way to the Russians. He reached a hand toward the Foreign Minister's arm to get his attention. "Maybe we should get together and speak privately. It might be more productive."

Sokolov and Balakin eyed the man suspiciously, both of them trying to figure out what Arnold was trying to accomplish.

"How about we meet in the conference room in ten minutes? The two of you along with me and a representative from the White House. We'll sit down and have a one-on-one discussion. Or two on two. Can't hurt."

Sokolov looked at Balakin, who nodded. "Fine," Sokolov said. "Ten minutes."

Arnold and Lawton hustled out of the chamber, and Arnold phoned the Vice President. "I got a meeting with Sokolov and Balakin in ten minutes. Send Alexandra to the conference room."

Alexandra arrived in five minutes.

"You ready?" Arnold asked.

"Yes. Anything I need to know?"

Arnold frowned. "No. Other than the fact that they don't look happy."

Eyeing herself in the large mirror on the wall, she swept the hair over her shoulders. Her blue skirt fell to her knees and hugged her curves, showing off her assets but not flaunting them, dignified but attractive. The matching three-inch heels would bring her close to Balakin's eye level.

When the Russian security team opened the doors to the conference room, they found two people—Arnold and Alexandra, both standing. After making sure all was clear, Sokolov and Balakin entered.

"Thank you for meeting with us, guys," Arnold said, greeting them. The handshakes were firm but awkward. Since the two Russians spoke English, there was no need for an interpreter and Arnold went straight into the introductions. "This is Alexandra Julian, Special Advisor to the White House here on behalf of the President."

Both men eyed her, Balakin holding the gaze longer than Sokolov. They were gentlemen enough to shake her hand.

Although the conference room had a table that could seat twenty, Arnold ushered everyone over to the four chairs spaced around a coffee table at the back of the room. Much more intimate. Arnold focused his attention on his diplomatic counterpart, Sokolov.

"I'm glad we were able to meet, Leonid. I hope we can come to an understanding. It goes without saying that President Schumacher was none too pleased with President Volkov and your bomber flights the other night. It was reckless and dangerous for both countries."

Sokolov, stodgy and rigid in his ways, acted like it was nothing. "President Volkov is his own man. He does what he wants. He has his own agenda."

"And what is that agenda?"

Sokolov did not hesitate. "To return Russia to its former glory as the world's greatest and most-feared superpower. I have no doubt he will succeed in his quest."

"How is his health? We have heard he is ill."

"His health is fine," he said, lying with ease. "Any suggestion to the contrary is a lie made up by our enemies."

As the diplomats went back and forth, Alexandra watched Balakin, noticing that he rarely took his eyes off her. The man was definitely handsome, well-dressed, and he carried himself with a swagger that was sure to attract the opposite sex. He knew what he was doing, and she knew he was doing it. She gave it right back. At that moment, she knew she could use it to her advantage.

She gestured her head to the left and mouthed the words "Let's talk" to Balakin. She noticed the sly smile that crossed his face. He nodded and rose.

At the opposite end and out of earshot of the two diplomats, Balakin was the first to speak.

"I'm sorry, but I must admit that I'm having trouble placing you, Ms. Julian. You look very familiar."

"I've done some work for the White House for a while now, Mr. Minister."

He reached out and touched her hand. "Please, call me Dmitri."

Alexandra nodded and smiled enough that she hoped to show a little blush. Such a ladies' man. She could almost feel the man ready to come on to her, maybe lean in and whisper in her ear. She didn't need her husband to teach her those tells. Any woman would notice them.

"Thank you, Dmitri. Perhaps my picture has crossed your desk from Russian intelligence."

"I must say I am at a disadvantage," he said, shaking his head. "I like to know the background of the people I meet with. Especially those as beautiful as yourself."

Another blush. She could feel it deepen this time as it flashed across her cheeks. She was reeling him in. "Thank you again, Dmitri."

"Have you ever worked for the State Department? I know I have seen you before. I just cannot place you."

"I was at one time the U.S. Ambassador to Egypt."

Balakin's eyes widened, the memory of Alexandra's ordeal that made headlines across the globe flashing through his mind. "Ah, yes. Now I remember. You were the American Ambassador who was kidnapped by the terrorists in Alexandria and then held hostage in Cairo."

"Unfortunately, that's correct."

"That must have been a harrowing experience."

"To say the least. It's not something I want to relive."

"Well, you are brave and heroic, Ms. Julian. I like that in a woman."

She noticed he kept referring to her maiden name. There were no diamond rings or wedding bands adorning her fingers that might tell a different story. She and Duke had done their best to keep their marriage quiet, but with the way secrets were kept in Washington, it was inevitable that the truth would come out someday. Not wanting him to ask if she was married or, if he knew, ask about her husband, she quickly steered the conversation to the current crisis facing their countries.

"I'm surprised to see you here. Normally the Defense Minister wouldn't sully himself by appearing before the U.N. Security Council. He usually leaves the dirty work to the diplomats."

Balakin shrugged. "The President asked me to attend with Minister Sokolov. I am honored to represent my country during such momentous times."

"Let me ask you, Dmitri. What is it that President Volkov really wants? Surely he does not want to get into a war with the United States. That cannot be in the best interests of Russia."

Balakin inhaled and then let it out as he considered his response. "My friend wants a lot of things, Ms. Julian. He is a man who dreams of having a legacy that will last for a thousand years. And as Minister Sokolov said, President Volkov wants to return Russia to its former glory as the most powerful nation on earth."

"And is that what you want?"

Alexandra noticed the look of lust vanish from his eyes. She had struck a chord.

"I want what's best for the Russian people, Ms. Julian."

Her mind worked in overdrive. *Should I mention his daughter? Would he consider it a threat? If I bring up Katia, will he tell her to flee the country and deprive Duke of the opportunity to grab her?* She decided to keep that ace up her sleeve in case her husband needed it.

"And what is best for the Russian people?"

"The end of sanctions against my country." His nostrils flared and his eyes narrowed—the lust replaced with greed. "And three billion dollars."

"You want three billion dollars?"

"You have stolen money from us for years, Ms. Julian," he said, playing hardball. "Your intentions are to ruin our economy. We cannot stand for that."

"I can assure you, Dmitri, we have no such intentions. You can sell your oil to whoever you want. We're not stopping you."

"But you have flooded the market with your own oil. It is no good to us if we only get twenty dollars a barrel for ours."

"That's not our problem."

"It is now."

She didn't like his tone or the tone of his demands. She thought he might be harder to figure out than expected. She decided to see if she could turn things around. She reached up and fingered the diamond necklace resting three inches above her cleavage. Once she saw his eyes go down, she knew she had another chance.

"Dmitri, this might be a little forward of me, but perhaps you and I could have dinner or a drink. Just the two of us."

She noticed how his eyes left her chest and then widened when he saw her coy smile. He was either surprised that she made the move or turned on by it.

"I'm listening."

Balakin reached up and centered the perfect knot in his tie, never taking his eyes off her. He looked like he couldn't wait to put the moves on her.

"Maybe we could have dinner tonight?"

"And what's in it for me? Besides the pleasure of your company."

"We could discuss the money and an acceptable path out of this crisis."

"Is that all?"

She played it as best she could by giving a little bite to her lower lip before saying, "I think you and I want the same thing, Dmitri."

She could almost see the man lick his lips.

"And what is that, Ms. Julian?"

She reached out and touched his arm. She could sense the jolt the touch sent through his body. "Peace."

CHAPTER 21

Near Gelendzhik, Russia

Late the night before, President Volkov left his Novo-Ogaryovo estate, the official government residence of the Russian President, in the Odintsovsky District west of Moscow. A large part of him knew he would probably never again step foot within the nineteen-foot-high walls that surrounded the mansion. Either the cancer would kill him before then or the Americans would pulverize it to the ground with its nukes. With what he had in mind, he had full confidence it wouldn't be the latter. He had every intention of making sure it was the White House that met its destructive end.

Under the cover of darkness, four modes of transportation departed Moscow destined for one of Volkov's many residences scattered around Russia, some secret, some not. The President's chopper flew northwest to the Konstantin Palace in St. Petersburg; his Ilyushin IL-96-300PU jet, the Russian equivalent of Air Force One, headed south to Sochi and the Bocharov Ruchey residence; his armored Aurus Senat limousine with an accompanying security contingent traveled west to the Yantar Palace in Kaliningrad; and a heavily fortified train went south to the outskirts of Gelendzhik. Hoping to throw off any American spies, Volkov had separate lookalikes take the chopper, the jet, and the limo.

He took the train.

Nearly a thousand miles south of Moscow on the Black Sea, the Gelendzhik residence cost the Russian people nearly a billion dollars, all of which Volkov had stolen and swindled from the treasury over the last half decade. The official word was that no state money went into building the property, that it was owned by a Russian oligarch, and that Volkov did not own it or even make use of it. They were all lies, and the massive security apparatus surrounding the estate operated by the Federal Security Service and the no-fly-zone above the massive grounds told everyone that the occupant was not some ordinary Russian billionaire splurging on opulence and grandiosity.

The entire complex sat on two hundred acres. With eleven bedrooms and nearly 200,000 square feet of living space in the main residence, the estate came complete with a train station, a home theater, an outdoor amphitheater, two pools, a casino, and an underground hockey rink. Situated on a cliff with the Black Sea on one side and a thick forest of pine trees on the other, Volkov saw the Gelendzhik palace as the most secure residence in the world.

This was where he would carry out his war.

With the fresh air from the sea and away from the congestion of Moscow, Volkov felt invigorated the whole day. He felt strong, stronger than he had in months. The cough remained but it was manageable. The upturn in his health allowed him to focus on the one thing that mattered—executing the plan to destroy the United States.

He was going strong at 8 p.m. when General Dernov entered his office.

"General, where are the ground troops?"

He offered no welcome to Dernov, who had arrived in secret late that afternoon. His head down, the President was standing at his desk, the maps of Russia, the United States, and other parts of the world strewn on top. Two computer screens off to his left showed satellite images with red diamonds denoting Russian defenses. Nearly all of the pieces of war were in place.

"They have been moved out of Moscow, sir," Dernov said, stepping toward the desk. "If the Americans strike, they will be out of harm's way and able to respond with force. And they are in position to repel any type of ground invasion."

"Good."

Volkov wished he had more troops. The Russian economy had necessitated the downsizing of soldiers and some of those in uniform had grown accustomed to getting their paychecks a month late. But what the Russians lacked in manpower was made up by an abundance of intercontinental ballistic missiles and nuclear warheads. Although they were aging ICBMs and needed to be replaced, they could still wreak havoc on the world.

And Volkov didn't plan on saving them any longer. He planned on using every last one of them. After nodding his head at his own thoughts, he looked up and then sat down in the leather chair behind him. "We are getting close, General."

"Yes, we are. And the military is ready to execute your orders."

"Where is the *Kuznetsov*?" Volkov asked of the Russian aircraft carrier.

"It is near Vladivostok in the Sea of Japan. It has eighteen Sukhoi Su fighters and six MiGs on board and ready for launch to the Pacific and the United States."

Volkov considered the report. He knew the carrier provided little offense against the U.S., but it would distract the Americans when the chaos started. The more the better."

"Mobile launchers?"

"In place and spread out for maximum effectiveness."

"Silo-based ICBMs?"

"Fully staffed. I took the liberty of making sure all of the missiles have been retargeted to match your strike plans."

"Good. What about the *Belgorod*?"

Dernov moved to the side of the desk and found the paper map of the United States. He pointed to a spot off the east coast of New Jersey and south of Nova Scotia. "The *Belgorod* is right here."

Volkov nodded twice as he considered his next question. "Where does it need to be?"

Dernov used his stubby index finger to trace a path further south and west to a spot directly east of Washington, D.C. "This would be the ideal place, sir. It will enable us to get so close to D.C. that the American defenses will be powerless to stop our missiles."

"What about the subs on the West Coast?"

"They are nearly in position, sir. Ready to take out Honolulu, Seattle, San Francisco, and Los Angeles."

"We are going to hit them from every angle, General." Volkov looked up, pleased with what he was hearing. "Well done."

"Thank you, sir." He pointed to the chair in front of the desk and said, "Mr. President, if I may."

"Please sit, General."

"Thank you, sir." Dernov took a seat, although he maintained his military posture. "Sir, I wanted to make you aware of a situation."

"Okay. What is it?"

"I was approached yesterday."

"Approached? What do you mean?"

"After my meeting with the commanders yesterday, I was approached by Deputy Minister Orlov from the Ministry of Energy. He wanted to speak privately, saying it was urgent and a matter of national security. I met with him in my office."

When Dernov's pause was too long, Volkov asked, "And?"

"He offered me a bribe, sir."

"A bribe?"

"Yes, sir. He said some people had come to him. He did not say who. But they want Russia to halt any plans of war, and Orlov wanted me to be the one who kept your orders from being executed."

"He asked you to defy my orders?"

"Yes, sir."

"How much did he offer?"

"Ten million dollars."

Volkov leaned back in his chair, letting it rock slightly as he thought about what was being said. Someone was trying to undermine the war effort. He was smart enough to know who was behind it.

"The Americans are worried, General. As they should be."

"That's what I thought, Mr. President."

"They are trying to turn our people against us."

"It appears so."

"They are desperate." Volkov gritted his teeth, his rage at the Americans' meddling rising. "What did you do? How did you respond?"

Dernov took a breath and let it out, like he was preparing himself for a response from Volkov that might not be kind. "I took the money, sir."

"You took the money?" Volkov stopped rocking. He gripped the armrests, looking like he was going to jump out of his seat and attack.

Before Volkov could call security, Dernov said, "And then I had the traitor thrown in jail."

Sitting back and digesting the news, Volkov broke out into a grin. General Dernov was a first-class scoundrel. Volkov liked the man across the table—devious, conniving, kindred spirits.

"Excellent. I have taught you well, General. Never pass up an opportunity to take someone's money. Especially the money of a traitorous fool."

"Yes, sir."

"Make sure everyone knows that Deputy Minister Orlov will not be treated well for his treasonous acts and that he will suffer greatly. Make his family suffer, too. We need to send the message to anyone else who might try to sabotage our efforts."

"I will make sure the people hear them suffer loud and clear."

The phone on Volkov's desk beeped. "Yes?" Volkov said into the speaker.

"Minister Balakin is on the line, Mr. President."

Volkov left the call on speaker. "Dmitri, I am here with General Dernov. We were discussing our latest plans. How are things going on your end?"

"Mr. President, the Americans are worried. Seriously worried. They know you are ill. They know you are determined to strike the U.S. They are scrambling trying to figure out what to do. I think we have them where we want them."

"Are they preparing for an attack, Dmitri?"

"Hard to say, sir. They are scared so I imagine they are taking precautions. But I don't get the sense that they are willing to go on offense. It's not in their nature. Their missile defense system test was meant to put doubt in our minds. We made sure they knew we were not impressed or intimidated." He cleared his throat as he prepared to switch gears. "I am meeting with a member of the U.S. delegation tonight. I think she might be able to give me some insight if I can draw it out of her."

"She?"

"Yes, sir. A woman. Her name is Alexandra Julian."

Volkov mouthed the name while looking at General Dernov, who shook his head like he didn't know her.

"She works for the White House. She was the U.S. Ambassador to Egypt who was kidnapped a few years back."

Volkov smiled, remembering her now. "Ah yes. Dark hair. Good looking. You do have a way with women, Dmitri."

Balakin took the compliment and then said, "She said we can talk money. I think I can get three billion from them."

The smile on Volkov's face grew wider. "Like taking candy from a baby."

"Yes, sir."

"Continue with the meeting, Dmitri. Take their money. As much as you can get. And then try to tamp down any concerns of war. I want to lull them into thinking I'm backing down. Then we will go for the kill when they least expect it."

"Yes, sir. I will."

Volkov saw Dernov raising a finger, like he wanted to remind the President of something. Volkov knew the signal immediately. "But be careful, Dmitri. General Dernov says he was approached yesterday by Deputy Minister Orlov in the Energy Ministry and bribed to stop the war. Ten million dollars. The General saw through it, took the money, and had Orlov arrested. It is clear that the Americans are trying to sabotage our plans. Be on your guard. Don't fall victim to the enemy's tactics."

"I won't, sir. I think I can have my way with Ms. Julian."

"Get the money and get back to Russia," Volkov ordered before ending the call.

Volkov sat back and rocked in his chair. It was all coming together. He could see his lasting legacy being written. The man who destroyed the United States. The history books would show he played the Americans like a fiddle. He coughed slightly, the first one in hours. He was feeling good, like he had all the power in the world.

And he was about to unleash it.

CHAPTER 22

The White House – Washington, D.C.

"Mr. President," Director Parker said over the phone. "We have a problem."

The President was upstairs in the Residence when the call came in. He knew if the CIA Director was calling during dinner time, it probably wasn't going to be good. The concern in Parker's voice confirmed it.

"Where are you?" the President asked.

"I'm at HQ."

"I thought you were in New York City with Ty and Mike."

"I was, but something's come up and I wanted to get back to Langley to find out what's happening. It's not good."

The President sighed. "Okay."

"I think we should meet."

"That serious, huh?"

"Yes, sir."

"Get to the White House as soon as you can."

"I'm on my way."

Twenty minutes later, the President was seated in his chair in the Situation Room at the end of the conference table. It had been a long day of wonder and worry, and anyone who saw him could see the toll it was taking by the absence of a tie. He kept the suit coat on. For now.

Alone with his thoughts, he wondered what Parker was going to tell him and what decisions he was inevitably going to have to make in response. Stubblefield had called earlier and mentioned that Alexandra was scheduled to have dinner with the Russian Defense Minister. He said she was cautiously optimistic that the man could be reasoned with and she might be able to get him to pause the start of any hostilities or at least slow them down. It wasn't much, but it was something.

His thoughts were interrupted when Parker came in carrying a briefcase and a frown. "We have a problem, sir."

"So you said."

Parker took a seat, placing his briefcase on the table. He still had a tie on, but the President noticed the knot had been loosened. He looked like an accountant behind on his work in the second week of April. Once Parker got situated, he said, "Mr. President, I am sorry to report that the plan failed."

The President tapped the table with his index finger, his mind going through all the possibilities. "Which plan are you talking about?"

"Well, I guess I should say the *plans* failed to be more specific. Two of them. The one where we tried to bribe General Dernov went nowhere. The guy's so corrupt that he took the bribe and then threw the man in jail. But it's the one regarding Volkov that has me deeply concerned."

"Let's hear it."

Parker opened his briefcase and pulled out a folder marked *Classified*. "Sir, what I'm about to tell you is only known by four Americans—me, the Deputy Director, the CIA station chief in Moscow, and our case officer in Moscow who recruited the agent. Obviously, this information is as sensitive as it gets."

The President nodded.

"We had someone inside the Kremlin, sir. About a year ago, we turned one of Volkov's secretaries. She's a young woman named Mila Kalashnika." Parker passed a file photo of her taken from her Moscow driver's license.

"She looks young for an Agency asset," the President said.

"Age twenty-nine. She had been with Volkov for three years. She's not a fan of his, had grown increasingly worried about his warmongering, and she has long dreamt of the days of starting a life of real freedom in the United States. She had done some work for us in the past, and our people on the ground were impressed with her results. Given the circumstances, we thought we'd give the plan a shot."

He took back the picture from the President and handed him a photo of the dragonfly brooch.

"Two days ago, our man in Moscow provided her with this brooch, which was filled with liquid Novichok. The tail could be unscrewed and the Novichok dropped into a cup of liquid. She made it through security and went about her duties without raising any red flags. When she was preparing coffee, she put the Novichok in the cups destined for Volkov, Balakin, and Dernov."

"All three of them?"

"Yes, all three of them were meeting in the Kremlin at that time. We only instructed her about Volkov. He was the target. She took it upon herself to split the poison between the cups to take out all three of them."

"Gutsy."

"To say the least, sir. Anyway, like I said, she placed it in each of the cups and was wheeling it into Volkov's office. She was probably less than a minute away from giving it to them, but . . . ." He stopped and shook his head, the strain evident on his face.

"But what?"

Parker gritted his teeth. "The security guards stopped her before she made it into Volkov's office."

"What did they do to her? Do you even know?"

"Oh, we know. And it's not what they did to her. It's what they did with the coffee. They didn't suspect a thing so they drank it."

"Drank it?" the President spat out. He then let out a curse. "You have got to be kidding me. All of it?"

"Yes, sir. Gulped it right down."

"Are you telling me that Volkov didn't get any?"

"From what we been able to piece together, she tried to put some residue from the brooch into Volkov's cup, but she's not sure if there was enough in there to have an impact or whether he even drank it."

"Well, what did she do?"

"She got the hell out of there. Told the head secretary that she was feeling ill and said she was going home."

The President sighed again. "So having heard nothing about Volkov's health, I guess nothing happened?"

Parker swallowed, the bad news about to come forth. "Not to Volkov that we know of. His whereabouts aren't known right now, but we haven't heard any chatter that he has shown any symptoms of nerve agent poisoning. But the problem is that something did happen to Volkov's security guards. Three of them. All of them are in the hospital right now with suspicious symptoms. One of them is close to organ failure. Pretty soon it's going to be known that they've been poisoned."

"And the finger is going to be pointed at the United States," the President said, running his hand over his face and cursing again.

"I'm afraid so, sir."

The President stood and started pacing the length of the conference table. He wanted to let a string of profanities fly, but he restrained himself in hopes of thinking clearly. He wondered if his decision to go forward with the plan would be the worst he ever made—for his presidency and the country.

"What happened to the young woman?"

"She was able to get a flight out of Moscow and make it to Amsterdam. We have her in protective custody so she's safe."

"They're going to know she's the one."

Parker held up a finger. "Perhaps, sir. That's what we're working on right now. Once word gets out about the guards, we'll be ready with our disinformation campaign. We'll make it sound like one of the guards tried to poison Volkov. We could even say it was Balakin or Dernov behind it. A power grab by those looking to replace Volkov."

The President rested his hands on top of the headrest of a leather chair, his finger tapping furiously. "We need a story for the secretary. They'll be looking for her, and they'll piece together pretty quickly that a secretary isn't going to have ready access to Novichok. They'll be looking at the CIA."

Parker stood, himself a pacer when in thought. After a single turn, he said, "In a day or two, I can have the CIA station in Amsterdam find a twenty-nine-year-old female in the hospital. We'll spread the word that the woman might be suffering from acute nerve agent poisoning. The Russians will investigate. They'll realize it's not her, but it will buy us some time."

The phone buzzed on the table. The President punched the button for the speaker and said, "Yes?"

"Mr. President, Secretary Javits is on the line," the duty officer said.

"Thank you." The President pushed another button and said, "Russ, I'm in the Situation Room with Director Parker. What's going on?"

"Sir, I wanted to let you know that the Russian aircraft carrier *Kuznetsov* has left the Sea of Japan and is heading east in the Pacific toward the United States."

The President felt like the world was closing in on him, and he needed some room to move and time to think. "Russ, what DEFCON level are we at?"

"We're at four, sir."

"What is your recommendation?"

"I think we should go to DEFCON Three. That puts the Air Force on notice that it needs to be ready to mobilize within fifteen minutes."

The President didn't hesitate. "Go to DEFCON Three and standby for a move to DEFCON Two. We need to be ready, Russ. Director Parker just told me that two of the CIA's plans have failed, and we could be looking at Russian retaliation in the very near future. I want everyone on alert."

"Roger that, Mr. President. I'll get right on it."

Borough of Manhattan, New York City

Alexandra Julian looked at the mirror in her hotel room at the Marriott near Times Square. She was feeling a little queasy. With the meeting with Dmitri Balakin looming, she chalked her stomach woes to nerves. This was going to be her first real time in the game since her days as Ambassador.

Except for a small detachment of Secret Service agents watching over her, she was going to meet with Balakin alone. She wasn't afraid. It was dinner and drinks in a public place. But a lot was riding on her and how the meeting went.

The better part of the afternoon had been spent huddled with Vice

President Stubblefield and Secretary Arnold in Stubblefield's suite. They discussed as many details as they could think of—whether the billions of dollars in bribes was on the table and whether Balakin had the power to prevent a war from starting.

It was a crash course in high-stakes diplomacy—the fate of the Western world hanging in the balance. She grabbed her stomach again, hoping to settle it.

She went with her short red dress. It ended just above her knees, allowing her to show off her tanned and toned legs. There was enough fabric missing from the upper half that Balakin wouldn't have any trouble knowing what she was hiding underneath. If the dress and her looks threw him off his game, it would be worth it.

Her phone vibrated on the edge of the bathroom sink. She tapped the screen and said, "Hey, babe."

"Hey," Duke Schiffer said. "Where are you?"

"At the hotel in New York. I'm getting ready for dinner with Minister Balakin."

"The whole delegation is meeting with the Russians?"

"No, it's just me."

"It's what?"

"It's just me and the Defense Minister, Duke." She could hear it in her husband's tone. He probably thought it was too dangerous. But she wasn't going to change her mind. And she sure wasn't going to let him change it for her. This was what she wanted to do. If he wanted to play that game, then she would demand that he leave the field and stay at home with her. She knew he wouldn't do it, and she wasn't going to either.

"The two of you? Alone?"

"Yes, Duke. I was able to convince him to get together during the meeting this afternoon. I think I might be able to get something positive out of it."

Schiffer took a second to respond before saying, "I don't like it. The guy's a snake. You and I both know it. We saw it in his dossier."

"Duke, the Vice President is making sure the Secret Service has me in sight the entire time. I'll be fine."

"Why don't you take Secretary Arnold with you?"

"Because Balakin and I agreed to meet, not Secretary Arnold and Minister Sokolov. Trust me, Duke. I'll be fine." She grunted into the phone and then blew out a breath.

"What's wrong?"

"Nothing," she said, aggravated. "I think I must have eaten something earlier that didn't agree with me. It doesn't help that I'm nervous. There's a lot riding on this meeting. Your lack of faith in me doesn't help."

"Babe."

Alexandra knew she got him. She knew how to play her husband. As she expected, his tone changed.

"You'll do fine," he said. "I know you will. Just be careful."

"Thank you, Duke. I will be careful." She looked at her watch. "It's almost time. I should get going."

CHAPTER 23

Near Gelendzhik, Russia

The door to President Volkov's bedroom blew open at 2 a.m. Startled from his sleep, the first thing he did was reach for his gun next to him in the bed.

Volkov's lead security agent, Andrey Levkin, rushed forward. "Mr. President, we have an emergency!"

Volkov pointed his pistol at the man, his dark figure framed by the white light of the hall behind him.

"It's me!" Levkin yelled out, slamming on the brakes. "It's me!"

Another man standing at the door turned on the lights, illuminating the room. With the gun pointed at the agent standing three feet from him, Volkov kept his finger on the trigger. The fright caused by the intrusion widened his eyes and sent his heart rate soaring. Agent Levkin had his hands raised, showing he was unarmed, and he took a step back to show he wasn't a threat.

"Sir, we have a problem."

Volkov's bleary eyes blinked fully awake, his chest rising and falling. He looked at Levkin and then toward the door where Anatoly Babkin, Volkov's personal physician, was standing. He pointed the gun at the ceiling, realizing they weren't out to kill him.

"What the hell is going on?"

"Mr. President," Levkin said. "We believe there has been an assassination attempt on your life."

Volkov glared at the man and then glanced at Dr. Babkin. He trusted no one, not even the two men in the room.

"What are you talking about?"

"At the Kremlin, sir. Three of the guards outside your office have come down with nerve agent sickness."

Stunned, Volkov lowered the gun. He flicked his hand at Levkin, motioning for him to back away. Volkov then threw off the sheet covering his lower legs and got out of bed, his gun still in his right hand.

"When did this happen?"

"They started feeling ill yesterday. Not long after you left. All three are in the hospital and under quarantine until further tests can be done. It has been confirmed, though. They were poisoned. We just don't know with what yet."

"Best guess?"

"We suspect Novichok, sir. We've seen similar symptoms before."

"How bad are the men?"

"They are deteriorating by the minute. Ivan is suffering from organ failure. It doesn't look good. They think he might have only a day or two left to live."

"What is he doing here?" Volkov asked Agent Levkin about Dr. Babkin.

"He's here to check on you."

Dr. Babkin stepped forward cautiously, not wanting to make any sudden movements that might cause Volkov to take drastic measures. Personal physicians could be replaced.

"Mr. President, I thought I would check on you and make sure you're not experiencing any symptoms."

Volkov stalked from one end of the spacious bedroom to the other, the gun still in his hand. "I feel fine, Doctor." At that exact moment, he stopped on a dime, braced himself with a hand on the wall, and proceeded to cough roughly.

With a final grunt and clearing of his throat, he said, "At least I don't feel any worse than normal."

His mind clearing and realizing what was happening, he cursed loudly, the rage inside him beginning to bubble up inside him.

"Has anyone else in my office come down with anything?" he barked.

"One of the secretaries claimed she was feeling ill and left early the day you met with General Dernov and Minister Balakin," Agent Levkin said. "She then called in sick yesterday."

"Is she in the hospital?"

"We don't know where she is, sir. We can't find her."

Volkov cursed again, louder than the last time. It was abundantly clear what happened. Incensed, he yelled, "It is the Americans! They have tried to kill me! This is an act of war!"

Volkov threw his gun on the bed and marched to the phone on the nightstand. He yanked the receiver off the cradle and punched the red button.

"Get me General Dernov! Now!"

Borough of Manhattan, New York City

Dmitri Balakin straightened his tie in the bathroom mirror. With his fine-tailored suit and perfectly styled hair, he looked like he could be in line to star as the new villain in the next James Bond film. And as a high-class swindler and ladies' man, he knew he could give 007 a run for his money.

He had initially agreed to have dinner with Alexandra at the Ritz-Carlton. But thirty minutes before the scheduled time, he called and said the plans had changed. Instead of the Ritz, Balakin said he had reserved a quiet space at the Plaza near Central Park. He claimed it was to throw off the members of the press who were staking out his hotel lobby and enable him and Alexandra to discuss matters with some semblance of privacy.

In reality, he changed locations so the CIA wouldn't have time to bug the dining area or fill the tables with its operatives. To his surprise, Alexandra did not balk at the change. Instead, she readily agreed and said she was looking forward to meeting with him. He was beginning to like her more with each passing hour. She was smart, gorgeous, and confident. All qualities that Balakin found sexy in a woman.

And in case she was feeling amorous and wanted even more privacy, he had a suite at the Plaza at his disposal. Balakin smiled at himself in the mirror, admiring his own talents, always thinking ahead. What a story it would be: Russian Defense Minister steals America's money, sleeps with White House Advisor, wins war against U.S., and becomes President of Russia—the world's greatest superpower.

Eat your heart out Bond.

He arrived early at the Plaza's elegant dining venue—the Palm Court—and waited near his table as his security agents made sure everything was secure. Situated in the corner with the restaurant's signature palm trees providing privacy, he welcomed Alexandra as she arrived at the agreed-upon time.

"Right on schedule," Balakin said.

"It helps when you have these guys providing the transportation," she said, gesturing to the two Secret Service agents accompanying her.

Balakin eyed the two men, who took up position out of earshot and near his own agents.

"Please, sit, Ms. Julian."

"Thank you, Dmitri. And please call me Alexandra."

"Very well, Alexandra. I hope you don't mind me saying you look stunning for a diplomat."

Alexandra smiled. "You look the part as well, Dmitri."

A waiter arrived and asked if they wanted to start with a drink. Balakin ordered a bourbon—Old Rip Van Winkle 12 year. Alexandra ordered an iced tea.

"Nothing stronger?" Balakin asked.

She shook her head. "Given the things that we have to discuss tonight, I prefer to have a clear mind."

Balakin nodded like it was admirable.

"No vodka for you?"

"Vodka is for the peasants. I drink better than that. I hope you don't mind, but I took the liberty of ordering some caviar."

"Russian, I presume."

"Osetra," Balakin said. "Imperial Russian. Harvested from the sturgeon in the Caspian Sea near my neck of the woods."

"But not beluga?"

"Your country for many years banned beluga caviar, Alexandra. It is only now legal again. Unfortunately, it is not on the menu."

The caviar arrived, but Alexandra begged off, saying she didn't care for fish or their eggs.

"I was hoping we could come to an agreement, Dmitri," she said as he took a bite. "The world is concerned with President Volkov's stability, and we all know that he doesn't have much time left on this earth. We need to think about the long-term future. What's best for the United States, Russia, you, me."

Balakin took a sip of his bourbon. He found the woman across the table highly attractive. Her red dress showed off her shapely curves and her dark hair hung down to her shoulders. The diamond necklace she was wearing earlier in the day was still there—still perched above what many men would consider the prize for that night's mission.

"You obviously have an eye on the presidency, Dmitri. You are the front-runner from everything I hear."

Balakin took another sip. After he returned the glass to the table, he asked, "Are you married, Alexandra?"

"Would it matter to you?"

He smiled. She definitely had something most women lacked. "I was just curious as to what the future held for you when this is all over."

"When will it be over?"

Balakin inhaled and then let it out. "I guess it depends on what President Volkov has in mind. He is a very determined man, Alexandra. And he usually gets what he wants."

Alexandra's cheeks rose. "Do you usually get what you want, Dmitri?"

He winked. "All the time."

With their eyes locked on each other's, neither one of them saw the Russian security guard rushing to the table.

"Sir," the man said, a phone in his hand. "It is President Volkov. He said it is an emergency. You must take this."

For a second disturbed at the intrusion, Balakin quickly recovered and grabbed the phone. "Yes, Mr. President." Fearing Alexandra could hear

Volkov's yelling over the phone, he raised a finger to her and excused himself from the table.

Balakin found a quiet place and listened. Halfway through the conversation, he turned and locked eyes with Alexandra. He wondered if he saw something in her look—a tell that she knew the facts Volkov was relaying to him. *Could she? Was she part of the American plot to undermine Russia?* His face hardened—the Russian blood in him beginning to boil. This was an attack on his country. His homeland. This was war, and he would not be duped.

He ended the call and handed the phone to the security agent. "Get the car ready," he ordered.

When he returned to the table, Alexandra stood. "Is something wrong, Dmitri?"

Balakin walked closer, close enough to her that she could probably smell the caviar and bourbon on his breath.

"You tried to poison my President, Alexandra."

"What?"

"I must return to Russia."

"Why, Dmitri? What are you talking about?"

Balakin's jaw clenched and he leaned closer to her ear. "Your future just took a turn for the worse, Alexandra."

CHAPTER 24

Palm Springs, California

Duke Schiffer rode shotgun while Ariel Segel was behind the wheel of the black Ford Explorer with tinted windows. Noah Wolfson sat in the back. The three had arrived in Palm Springs late that afternoon once they confirmed that Katia Balakina was on the move east from Los Angeles. Given that she had her phone on her that Schiffer could track, Segel kept a safe distance from the Range Rover occupied by Katia and her three Russian bodyguards as it traveled Interstate 10 toward the California desert resort town.

Still in the late summer, the temperature in Palm Springs had topped out at just over a hundred degrees with plenty of sunshine and no chance of rain. The three men welcomed the growing darkness, hoping the temps would drop enough after the sun went down to not cause any heat-related problems on the night's mission.

They followed Katia until she reached Southridge Drive and her destination at the home of Sam Rothstein, the head honcho of one of Hollywood's biggest movie studios, and the current owner of the iconic Hope residence. She was set to stay the night, giving Schiffer the opportunity he had been looking for.

After a light dinner at a Mexican restaurant, they went over the plan once again. The fact that the house had received so much press over the years made it ideal for planning purposes. Schiffer loved it when the rich and famous liked to show off their fancy mansions, offering the world not only a glimpse into their lavish lifestyles but also, for people like him, the locations of access points, security cameras, and hiding places. It was like the homeowners were doing his homework for him.

The old Hope home, the one that some said looked like a giant mushroom but others thought more closely resembled an alien spaceship, came complete with 23,000 square feet, six bedrooms, ten bathrooms, an indoor/outdoor pool, tennis court, and a putting green. And the best part were the hills above that would hopefully give Schiffer and Wolfson a bird's-eye view of the place.

In the corner of a department store parking lot and out of the eyes of security cameras, the three men waited for the darkness to envelop the hills above the Coachella Valley. Schiffer and Wolfson changed into their black tactical pants and shirts and laced up their hiking boots. Each readied a backpack with the gear they thought they would need—including suppressed Sig Sauer Rattler rifles with folding stocks, plastic flex-cuffs, duct tape, and a hood. They each carried water to keep themselves hydrated, even in the dark of night.

Schiffer didn't want things to get loud, and he hoped to keep the gunplay to a minimum. But with the stakes as high as they were, pulling the trigger was an option on anyone other than Katia Balakina.

Segel's investigation of the three Russian bodyguards revealed the men were former Russian mercenaries, all of them suspected of doing some dirty work in Ukraine and Georgia on Russia's behalf. Dmitri Balakin had hand selected them to provide protection for his daughter, knowing their ruthlessness knew no bounds and they would take any and all actions to keep her safe. Segel remarked more than once that the three men deserved any fate that Schiffer sent their way.

Nearing the time to move, Schiffer pulled the phone out of the thigh pocket of his pants. He tapped the screen and went to his tracking app. Katia's phone was still at Rothstein's house. It hadn't moved since she got there. He made a couple swipes and hit the speed dial for his friend Dustin at the NSA.

"Yes?"

"Dustin, are you ready?"

"Yes, sir." He sounded like he had no choice but to be ready to do anything that Schiffer asked.

"I need camera views from the Rothstein residence. The one I told you about earlier."

"There are only two, Mr. Schiffer. One at the front gate down the hill and the other out from the main entrance to the house."

Schiffer frowned. He was hoping for some on the interior. "No web cameras you can hack into?"

"No, sir, none. There are three vehicles out front. One of them is the Range Rover."

"Okay, good. Dustin, I need you to patch me into what you're seeing so I can access it."

"Yes, sir. I'll have it ready in two minutes."

"Good work, Dustin."

As soon as he ended the call with Dustin, the phone vibrated in his hand. "Yeah, babe, go ahead."

"Where are you?" Alexandra said.

"Palm Springs. I have you on speaker with Ariel and Noah. We're about ready to move."

"Duke, Volkov knows."

"Knows what?"

"Knows about the plot. I don't know if he knows it's us, but he thinks it is."

"What happened with Balakin?"

"I thought things were going well, but he took a call from Volkov during dinner. I could hear Volkov yelling. Once Balakin ended the call, he accused the United States of trying to poison the Russian President. Things went south in a hurry, Duke. He got this crazy look in his eyes and then stormed out. It's been confirmed that Balakin is on his way back to Russia."

Schiffer cursed.

"We're at DEFCON Three, Duke," she said whispering. "And the President has told people to be ready to go to DEFCON Two."

Schiffer made eye contact with the two Israelis, both of them looking like they realized the mission that night just took on a greater sense of urgency.

"Where are you, Alexandra?"

"I'm with the Vice President on Air Force Two. We're about ready to land at Andrews. The President wants us to head straight to the White House. I'm afraid things might be spiraling out of control."

Schiffer checked his watch. They needed to get moving if they wanted to maximize the darkness. "Alexandra, I need you to convince the President to let us grab the daughter. Tell him we have no other choice now. I think the Vice President agrees with me so use him to help convince the President. This is our best shot at stopping all of this. We can do it tonight."

"What would you do if you got her?"

"Take her somewhere where she can talk to her father."

"The President has been insistent that it's a nonstarter. I don't think he's changed his mind."

"Well, try to convince him."

"I'll try, Duke. Please be careful."

"I will. I'll contact you when I can."

Schiffer ended the call and put the phone back in his pocket. He turned in his seat and looked at Wolfson. "You ready?"

"Of course I'm ready."

Segel started the Explorer and left the parking lot headed east on Palm Canyon Drive until he came to Southridge Drive and Rim Road. He pulled to a stop in a dusty parking lot at the trailhead to the Araby Trail and turned off the headlights. All three sat still in the silence. They didn't expect anyone to be following them, but in their line of work, paying attention to your surroundings at all times was a must. The traffic was light on Palm

Canyon Drive, and no traffic was allowed up Southridge Drive unless it was a resident. Anyone wanting to go up the mountain had to hike. There were no cars left in the parking lot of the trail.

Schiffer put on his black balaclava and then his night-vision goggles, keeping them tilted above his head. They all checked their comms, and Schiffer and Wolfson put on their black gloves.

"It should take us about forty-five minutes to get into position," Schiffer told Segel.

"I'll be at the rendezvous point unless I hear otherwise," Segel said.

"If you get the emergency signal from one of us, call Ty immediately," Schiffer said.

"You got it."

"Hopefully it won't come to that."

Having unscrewed the dome lights in the Explorer, Schiffer and Wolfson opened their doors keeping the interior dark. They slipped on their backpacks and secured the straps across their midsections. Each took one last drink of water before securing their bottles.

"Watch your step, guys," Segel said. "And be safe."

Schiffer and Wolfson responded with nods and then quietly shut their doors.

"Let's move," Schiffer said.

CHAPTER 25

Palm Springs, California

Schiffer and Wolfson hugged the wall of rock on their right until they had to hustle across the road to the start of the Araby Trail, a dirt path that made its way up into the Santa Rosa and San Jacinto Mountains National Monument. The trail maxed out at 3.4 miles with 1,200 feet of climbing to a high point of 1,360 feet. A favorite of early morning hikers hoping to beat the heat, Schiffer and Wolfson, with the help of their night-vision goggles, had the trail to themselves.

The narrow path littered with rocks made the trek slower than they would have liked. A twisted ankle would do them no good. Schiffer took the lead and Wolfson, who was in peak physical condition, had no trouble keeping up with the pace.

Although they couldn't walk and talk side-by-side, their comm units worked fine.

"This sure beats swimming in a cold Swiss lake in the middle of the night, doesn't it, Wolf?"

Schiffer heard Wolfson's grunt in his earpiece.

They stopped at a ridge and took a break, each of them taking on some water. It wasn't much farther, and when they got to their location, they wanted to keep their movements to a minimum. Both of them unzipped their backpacks and pulled out their Sig Rattlers. They used the guns' slings to keep them in front of their chests.

"About a quarter of a mile to go," Schiffer said, slinging the backpack over his right shoulder.

The higher they went, and with it the less light pollution around them, the more the night-vision goggles took effect. They kept to the trail, the signs pointing them in the right direction.

A crack of a twig stopped Schiffer in his tracks. He raised a fist, stopping Wolfson behind him. The two men crouched, ready to take cover in what little cover there was.

Schiffer heard another crack. Movement up ahead. He glanced back over his right shoulder with his goggles and saw Wolfson moving his hand to his gun and thumbing the safety.

Was there someone up there with them? Was it a lost hiker? Someone hiking at night? Or was it one of Katia's Russian mercenaries out on the hunt for them?

Holding up a finger, Schiffer turned his head to the left and raised up his goggles, willing his eyes to adjust to the darkness and looking for any headlamps or flashlights coming their way.

He strained to hear. It sounded like footsteps. Scratchy footsteps. Louder. Getting closer now.

He lowered his goggles and then turned his body to the right, giving his left side room to grab his gun. He flipped the selector with his thumb and put his index finger on the trigger. He reminded himself to relax, to let out the breath that was building inside him.

A thousand thoughts raced through his mind. He needed to identify the source of the noise, assess the threat, and then figure out a way to neutralize it. He had a badge on him. He always carried a badge of some sort in case he needed it. The one in his pocket was from the FBI.

If it was a hiker, he could flash the badge, tell the hiker he wasn't supposed to be on the mountain at that time of the evening, and order him to get lost. If it was one of Katia's Russian goons, well . . .

The footsteps continued along with a clicking, like heels scraping on a rock. Schiffer thought he heard a grunt, and then there was movement behind a bush in front of him.

He pulled the gun up and aimed, the red dot in the scope landing right in between the eyes of a bighorn sheep. The move startled the sheep and it froze in its tracks.

"Git!" Schiffer whispered loudly before flicking his hand at it. "Get out of here."

The sheep turned tail and took off up the trail. Schiffer never saw it again. He turned to see Wolfson taking a breath and thumbing the selector to secure his weapon.

"Let's go," Schiffer whispered. "It's only a couple hundred more yards."

As they neared the Rothstein residence, they took cover behind a large rock on the side of the trail. Lying side-by-side on the dirt path, they had a good vantage point over the rock looking down on the massive house and surrounding grounds.

After removing his goggles, Schiffer scooted back, lowered himself behind the rock, and powered up his phone. Careful to keep any light from the screen being visible, he looked at the two camera views Dustin had provided him with.

"Three cars still out front." He made two swipes and then said, "Her phone's still there."

He turned off the phone and unslung the backpack from his shoulder. Wolfson did the same.

"You want the drone or the binoculars?" Wolfson said.

"Give me the binoculars," Schiffer said. "You can play with your toys."

Wolfson set the miniature drone on the rock in front of them, flipped a couple switches, and used the remote control to put it into flight. Nearly silent, the drone rose high above the mountain and over the house. Using an app on his phone, Wolfson was able to watch the drone's camera feed appear on the screen.

"Three Russians," he announced.

"Where?"

"Outside the Range Rover in front of the house. All of them smoking."

"Armed?" Schiffer asked.

Wolfson peered at the screen, trying to keep the drone at a safe distance. "Unclear. More than likely, though."

It was what they expected. They didn't think the Russian bodyguards would be let inside the house. They'd be forced to stay outside like the servants they were. No one was going to harm Katia inside, they were told.

Of course, no one told them about the two men watching from above.

Wolfson brought the drone back and secured it. He then contacted Segel and told him they were in position.

Schiffer had the binoculars focused on the house, checking the putting green, the tennis court, and the swimming pool for movement.

"Here we go," he whispered to Wolfson.

Even from the distance, Wolfson could see two people walking around the pool—one male, one female. Schiffer had the better view. On the left, Sam Rothstein, age sixty-two, wore white swim trunks and nothing covering his hairy chest. He toed the water checking its temperature before stepping gingerly into the pool one step at a time.

On the right, Katia Balakina wore Daisy Duke blue-jean shorts and a skin-tight white T-shirt. She said something to Rothstein who was now up to his shoulders in the water looking up at her. He waved her in.

Katia unbuttoned her shorts and slid them down her legs, revealing a red bikini bottom. The landscaping lights surrounding the pool highlighted her legs. She said something to Rothstein and he held up both hands. She shimmied out of her bikini bottom and tossed it aside.

Through the binoculars, Schiffer watched as Katia pulled the T-shirt over her head. There was no bikini top in sight and she was content to let it all hang out. She stretched her arms high above her head, giving Rothstein . . . and Schiffer . . . wonderful views of her breasts. Even without magnification, the eagle-eyed Wolfson was getting a decent show at that distance. She turned left and right, showing off her curves from every angle. Rothstein started clapping. Schiffer almost did the same.

"Hey," Wolfson whispered, trying to get Schiffer's attention. He tapped him on the forearm and whispered louder. "Hey."

Reluctantly, Schiffer took the binoculars away from his eyes and looked at him. "What?"

"You're a married man. You shouldn't be looking at hot naked women."

Schiffer made a face as if he was looking at a crazy person. "It's surveillance." His cheeks rose before he put the binoculars back to his eyes and adjusted the focus.

"Let me have a look."

"Use your scope, Wolf."

Wolfson flicked him on the arm with the back of his hand. "Come on man." He then flicked him a second time.

Cursing under his breath, Schiffer handed the binoculars to him, and the man hurried to put them to his eyes and give the woman a good long look.

"Wow," he said, a rare moment where he lost his assassin's demeanor.

As Wolfson ogled the Russian movie star, Schiffer powered up his phone. If there was a time to get Katia, that was it. If they could get into the residence from the rear, the Russian bodyguards wouldn't even know it. The balding man with the rich man's paunch she was currently with wouldn't offer much resistance. And she, of course, from all that they could see, was unarmed at that moment.

"Segel," Schiffer whispered into his comm unit. "Standby. Target in sight."

"Roger that."

"Get ready to move, Wolf."

Wolfson kept the binoculars on Katia as she paraded around the pool's edge.

Schiffer switched to the messaging app. He had never used it before, but the President said he could contact him anytime, anywhere. Now was the time, and Schiffer needed the go-ahead.

He typed out a message with his thumbs. *I can pick up the package.*

Schiffer knew it would take time for the President to decipher the message and make the decision. But with everything Alexandra told him, the President had few options remaining. Time was running out. And the option to grab Katia was looking like it had a high degree of success. Schiffer could make it happen right then.

Repeat: The package is in sight. I can pick it up now.

Schiffer wondered if the President was in the Situation Room. Outside communications didn't always make their way in, but it was the President's phone he was contacting. He needed the order, and he needed it right now.

A bubble popped up. Finally.

Where? was the response.

Cali.

Schiffer waited. He looked over the rock and saw Rothstein and Katia canoodling in the pool. They wouldn't be in there forever. The guards were still out front. This was the best chance they'd ever get to grab her.

"Come on, come on," he whispered.

He had thought about grabbing Katia without the President's permission, forcing his hand. He knew it was the best option, and he knew he could make it happen. Right now. He wanted to tap Wolfson on the shoulder and tell him they were moving. Get it done and over with, and then let the President use her as a bargaining chip. The President would forgive him.

Unable to wait much longer, he exited out of the message with the President and put the Vice President and Alexandra in a group text message. *I can pick up the package. It needs to be now.*

Alexandra was quick to respond. *In the limo. The VP is on the phone with him. POTUS is thinking about it. Hold on.*

I can't hold on much longer. Running out of time.

Alexandra responded. *Standby.*

Schiffer looked over the rock. Katia used her arms to hoist herself out onto the pool's edge. She sat there, the water dripping off her naked body. She playfully kicked water in the face of Rothstein.

"Come on," Schiffer said in a low growl.

He was about to type out a new message when the bubble from the President's response popped up.

Red light. No go.

Schiffer looked at it twice before spitting out an expletive. A part of him wanted to ignore it, tell the President he didn't get the message. He made one last attempt.

I can pick up the package safely.

The response was quicker than Schiffer would have liked. The President had made his decision and it was final.

The Commander-in-Chief gave a one-word response. *Negative.*

Schiffer cursed again, pounding the rock with his fist. He couldn't believe the President passed up the opportunity. The best bargaining chip in the world when it came to Dmitri Balakin was right in front of him in all her glory. And Schiffer couldn't do a dang thing about it. He wondered what it meant for the world.

He sighed and looked to his right. Wolfson was still enjoying what he was seeing.

"Hey," he said, waving his hand in front of the binoculars and obscuring Wolfson's view. "Show's over. Let's go."

CHAPTER 26

The White House – Washington, D.C.

The air conditioner for the Situation Room was straining to keep the temperature cool with the growing crowd. Every seat was filled around the conference table, and high-level staffers were lining the walls ready to take their bosses' orders and put them into action.

The President had called the emergency meeting upon hearing that Minister Balakin had abruptly left New York. From all accounts, things were not looking good. Vice President Stubblefield and Alexandra both were concerned that the Russians' leaving the bargaining table meant the United States could be in for a rough go of it in the very near future. Their motorcade was currently entering the White House grounds.

The press was beginning to catch wind of what was going on. Unconfirmed reports were filtering out of Moscow that an assassination attempt had been made against Volkov. There was confirmation that three of his security guards were currently in the hospital after being poisoned and a secretary had gone missing. Whether they were in on the plot was still unknown as even the Russians were still trying to put the pieces of the puzzle together.

For its part, the CIA had skillfully spread the false narrative through several back channels that it had been an inside hit job on Volkov—with either the KGB or the military attempting a coup to throw him out of power. The narrative had carried the day so far, but it wouldn't last long once Volkov did his best to pin all the blame on the United States. It would come, and it would come with raging fury.

Once Vice President Stubblefield and Alexandra arrived, the President asked that the room be cleared except for the national security brain trust—Stubblefield, Secretary Javits, Secretary Arnold, Chairman Cummins, Director Parker, NSA Harnacke, and Alexandra.

Stubblefield opened a bottled water and took a big gulp. He motioned for Alexandra to take the seat next to him. Both of them had harried looks on their faces, and the long days were starting to wear them down.

Unfortunately, there would be little rest for the weary.

The President wasted no time. "Alexandra, what can you tell me about Balakin? You met with him. Looked him in the eyes. What's your take on him?"

"I thought I had something going, Mr. President. We were getting to know each other and building a rapport. It all changed when . . ." She stopped and looked around the table, making sure everyone there was in the know on the plot. "When Volkov called and said we tried to poison him. Balakin, obviously, didn't take too kindly to us trying to take out a fellow Russian. And his friend for that matter. He stormed out."

The President rapped his fingers on the table as he thought.

"Any word from him since?"

"No, sir."

"Thoughts?" he said, looking around the table. "Anyone?"

Secretary Arnold spoke. "We need to get the Russians back to the bargaining table. If nothing else, it will buy us some time. It will help slow the momentum before it gets out of control."

"What do you think, Alexandra?" the President asked. "You think the Russians would do it?"

"The French were the ones behind the talks at the U.N.," she said. "They might be open to having another meeting. We could ask them to set one up in Paris."

"Mike?"

"It's worth a shot."

"I agree," the President said. "I'll call President Pinot as soon as we're done here. I'll ask him to set up a meeting to bring both sides together. I'll make sure he knows it's urgent."

"I think I should go, Mr. President," Stubblefield said. "It will show the Russians that we're serious and that we want to find a way to have peace."

"Yeah. That sounds good."

Stubblefield gestured to his right. "I'll take Alexandra with me. Maybe they can reconnect and give us another chance at convincing him that war is not the answer."

Near Gelendzhik, Russia

"Where the hell have you been?" Volkov thundered. "What took you so long?"

Dmitri Balakin had to catch his breath on receipt of the verbal blows. He had flown ten hours straight from New York to Moscow and then took a chopper to Volkov's residence on the Black Sea. He had slept little during the flights, wondering what had happened with Volkov and what he had planned to do in response. He didn't even have time to change clothes. The tie was off, and the white dress shirt's top button undone.

"I got here as fast as I could, Mr. President."

An agitated Volkov stalked around his office, pounding his fist in his palm. Balakin thought Volkov looked thinner than the last time he saw him, but he was not lacking in energy.

"What is going on?" Balakin asked.

"Three of my guards have been poisoned. Babkin says they got it from drinking coffee. The tests confirm it was in the cups." He looked at Balakin. "Those cups were destined for me!"

Balakin stepped closer, trying to process the information. Were the cups destined for him, too? And Dernov? When all three of them were together in Volkov's office?

"This has all the hallmarks of the Americans!" Volkov spat out. "Their CIA tried to kill me! This is an act of war!"

Was it? Balakin wondered if someone else might have been involved. It would not be out of the question for one Russian to stab another in the back. All he knew was it wasn't him behind the plot. For that and for his own safety, he was thankful.

"Are you sure, Mr. President? Are you sure it was the Americans?"

"Don't doubt me, Dmitri. This is the CIA's handiwork. The Americans are trying to take me out before I can launch." He glared at his Defense Minister. "And frankly, Dmitri, I'm surprised that you would even question it. That concerns me. It makes me wonder what's going on in your mind."

Balakin held out his hands, wanting to put an end to any talk of being in on the plot. "Mr. President, you know I share your concerns. If the poison was in all three cups, I was also a target. General Dernov as well. And we have been friends for far too long to question my loyalty to you, sir. I don't know who was behind it."

"It is the Americans, Dmitri! I know it and you know it. I can't believe they would even try it."

"I can't either, sir. They have crossed the line."

Volkov punched his fist into his palm again. "Well, they are going to regret ever messing with me. If it's the last thing I do, I will make them pay."

"They seem desperate. Maybe you can get more out of them. Let the world know what they did, and then try to exploit it for all it's worth."

"Oh, I'm going to exploit it, Dmitri. I am going to use it as reason to strike the United States. This is war and the Americans have fired the first shot. I have the upper hand now and I am going to bring it crashing down on the Americans."

"Sir, the French President just called before I arrived. He wants both sides to get together in Paris."

Volkov shook his head like it was a nonstarter. "The Americans are stalling, Dmitri. Don't fall for their lies. It is only a ploy to buy time, but their time is up."

"It might help us, Mr. President."

"No. I've made my decision." Volkov stalked over to his desk, picked up the receiver, and punched a red button. "Get General Dernov in here now!"

Dernov was quick to appear. And like Balakin, he had a look of concern on his face, like he wasn't sure if Volkov was going to yell at him or shoot him. He had no reason to fear, but Volkov had been known to believe rumors and take out his revenge on the innocent.

"Yes, Mr. President."

"General, the time has come. The Americans have started the war. I want to launch as soon as possible."

Dernov glanced at Balakin, as if wondering if Volkov was serious. Seeing no response, he said, "Yes, sir. Where do you want to start?"

"Three places. D.C., New York City, and Los Angeles. If we hit them there, it will be a devastating blow. Millions of Americans will suffer, as they should. The American military will be unable to respond. We will cut them to the bone, and then we will go for the kill with our second wave of attacks."

Balakin bit the inside of his lip and looked at the floor. This was really happening. Even with all the bluffing, the posturing, and the threats, he never thought it would come to this. He thought his friend would succumb to his cancer before it happened. And he never thought the Americans would try to take him out. But now Russia was on the verge of starting a nuclear war with its sworn enemy.

And all Balakin could think about at that moment was one thing.

His daughter.

His thoughts envisioned her being vaporized in a mushroom cloud, caused in part by the order given by her father and her "favorite uncle." His lovely talented daughter gone. Never to be seen again. Never to grace the big screen with her beauty.

He had to do something.

"Dmitri, are you listening to me?" Volkov snapped. "I want everyone in place. Bombers, troops, warships, missiles—I want them all ready. This is going to be the most powerful military strike in history. Overwhelming force the likes of which has never been seen before."

Balakin tried to swallow. He couldn't remember the last time he had a drink. He would take water, but he really wanted something stronger.

"Dmitri!"

Balakin looked at Volkov and geared himself up for what he needed to say. He had to. He would never forgive himself if he didn't.

"Sir, it is Katia. She is still in the United States."

Volkov cursed and flicked his hand at the man. "That is not my problem."

"But it is *my* problem."

"Dmitri, I am ready to launch!"

"Mr. President, that is my daughter!" Feeling emboldened by his response, Balakin added, "She is your *kotenok*. You have known her since she was a baby. Do you want to see your *kotenok* again? Do you want her dead!?"

Volkov glared at him, although Balakin thought the look had something sinister behind it. Like Volkov definitely wanted to see his *kotenok* again and someday he would, but not for the right reasons.

Balakin licked his lips. He was running on empty, and his concern for his daughter and his outburst at Volkov had zapped him of energy. The only thing he had left was to beg. "Please, Mr. President," he said softly. "Send me to Paris to meet with the Americans. It will give me time to get my daughter out of the United States before the bombs start falling."

The two other men in the room could hear Volkov grinding his teeth.

Dernov broke the silence. "Actually, sir. If I may. If we could get the Americans out of the U.S., it might help us. Their Vice President and Secretary of State were in New York City. If they go to Paris, it will make it that much harder for them to respond once we attack. They would be away from their command-and-control facilities. It would give us an advantage."

After thinking it over, Volkov exhaled loudly. "Fine, you can go to Paris, Dmitri." He then focused on Dernov. "General, how much time until the *Belgorod* is in position?"

"Two days, sir," Dernov said confidently. "Two days and the *Belgorod* and every sub we have in our arsenal will be ready to initiate the attack and answer any response from the Americans."

Volkov nodded, happy to hear it, and then pointed a finger at Balakin. "There you go, Dmitri. I will give you forty-eight hours to get my *kotenok* out of the U.S. If she's not out by then, I can't help her." He stepped forward and thumped his index finger in the man's chest. "And then I expect you to execute my orders."

Balakin could do nothing else but nod and say, "Yes, sir."

CHAPTER 27

Over the Atlantic Ocean

Vice President Stubblefield sat behind his desk in his office onboard Air Force Two with Alexandra seated across from him. Neither had the luxury of relaxing. The President had sent them on the most important mission they would ever be on—trying to save America from a Russian nuclear attack. The two were hyper-focused on figuring out a way to make it happen.

For security purposes, Secretary of State Mike Arnold was traveling on a separate plane, but once they arrived in Paris, they were tasked with bringing the two countries back from the brink of war. The President remained at the White House and Secretary Javits at the Pentagon, both of them hoping that they didn't have to launch an attack if the three Americans in Paris failed in their mission.

Alexandra looked up from her phone. "There's an article that Foreign Minister Sokolov and Defense Minister Balakin are heading to Paris. The quotes from them don't sound positive. They're blaming us for the escalation of hostilities and saying they have a right to respond."

Stubblefield took off his reading glasses and rubbed his eyes. "That's not what we wanted to hear. At least they're coming to the table."

"How do you want to handle this?" Alexandra asked, turning off her phone. "Do we go after Sokolov or Balakin?"

"I think we let Mike meet with Sokolov—they're both the head diplomats for each country. But I think we need to stick with Balakin. You have a relationship with him, short as it may be, so maybe something can come of that."

"What are you thinking? What do you want me to do?"

Stubblefield sat back in his leather chair, his eyes glancing down to his chest and the pistol strapped in the shoulder holster on his left side. Usually in these types of situations, he had Duke on the other side of the desk. Duke had skills that most could only dream about, and Stubblefield knew what the man was capable of and how best to use him when it counted.

But now he had Alexandra—a beautiful, intelligent woman who

wasn't afraid to insert herself in compromising situations. There was a lot to work with, and she had assets that Duke didn't have. *How can I use her for the good of the country?* That's the question he had spent the last hour trying to answer.

But there was one nagging thought that kept popping up in his mind.

He remembered back to his time walking to the chopper with Duke after their meeting at the house. He had promised that he wouldn't put Alexandra in any dangerous situations. Duke wanted her to be safe so they could start a family and enjoy life. Stubblefield had thought it admirable, and Duke and Alexandra had certainly earned that right.

But that was then and this was now. Times had changed, and the United States was on the verge of nuclear war unless Stubblefield and Alexandra could figure out a way to stop it. He couldn't not use her. He had to use every weapon in his arsenal to stop the threat. And if that meant putting Alexandra to good use, so be it. She was a grown woman after all. She was entitled to make her own decisions.

"Any ideas?" she asked.

Stubblefield looked up and folded his hands in front of him. "A few weeks ago, Secretary Javits told us that Russia's three nuclear decision makers are Volkov, Balakin, and Dernov."

Alexandra nodded. "I remember you telling me and Duke that. Nothing can happen without all three of them."

"That's right. Volkov and Balakin each have a card of nuclear codes that are used to authenticate the launch order. It's similar to the one the President carries with him and can use with the nuclear football." He reached into his chest pocket of his shirt and pulled out his own card. "Just like mine in case the President is incapacitated and I have to give the order."

"Okay."

Stubblefield gave Alexandra a look, like she should take what he was about to say and run with it. And she could run with it any way she wanted.

"According to our intelligence, Balakin carries the card with him. We are pretty sure of that. But he can't authenticate a launch if he doesn't have his card."

"So we need to steal the card from him."

Stubblefield bit the inside of his lip, trying not to smile. He liked her style. He always thought he and Duke were on the same wavelength, so much so that they didn't even have to say what they were both thinking. And now he was beginning to believe the same about him and Alexandra. She was quick on her feet and knew desperate times called for desperate measures.

"Short of getting him to convince Volkov to back down, I think that is our only option. We need that card."

Alexandra leaned forward, her eyes wide with anticipation. "How are we going to get the card away from him?"

For a split second, Stubblefield hoped what was about to be said never made its way back to Schiffer. But, if it did, Stubblefield figured he'd deal with it then.

"I think the real question is," he said before pointing his finger at her. "How are *you* going to get the card away from him?"

* * *

Dmitri Balakin sat by himself in the back of his Russian Defense Ministry jet. He was running on fumes, and the contents of the glass of bourbon in his hand had done little more than dull his already frazzled senses. Once Volkov told him to go to Paris, he took the chopper back to Moscow. Given the importance of the meeting, he did take the time to shower and put on a fresh suit. He took his time. The meeting with the Americans wasn't until later that evening, and it was less than a five-hour flight to Paris.

Russia was going to war.

That was the realization that his mind was coming to grips with. Volkov was adamant, and there was no use trying to reason with him. The fact that the Americans tried to take him out was enough justification for him to unleash his hell on earth. And Balakin knew that if war started, Russia would have to go all in. If he wanted to become President someday and have the same power enjoyed by Volkov, Russia would have to win the war.

He took another drink, the bourbon washing down the back of his throat. He had come to the conclusion that war was inevitable. And as Defense Minister, he had to follow orders. Otherwise he would never become President. Or worse, Volkov would have him killed for being a traitor.

The only thing left to do was get Katia out of the U.S.

He had tried calling her three times already, but she never answered. It was the middle of the night in California, but he expected her to pick up. The messages he left on her voice mail had become increasingly agitated, a product of the booze and his nerves.

He pushed the speed dial for her and tried again. Finally, she picked up.

"Hello?"

"Katia, I have been trying to contact you, why haven't you picked up?"

It took her a second to respond, no doubt trying to figure out what was going on and how to respond. "Father, I have been asleep. I didn't hear the phone ring."

"Where are you?"

"I'm at my house in Los Angeles."

Balakin cursed, although he didn't know why since he wasn't surprised. She had not listened to his warnings. "Katia, you need to come home to Russia."

"Father, we have been through this," she said, sounding groggy to him. "I am working on my current project. Once it's finished, I'll try to come home to visit."

"No," he snapped. "You must come home now."

"This is my life, Father," she shot back. Her voice was clearer now and much more defiant. "I am entitled to make my own decisions. I love what I'm doing. I love being an actress. This is the life—"

"Katia! The war is going to start tomorrow!"

"What?"

Balakin cursed, in part because he had let the word out. But, at that moment, he didn't care if the Americans were listening, he only cared about his daughter.

"Katia, the war is going to start tomorrow," he said, softer this time. "You need to leave the United States immediately. You are not safe in Los Angeles."

"Father, you're scaring me."

"You should be scared. It is very serious."

"Can't you do anything about it? Can't you stop it?"

"Katia, the Americans tried to poison President Volkov. They tried to poison me. It is an act of war. We have every right to retaliate. Russia must stand up and defend itself."

"But war? Must we go to war?"

"We have no other choice. That is why you must leave now. Right now."

Balakin heard nothing but silence on the other end of the phone. *Why is she taking so long to respond? She is obstinate like her mother.*

"Katia?" He waited another few seconds. "Katia? Are you there?"

The call dropped. Disgusted, he threw the phone to the floor. Then he leaned forward and sunk his head into his hands.

"What the hell am I going to do?"

CHAPTER 28

Paris, France

Within minutes of Air Force Two touching down on the tarmac at Charles de Gaulle Airport on the outskirts of Paris, the Secret Service hustled the Vice President and Alexandra to the Ritz Paris, a luxury hotel four blocks from the American Embassy just off the Plaza de la Concorde.

Across the street on the Rue de la Paix was the Park Hyatt Paris-Vendôme, a five-star hotel that would house the Russian delegation. The meeting that evening was scheduled to take place at the Élysée Palace, the official residence of French President Marcel Pinot.

Stubblefield and Alexandra rode the elevator before heading to their separate rooms.

"We've got five hours to rest up," he said before parting ways with her. "I'm going to call the President to see if there's any news. Let me know if you have any ideas."

Alexandra said she would, but she had no intention of telling him about what she had planned. She shut the door to her room. Her bag was already on the bed. She opened it, grabbed her toiletry kit, and headed for the bathroom. She needed some time to herself. She thought it would help clear her mind. Or maybe it would muddy it, she wasn't sure.

After a few minutes to confirm what she already knew, she splashed water on her face, cooling her cheeks. Grabbing the towel, she looked at her reflection in the mirror. She knew she had to make a decision. She was either in or out. She couldn't help but think she had to take the chance. It was now or never.

She leaned forward, her hands bracing herself on the vanity. The U.S. was on the verge of nuclear war, and she was one of the few people on the planet who could have a hand in stopping it. What would she think of herself if she didn't take the chance to save the world? Chickening out now would haunt her for the rest of her life. If there was even a life to look forward to.

She knew what she had to do. It had to be done. She knew Duke would be mad, but he would forgive her once she explained herself. He would come to understand that she had no other choice but to give it a shot.

She knew he would do the same.

Alexandra raised her head and looked at herself in the mirror. She couldn't contain the smile that was forming. The decision had been made.

"Let's do this."

She reached for her phone, powered it up, and scrolled through her contacts list until she came to the name of Secretary of State Mike Arnold. She took a deep breath and then tapped the speed dial.

"Mr. Secretary, I'm sorry to bother you, but I need another favor."

Speaking from his hotel room one floor below, Secretary Arnold said, "Sure. What can I do for you?"

Alexandra licked her lips, wondering how he would take what she had to say. Only one way to find out. "I need a plane."

"A plane?"

"I need to get to Milan."

"A plane to Milan? What are you talking about?"

"I can't explain everything, Mike, but I need to go to Milan. There might be someone there who can help us with Balakin. But I don't have any time to waste. I need to get back before the meeting so I have to go now. I can't wait on a commercial flight or the train."

"Well," he said, thinking it through. "I guess I could let you take the State Department's plane. As long as the Vice President and Air Force Two are here, I could always hitch a ride with him if something happens."

"Thank you, Mike, but let's hope that doesn't happen. And I'd appreciate it if you keep this between us for now. No sense worrying the Vice President if there's nothing to worry about."

"Is there something to worry about, Alexandra? If something's going to put you in danger, I don't know if I should let you do whatever it is you're wanting to do. The President . . . the VP . . . your husband . . . I don't think they'd be too happy with me if something goes wrong."

"It's not dangerous, Mike. It has to do with that favor I asked you earlier. Nothing's going to go wrong. I just need to find an old friend who might be able to have an in with Balakin and I need to do it quick."

"Okay, I'll have my car take you to Charles de Gaulle, and I'll let the consulate in Milan know you're coming."

Alexandra smiled in the mirror. It was happening. She was doing this. "Thanks, Mike. I owe you another one."

Once the call ended, she hurried to change her clothes. She had brought five outfits with her and she went with one of her designer dresses. She left her hair to hang to her shoulders and threw on a little blush to color her cheeks. After she grabbed her purse, her phone, and her sunglasses, she was ready. She shut the door quietly and hurried past the Vice President's room. After telling the Secret Service agents guarding the floor that she had a meeting, she took the elevator down to the lobby and found an embassy car waiting at the curb.

On the way to the airport, she prayed her phone wouldn't ring. She hoped Stubblefield didn't call and ask to meet. Otherwise, she'd either have to lie or explain herself over the phone. She rather do it when she got back. She didn't think Secretary Arnold would tattle on her. She just needed to be careful that nothing went wrong.

The plane was waiting for her and she finally took a breath when the wheels lifted off the runway for the ninety-minute flight to Milan.

Her mind ran through all the possibilities. *What if I can't find who I'm looking for? And if she does, what if the person doesn't want to help? I guess it'll be Plan B then.*

Her phone vibrated and looking at the screen caused her to curse under her breath. Her husband. She debated whether she should take it. She could wait and say later that she was in the shower or in a meeting. But that excuse probably wouldn't fly for three hours. And telling him her phone was off wouldn't work—her phone always had to be on. She reluctantly tapped the screen to accept the call.

"Hey, babe," Duke Schiffer said.

"Hey."

"I just got off the phone with Ty. I'm still trying to get him to convince the President to go after the daughter."

"Uh huh," she said, hoping not to prolong the call any more than necessary.

"I think it can be done, but he still says the President doesn't want to do it."

"Yeah, that's what I'm hearing."

"What have you guys come up with for the meeting?"

"We're still working on it. Sokolov and Balakin are supposed to be in Paris, so we'll see if an agreement can be made." She left unsaid her conversation with Stubblefield regarding Balakin's nuclear card or the fact that she was currently thirty-thousand feet over France heading toward Italy. "We have a few more hours to strategize."

"Where are you?"

Her stomach dropped at the question. *You have got to be kidding me.* She had to think fast. Deflect and change the subject. "Where do you think I am? We landed in Paris an hour ago. Where are you?"

Unfortunately for Alexandra, her husband didn't take the bait. "It sounds like you're on an airplane. I thought Ty said you were at the hotel."

Alexandra cursed to herself. She should have expected nothing less from her husband—always observant of the surroundings, even hers, even when they were over five-thousand miles apart.

Son of a...

"Alexandra, where are you?"

Thankful there was no one else in the cabin with her, she didn't know whether to lie or come right out with it. Figuring he would find out one way or the other and he couldn't do anything about it now, she said, "I'm going somewhere, Duke."

"Somewhere?" His voice rose. "What are you talking about? Alexandra, where are you?"

"I'm going to Milan."

"Milan? What the hell are you going to do in Milan?"

"I'm hoping to meet with someone who can help with Minister Balakin," she shot back.

"Alexandra, how many times do I have to tell you? You are not a spy! You don't have the training!"

"You don't even know what I'm doing, Duke!"

"Who are you with? How many agents do you have with you?"

"I don't have anybody with me. I can't take agents away from the Vice President. I can take care of myself."

Schiffer cursed. "Alexandra, you don't know what you're doing!"

"I'll figure it out!" she yelled back.

"You don't have anyone to back you up! Are you out of your mind?"

"Hey! Don't yell at me! This is my life, Duke! I can do what I want when I want!"

Schiffer cursed again. "You're going to get yourself killed!"

She spat out an expletive in response. "I'm not going to get myself killed! It's not like I'm going to Baghdad." She rose from her seat and pounded the headrest with her fist. She had never been so mad at her husband. She didn't care if he was trying to protect her. She knew full well that he wouldn't back down if she was the one complaining that he was putting himself in danger. Well, two can play at that game.

"Alexandra, listen to me."

"No, you listen to me, Duke," she snapped in defiance. Now fully ticked, she added, "I'm going to Milan and you can't stop me."

"Alexandra."

Before she ended the call, she had one more thing to say. One last little nugget that she had intended to share with him in private but now thought she'd go ahead and throw in his face to piss him off some more.

"Oh, and by the way, I'm pregnant."

Click.

Milan, Italy

Luckily, Alexandra had thirty minutes remaining in the air before she landed at Milano Linate Airport. It gave her a chance to pace back and forth in the cabin in an attempt to calm down. After a few minutes, she was able to catch her breath and let her heart rate return to normal. She wondered what the pilots thought about her little outburst. After she had composed herself, she put it behind her when the wheels touched down on the tarmac. Once the plane came to a stop, she stepped down the airstairs and found a man standing in front of a black vehicle waiting for her.

He said his name was Chad. She was still new enough to the game that she wasn't sure if he was lying. He claimed he was an employee at the U.S. Consulate in Milan and he said his orders were to take her wherever she wanted to go.

"Do you have any bags?"

"No," she said, showing her purse and phone in her hands. "This is all I have. I won't be here long."

He held the car door open for her and she took a seat in the back. Once he was behind the wheel, she handed him a scrap of paper that contained the address of her destination.

He grabbed the note over his shoulder, looked at the street name and then her in the rearview mirror before saying, "This is where you want to go?"

"Yes. Do you know where it is?"

"Oh, yes. It's a popular area. Actually it's not far from the consulate. It won't take long."

"Good. Because I'm kind of in a hurry."

In the back seat, she kept her head on a swivel. The phone was in her hand but the ringer was off, not wanting any audible distractions. Duke had called twice after their little dustup, and she let the calls go to voice mail. She wanted no part of him at that moment. She needed to focus. With her mind running at what felt like a hundred miles per hour, she ran through every tip, trick, and rule that Duke had taught her.

It was time to put her training to good use.

Her eyes darted around, checking her surroundings. The car was a four-door Audi A3 with an automatic transmission. According to the dash, the gas tank was full. From what she could tell, "Chad," if that was his real name, was not armed, and she didn't see any pistols mounted under the dash or sawed-off shotguns stashed in the door.

Still, she surreptitiously opened her purse and made sure her tactical pen with the glass-breaking tip was within reach, just in case she had to break the door glass or plunge the tip into Chad's temple. The man wore glasses, and they were thick enough that Alexandra thought he might be at a disadvantage without them. She could get those off him fairly easily. Toss 'em to the floorboards and he might be blind as a bat. Seated behind him, she also knew she could stretch her seat belt far enough forward to wrap it around his neck and choke him to death.

She gasped silently. *My goodness, what has my husband done to me?*

Chad kept glancing up at her in the mirror, and she was glad she had brought her big sunglasses. Was the man acting suspicious? Was he really from the consulate? *Why are you looking at me, Chad? You got a problem? Keep your eyes on the road, bud.*

She decided to keep his focus where it needed to be. "How much longer?" she asked.

"Ten minutes if there's no traffic." He looked at her again. "Is it cool enough back there for you?"

"Yes, it's fine. Thank you."

At the red light, she noticed Chad rolled to a stop, nearly kissing the bumper of the car in front of him. Alexandra looked to her right and glanced out the back window in time to see a car pulling up close behind. Chad had allowed himself to get boxed in.

Idiot.

Realizing the automatic locks had engaged when the car was in gear, her left hand slowly reached toward the door and quietly raised the lock. Now she could bail out if need be. Although if she had to make a run for it, she wished she hadn't worn her heels. They would have to come off if there was a chase. She'd keep one as a weapon in case she needed to plunge the heel into someone's eye socket.

She wondered if this was what Duke felt like when he was on the hunt. *Control your breathing*, he always told her. She inhaled, held it, and then let it out. It helped so she did it again. Feeling loose, she wiggled her fingers to keep the blood flowing in case she needed to strike. She wished she had a gun, although she had no thought that she would need it where she was going.

"We're almost there." Chad pointed out the front windshield. "Coming up here on the right."

Alexandra unbuckled her seat belt as Chad pulled to the curb outside the Dolce & Gabbana store.

"Picking something up for yourself?"

"Not exactly. Wait right here."

Once out of the car, she straightened her dress, put her purse over her shoulder, and walked across the sidewalk and through the door. Once inside, she kept her sunglasses on. The rich and the famous always did it to keep their identity hidden, so she figured she wouldn't stick out. There would be plenty of rich female customers in there, too. With the way she was dressed, she'd fit in fine. She walked around the racks and the mannequins, not looking at the merchandise but praying that she would find what she was looking for.

And then she found the target.

Seated behind the desk, the sight of the woman brought back a flood of memories rushing through Alexandra's mind. It was good to see her again. With her yellow dress and tanned face, she looked like a ray of golden sunshine. Beautiful and gorgeous as ever. And, most importantly, safe since the last time they'd been together. Alexandra then felt a pang of worry flash through her gut, wondering if she was about to ask the woman to go into harm's way. Was she on a fool's errand? Was she wasting her time?

She had come too far to turn around now and the stakes were too high not to ask. Only one way to find out if the woman was up for it.

"Good afternoon," Alexandra said to the woman seated behind the desk.

"Good afternoon," the woman said in near perfect English. "Can I help you find something?"

"No, I believe I have found what I'm looking for."

When Alexandra removed her sunglasses, the woman's angelic face went white, like she was seeing a ghost of a former acquaintance in front of her. It didn't take but a second for her to realize who was speaking to her. Her chair rolled back as if an invisible force had slammed her in the chest.

"It is you! It is really you!"

"Yes, Gisella, it's me."

Gisella hurried out of her chair and rushed around the desk. She was about to go for a hug when she stopped abruptly to take a good long look at Alexandra. She still couldn't believe it.

Finally, realizing it wasn't a ghost staring her in the face, Gisella wrapped her arms around Alexandra. "I cannot believe it. I did not know whether you were dead or alive."

Alexandra held the hug until Gisella released.

"I'm very much alive, Gisella."

The two had first met at Karl Bonhoff's residence at the Odéon Tower in Monaco. Gisella and a dozen other models had been flown in from Milan to entertain Bonhoff with whatever he and his guests desired. Alexandra had been there for different reasons—to kill him.

For the short time they were together, Gisella had become a friend, a starry-eyed dreamer who thought her invitation to Bonhoff's would be the start of a blossoming career in the industry. They had chatted on the way up, and Alexandra found her to be nothing like the catty, backstabbing gossips that she expected of high-end models and call girls. Somehow, they had connected. But things went south quickly when Bonhoff fell to his death from the 47th-floor balcony after trying to kill Alexandra and her husband.

The last time Gisella saw Alexandra they were both rushing out of the building and running for their lives.

Alexandra escaped with Duke and the Israelis to make it back to the U.S. Gisella had no choice but to return to Milan in hopes of making her dream of becoming a fashion model come true. But, as is so often the case in the ruthless world of fashion, her career hit the skids when she turned the ripe old age of thirty. Now she had to compete against women with bigger boobs, tighter rears, and longer legs, and there was always someone younger, prettier, and perkier who was willing to do whatever it took to claw their way to the top.

She picked up modeling gigs when she could and spent the rest of her days as a "fashion associate" in one of Dolce & Gabbana's Milan stores.

"I could never find out what happened to you," Gisella said. "I looked in all the papers and the stories were so very vague. I could not believe it. It felt like something out of a movie. And then it was like you vanished into thin air."

"I can see how it would seem like that."

"I was so worried about you. People claimed it was the Israelis behind Bonhoff's death."

"I have heard that, too."

"It all made me wonder." Gisella looked both ways before whispering, "Were you with them? Are you an Israeli spy?"

Alexandra felt a tingle ripple up and down her spine but she kept the smile hidden by biting the inside of her lip. Someone wondered if she was a spy—a spy! *What would Duke think?*

"I'm not Israeli," she said, letting it hang out there that she might be an American spook.

"What are you doing here?"

"I wanted to talk with you and see whether you're interested in helping me."

"Helping you?"

Alexandra looked at her watch. "How much longer are you working?"

"We are about ready to close. Why?"

"How would you like to go to Paris with me?"

"Paris?"

"Yeah."

"When?"

"Right now. I've got a plane and I'll explain on the way." When Gisella hesitated, looking like she wasn't up for it, Alexandra hoped one last question would convince her. "Gisella, how would you like to help me save the world?"

CHAPTER 29

Paris, France

When the plane from Milan landed in Paris, the round trip had only taken a little over three-and-a-half hours. Still time before the meeting with the Russians.

With Gisella right behind her, Alexandra unlocked the door to her hotel room and walked in . . . to find a six-foot-four black man sitting on her bed.

"Jeez!" she yelled, throwing a hand to her chest. She blurted out a profanity. "Ty!"

"Good evening, Alexandra."

With his back against the headboard, Vice President Stubblefield, a stern frown on his face, sat on top of the made bed in his suit and tie, his hands across his stomach, his dress shoes crossed. Thankfully, his pistol was still in its holster. Her absence had not gone unnoticed, and Stubblefield had every intention of making sure she knew the problems she had caused.

"How did you . . . ?" Alexandra felt a hand behind her, but she waved off Gisella's concern. "It's okay," she told her. "He's with me."

Stubblefield chuckled, amused at the claim. "Yeah, *I'm* with *her*. Although it would probably be more accurate to say that *she's* with *me*. At least that's the way it was supposed to be." He pointed at Gisella. "And who is this?"

"This is Gisella. She's a friend of mine." She turned and said, "Gisella, this is the Vice President of the United States."

Stubblefield threw his legs off the bed and stood. He extended a hand to her. "Gisella, a pleasure."

Gisella had a look of disbelief on her face, as if wondering what in the world she had gotten herself into. She was in a Paris hotel room with a possible American spy along with the man who was next in line to the presidency. Still in shock, her shaking hand got lost in Stubblefield's and she said something incomprehensible to him, possibly an Italian expletive.

Stubblefield turned his focus back to Alexandra. "And you, young lady, have some explaining to do." He held up his phone and then in his deep voice lit into her. "I just spent the last half hour getting my ass chewed out by your husband."

Alexandra's shoulders drooped and she let out a groan.

"Oh, yeah. He reamed me a new one pretty good. Blamed me for letting you jet off to who knows where for who knows what. It's lucky he's not over here. He's so ticked off he probably would have shot me. Then he'd go looking for you."

She held out her hands to stop him. "I have an idea."

"Oh, you do? Well, hell's bells, would you care to share it with me?"

"It has to do with Minister Balakin."

Stubblefield put his hands on his hips and grimaced. He then grabbed Alexandra's triceps, firm enough that it had meaning. They were going somewhere. "If you'll excuse us, Gisella, Alexandra and I need to speak in private."

Once Stubblefield marched her down to his suite, he shut the door. "Duke's not happy."

"Trust me, I know. I heard it from him on the phone, and I don't need to hear it from you. I can handle myself, Mr. Vice President. You two act like I'm a defenseless little girl who doesn't have a clue what's going on. For goodness sakes, I was once the Ambassador to Egypt."

"With a security detail."

"I made it back here, didn't I?"

Stubblefield shook his head, not appreciating the sass and she was spewing forth a lot of it. He didn't know whether he should be mad at her or impressed that she took some initiative. There was one thing that was bugging him, though.

"And you're pregnant?" The head shaking became more adamant. "Huh? You didn't think to tell me that little bit of information when we were discussing what we were going to do on the flight over here? Did it just slip your mind? Did you happen to think I might have wanted to know that before I let you go into harm's way?"

"I didn't know, Ty," she snapped back. "Not until after we landed and I got to the hotel room. I haven't been feeling well in the last week. I thought it might be because I was pregnant, so I finally took the test. The stick was positive. I guess I am."

After an audible sigh, Stubblefield ran his hand over his bald head, his jaw clenched. Now he had two people to worry about instead of just one. Yes, she was a grown woman, but now she was a grown woman with child.

Nothing he could do about it now. And they still had other important matters staring them in the face. He tried to refocus.

"Who is the woman? This Gisella."

"I met her at Bonhoff's penthouse in Monaco. She was one of the models that was brought in. We hit it off. I think she might be of use to us."

"Use to us?"

"Yeah, I have an idea."

"Can we trust her?"

"Yes. She has a great heart and she wants to do some good. I can tell. I haven't got into too many specifics with her, but I think she can help."

"What are we going to do? What's your plan?"

For the next several minutes, Alexandra laid out her idea. It was a bold plan, and one that had some chance of success, especially given Balakin's history. It could also go the other way and quicken Russia's pace to start the war. But it showed promise.

Stubblefield cursed, realizing the plan was good enough that he had to okay it. He cursed again. "Duke is going to kill me."

Near Gelendzhik, Russia

President Volkov took a step outside of his office to breathe in the salty air rolling off the Black Sea. The coughing fit had returned, painful and worse than ever. He could almost feel his lungs wasting away. He knew he had a dwindling number of breaths left in life.

But he felt good, strong in fact, better than he had felt in years. He knew his time had come. It was time to change the world and make his permanent mark on history. It would be glorious, and he would soon be revered more than Stalin and Lenin combined. The Americans couldn't stop him. In fact, it was the Americans who would be blamed for giving him no choice but to strike a death blow to the United States. He hoped he lived long enough to see the American people suffering through the ravages of a dying country, having been defeated once and for all by the mighty Russians.

Rejuvenated even more, Volkov headed into his office and picked up the phone. "General, are you ready?"

"We are almost ready, sir," General Dernov said. "But preparations to strike can begin on your orders."

"The *Belgorod*?"

"Sir, I think it is time to let the Americans know they are no match for our *Belgorod*. We have been toying with them. Now it's time to vanish and get into launch position."

Volkov smiled, pleased at what he was hearing. "Good. Let's do that. Get the bombers fueled and ready."

"Already done, sir. Missile sites are locked and loaded."

"You have done good work, General. Soon we will be celebrating this amazing achievement. Make sure you let your counterparts in China and North Korea know that we are ready to launch in case they want to get in on the fun. It can only help us."

Volkov ended the call. There was only one other person he needed to talk to. He ordered his secretary to get Minister Balakin on the phone.

He waited, standing at his desk. The coughing returned, and he grunted in pain as the phlegm rose from his chest and into his throat. Nearly gagging, he spat it out into the trash can and grunted again. Weakened by the episode, he yanked the phone off the cradle.

"Where the hell is Minister Balakin?" he yelled.

"He's not answering his phone, sir. It's possible that he is en route to his meeting with the Americans."

Volkov pounded the desk with his fist. He needed Balakin to launch the nukes.

"Try him again."

Another minute passed before the secretary returned on the line and said, "Still no answer, sir. Shall I try his security detail or Minister Sokolov?"

Volkov clenched his fists. He wasn't surprised that Balakin would be hesitant. The man had his sights on the presidency, and that meant he did not always have Volkov's interests at heart. Or, at least, they weren't his number one priority.

But Volkov knew how to change that.

"Shall I call them, sir?"

"No," Volkov answered. "I will make the call myself."

Volkov stabbed the button on his desk phone to end the call. He then reached into his pocket and pulled out his cell phone. He found the number and tapped the button. Oleg Roznak picked up.

"Oleg, where are you?"

"I'm in the air over France."

"Are your men ready?"

"They are ready on multiple continents, Yuri. Europe . . . America. Just as you requested and expected. You have many options before and after the bombs drop."

"That is good to hear."

"What do you need from me?"

Volkov liked the man, always eager to get his hands dirty. He was a bully and didn't have an agenda. He simply liked to hurt people. Exactly what Volkov needed. He had learned early on that he couldn't simply rely on political and military leaders to carry out his orders. He needed thugs and assassins—violent men who could break legs and slit throats.

Now was the time.

"I'm having trouble contacting Minister Balakin. I want you to let him know that it is time to execute the plan to strike the United States."

"Yes, sir."

"He must know the severity of the situation. He has to act to enable us to strike."

"I can make sure he has no other option but to execute your orders, sir."

"Yes, just like we discussed."

"I can make it happen quickly, Mr. President. I will see to it personally."

"Good." Volkov took in a breath. He waited for the cough but it didn't come. He felt good again, his spirits buoyed by his plan. Threats always worked. And he knew the one threat that would strike Balakin in the heart. It would give the man no choice but to execute the President's orders.

"You will be richly rewarded for your loyalty, Oleg. Now go make sure Minister Balakin gets the message loud and clear."

CHAPTER 30

The White House – Washington, D.C.
 "Ty, what's going on?" the President asked over the secure video chat.
 From his hotel suite, Stubblefield sat in his shirt and tie, his pistol at the ready. "We're about to head to the meeting with Sokolov and Balakin."
 "Have you heard anything from the Russians? Any movement?"
 "Negative. Mike hasn't heard anything either."
 "You come up with any plans?"
 "We have some ideas. It all depends on the circumstances."
 "We're running out of time, Ty."
 "We're trying, sir."
 The President's eyes were drawn to another screen on the wall. The graphic for the Defense Department was replaced by Secretary Javits, his suit coat off and his tie loosened. He looked like he hadn't slept in days. He glanced off screen before focusing on the camera in front of him.
 "Mr. President, can you hear me?"
 "I can hear you, Russ. Where are you?"
 "I'm at the Pentagon. Chairman Cummins is meeting with the Joint Chiefs. Sir, we have spotted four Russian bombers in the air over Cuba. We're also seeing increased air traffic from the Russian aircraft carrier in the Pacific. I think this is it, sir. The attack is about to start."
 Another screen flickered with activity. The screen was filled by the big-bodied Chairman of the Joint Chiefs of Staff, Hugh Cummins. He didn't wait around to see if the President could hear him or politely find a moment to insert himself into the conversation.
 "Mr. President, we have a problem."
 The President ran a hand over his head. He felt like he was trying to drink from three different fire hoses at once. "What is it, General?"
 "We've lost the *Belgorod*."
 "What?"
 "The *Belgorod* has fallen off our sonar screens. We don't know where it is."
 "Ty . . . Russ, are you hearing this?"
 Stubblefield and Javits confirmed they had heard the Chairman's

report.

"Last known location?" the President asked.

"South of Nova Scotia heading southwest toward the United States."

"What is your best guess of its path?"

"Off the coast east of Washington, D.C."

Javits chimed in. "Sir, with bombers in the air and the *Belgorod* missing, I think this confirms the attack is about to start. You need to get ready to launch."

Special Agent Mac Clark took a step toward the President. "Sir, we have to go."

The President looked at him but made no verbal response. The fact that he didn't tell him to back off because he wasn't leaving the White House said something. But still, the President didn't move, contemplating how to respond.

"Sir, I know what you're thinking," Javits said, interrupting. "But you are not running away. You are not abandoning the fort. You are getting a bird's-eye view of the fort so you can have a clear vision of what decisions need to be made. And if the Russians are successful in knocking out communications at the White House, it will be that much more difficult to issue your orders. That's if you're still alive. The country needs you where you can see the big picture and give the orders. And it looks like you're going to need to give those orders within the next several hours."

"I agree with Russ, Mr. President," Stubblefield said. "You have a duty to the American people to get to a place where you can safely run the war. You need to get to a more secure location."

When the President didn't respond, Javits added, "I think I should go to the mobile command post, too. Chairman Cummins is getting ready to go to Site R. He can conduct emergency operations from there. If the nukes start falling, we all need to be in positions to respond, preferably away from Washington."

The President closed his eyes and took a few seconds to breathe. If Javits was ready to move and General Cummins was heading to the Underground Pentagon at the Raven Rock Mountain Complex in Pennsylvania, it was obvious both men believed the excrement was about to hit the fan. The President needed to do the same.

Still, the last thing he wanted to do was run. It looked like he was going to have to make the most momentous decision of his presidency—either launch an initial nuclear strike or retaliate in response. He would be no good if a Russian nuke buried him in the bunker of the White House.

Rubbing the back of his neck, he opened his eyes when he felt movement next to him.

"Sir," Agent Clark said, reaching out a hand but stopping short of grabbing him. "We can't wait any longer. We need to go."

The President nodded but not before thumping the table with his fist. He looked at Javits. "Russ, implement the continuity of government procedures. Get the cabinet, congressional leaders, and Supreme Court Justices where they need to be."

"Yes, sir, I'm on it."

Knowing nuclear war could be imminent and an immediate response required, the President added, "And go to DEFCON One."

"Roger that," Javits said. He twirled a finger to someone off screen before returning his focus to the President. "It's done."

Before another ninety seconds could pass, LGM-30 Minuteman missile silos in Montana and North Dakota would be readied for launch, B-2 Stealth bombers would roar off the runway in Missouri and take to the skies over the heartland of America, and Ohio-class Trident submarines in every corner of the globe would prepare for nuclear war.

"Ty, stay in contact. Get a deal in place that will buy us some time. If you can't, get in the air."

"Yes, sir."

The President stood and looked at Agent Clark. "Where's my wife?"

"We have her packed and ready to go."

Before the President left the Situation Room, he picked up the phone. "Get me the Secret Service Director."

"Yes, sir," the watch officer said.

Within twenty seconds, Director Defoe was on the line. "Yes, Mr. President."

"Allen, I want you to increase the security around my kids."

"I can do that. Is everything all right?"

"No, everything is not all right. I just want it done immediately."

"I'll get right on it."

The President hung up and looked at Agent Clark. "Okay, let's go."

With four agents leading the way, the President and Agent Clark hurried up the stairs from the Situation Room. Clark was on his mic, quietly giving orders and letting all agents know that Shadow and Sunshine would soon be on the move.

The President found the First Lady in the Oval Office.

The look in his eyes must have given something away because his wife asked, "What's wrong? What's going on?"

"It's going to be okay," he said to her.

"What about the kids?"

"I've taken care of it. They'll be okay. We just need to go."

As the President and First Lady left the White House to the waiting chopper, their ears told them something out of the ordinary was going on. The sound of sirens were common to those who lived and worked in D.C., but the sheer volume coming from every direction was almost deafening. Secret Service tactical teams were stationed inside and outside the fence on the South Lawn and snipers were on the roof of the White House pointed in every direction. The sky above thundered with the sounds of jet fighters conducting combat air patrols. Three decoy Marine One choppers were already in the air near the Washington Monument waiting for the President's to join them and begin the shell game to thwart any attempted missile attacks on the way to Joint Base Andrews.

Across D.C., the skies were littered with Black Hawk helicopters, a line forming on the East Front of the Capitol as high-level members of Congress and Cabinet secretaries were being picked up and whisked away to secure locations. Streets were being blocked off, and Patriot missile batteries took position up and down the National Mall from the Lincoln Memorial to Capitol Hill.

The press was told nothing other than the President and First Lady were leaving the White House. No reporters or cameras were allowed to watch or record the departure, and those at their fixed camera positions were ordered to evacuate the grounds because the White House was being locked down.

The nation's capital was preparing for battle.

As soon as the Marine crew chief secured the door, Marine One's blades began to turn. Sixty seconds later, it was in the air and clearing the fence at the edge of the South Lawn.

The cabin was eerily quiet, despite the two General Electric turboshaft engines running at full song. The cacophony of noise that had surrounded the President over the last few minutes was gone. He knew it wouldn't last. This was the calm before the storm. As the chopper flew southeast, the Jefferson Memorial passed by underneath, the Capitol Building off to the President's left. He wondered if they'd still be there when he returned. If he ever returned. He tried to burn a mental image into his brain just in case.

A bolt of fear shook him out of his thoughts.

He hurriedly reached down to the pocket of his suit coat, searching for his nuclear authentication card—the so-called biscuit. He had a fleeting worry that he had forgotten it in the rush to the leave the White House. He let out a breath when he fingered the card and took it out. There was a good chance he was going to have to use it in the very near future.

The President took a breath. He needed to clear his mind for the decisions that would have to be made. *See the play*, he thought to himself. *Then make the decision and execute the plan. Let the people around you do what they've been trained to do.* He put the card back in his pocket and balled his fists to release the tension. It was time to lead.

Joint Base Andrews – Camp Springs, Maryland

With the three decoy choppers peeling off, Marine One touched down at Joint Base Andrews in less than twenty minutes, and it immediately headed for one of the hangars to keep the President from being exposed to the open air as much as possible.

After he saluted the Marine at the foot of the stairs, he helped his wife down and they headed inside to find a white Boeing 747 with a single blue stripe across its fuselage and below the stenciled *United States of America*. An American flag on the tail was the only other thing that provided some color.

Colonel Max Petitt, the commander of the 89th Airlift Wing in charge of airlifting the President around the world, met him. They shook hands. There were no smiles, just determined looks on the faces of everyone in the hangar. The President pointed to the 747.

"Where's Air Force One?" he asked Colonel Petitt in the absence of the usual, blue-bellied jumbo jet that ferried him all over the world.

"This is it, sir. It's the E-Four B. This is Air Force One today."

The President quickly nodded, realizing why he had been mistaken. The call sign for any plane he steps on board is referred to as Air Force One. But, given the circumstances, his usual plane was being swapped out for one of the most secure planes ever constructed.

The Air Force's E4-B, dubbed the "Doomsday Plane," was a heavily modified Boeing 747 that contained every type of communication system imaginable and was shielded to protect those systems from a nuclear blast or an electromagnetic pulse. Capable of in-flight refueling that allowed it to stay aloft for a whole week, it acted as a mobile command post for the National Command Authority—the President and Secretary of Defense.

With a battle staff of nearly sixty, including communications specialists, launch system operators, and support personnel, they could conduct the war from anywhere. Secretary Javits was currently making his way to the Navy's own "Doomsday Plane," the E-6 Mercury.

"Colonel Hauser is at the controls, sir. He's ready to roll when you say the word."

"I'm ready. Let's go."

As soon as the President, the First Lady, a handful of White House staffers, and the Secret Service agents were on board, the hangar doors were opened. In less than three minutes, Colonel Sam Hauser had the E4-B's giant GE turbofan engines roaring off the runway before putting it into a steep climb and heading west.

"Where are we going?" the President asked Agent Clark.

"We're going to Offutt," Clark said, referring to Offutt Air Force Base near Omaha, Nebraska, and the home of the 1st Airborne Command Control Squadron. "That's where the E-Four-Bs are based, and middle America is the safest place for you right now."

Given that the E-4B had a specific purpose in mind, keeping the National Command Authority safe so it could send orders of war around the world, the furnishings were spartan. The President found the conference room and waited for the screens to come to life.

"Russ, can you see and hear me?"

"I read you loud and clear, sir."

"Let's hope our communications don't flame out up here."

"They won't, sir. We tested them within the last week. Every one of them. Even the VLF communications with the five-mile trailing wire antenna. You'll be able to communicate with any sub anywhere on the planet. I have full faith in the E-Four-B's capabilities and that of the crews."

"Roger that, Russ. Let's pray you're right because we're going to need them"

CHAPTER 31

Paris, France

The thunderstorm that was pummeling Paris did little to lessen the tension in the air. With news reports indicating war between the United States and Russia was imminent, the rumbling thunder and flashes of lightning gave many additional reasons to scurry for cover. Parisians worried their country would be drawn into war, maybe even invaded, and a few of them were old enough to shudder at the thought of foreign armies marching up and down the Champs-Élysées.

President Pinot was waiting at the main entrance to the Élysée Palace as the Russian and U.S. delegations began to arrive for the last-ditch effort at peace. Secretary Arnold arrived first, and he wore a somber look as he shook the hand of the French President. He was then whisked off to a holding room. Minister Sokolov arrived next, and the hardened look of an ex-Soviet communist told the world that the chances for peace were miniscule.

From the Diplomatic Security Service agents guarding Secretary Arnold, Vice President Stubblefield was being fed constant updates on those in the Russian delegation. There had been no sign of Minister Balakin.

Stubblefield held his hand over his phone as he spoke to Special Agent David Rose, the head of his Secret Service detail. "Any movement from Balakin?"

"No. Our guys watching the Hyatt haven't seen him."

"Do you know if he's still in the country?"

"We believe so. His plane is still at the airport."

Stubblefield then told the DSS agent to keep him posted if anything changed. He ended the call and focused on Alexandra.

"Balakin hasn't showed up yet." He looked at his watch. "The meeting has started. He's either late or he's not coming."

"It could be they're holding him in reserve like we're doing with you. Bring him in at the last minute to get a deal done."

"I don't know if we can wait around hoping that's the case. It could all be a bluff on the part of the Russians to distract us. If nothing else, they succeeded in getting me and Secretary Arnold out of the U.S."

"What do you want to do?"

Stubblefield stood and turned his back to her. He could feel his teeth grinding as he knew a decision had to be made. He told himself to put the threats from Schiffer out of his mind. Alexandra wasn't going to be involved in any gunplay . . . at least he didn't think so. He winced at the thought. What if something happened to her? To the baby? He shook his head to clear the thoughts from his mind. What if the Russians launched their nukes? What would that mean for the U.S.? For Alexandra? For the baby?

"Ty?"

He turned around, and their eyes met. "Are you up for this?"

"Yes," she said without hesitation. She stood, like she was ready to go. "I can do this." She gestured to her room on the other side of the wall. "It's why I brought Gisella here. We can get in there. Knowing Balakin like I do, I'd bet my life on it."

Stubblefield's face hardened, ready to give her the mission instructions. It was pretty simple. "We need his nuclear card, Alexandra."

* * *

Alexandra hurried to her room. This was the moment she had been waiting for. She knew she had to come through. She opened the door to find Gisella seated on the bed reading a fashion magazine. Taking a seat next to her, Alexandra ran through the plan with her, giving her reasons why they were doing it and what was at stake. Alexandra hinted at how Gisella could play her role, offering ideas that she could use on Balakin.

"I'm not asking you to do anything illegal, Gisella. And if you don't feel comfortable doing something, you can leave the room. All you need to do is be yourself. I just need a few minutes to get that card from Balakin."

"That card is important?"

"Yes, the Russians can't launch if Minister Balakin can't authenticate himself with that card."

"Do you know where he keeps it?"

"Not exactly. I would imagine it's somewhere that he can get to it quickly. Either in his pants pocket, his suit coat, or near his phone."

"If it's in his pants pocket, how are you going to get it?"

Alexandra raised her eyebrows, not needing to utter a verbal response.

"Oh!" Gisella said, getting the hint.

"Like I said, you don't have to do anything you don't want to do. And you can leave at any time. I'm not going to let Minister Balakin hurt you. He's not that kind of guy. I just need you to distract him long enough to give me time to find it."

"I can do it, Alexandra. I know what to do. I know how to take a man's mind off things."

With the driving rain pelting the streets of Paris, the Secret Service drove Alexandra and Gisella the two blocks to the Park Hyatt.

"Are you sure you don't want us to go with you?" the agent in the front passenger seat asked Alexandra.

"No. We'll be fine. I'll call if we need you."

Entering the hotel, Alexandra said she needed to go to the bar. Once inside, she headed straight for the bartender.

"Do you have a bottle of Pappy Van Winkle?"

The bartender could not control his snicker, the typical haughty French look he reserved especially for American tourists. "*Oui.*"

"I want it."

At six-foot-three, the man looked down on her, sneering as if she was a redneck rube just up from the holler after a dip in the crick. "Madame, it is very expensive. People buy it by the glass not by the bottle."

"I want the whole bottle." She slid her credit card across the bar.

"Like I said, it is very expensive."

"How much?"

"Twenty-four-hundred euros."

She slid the card closer to him. "I want it, and I want it now."

The man eyed her derisively, like he either didn't want to sell it to an American or was kicking himself for not charging her more.

"And a bottle of sparkling champagne, too. Non-alcoholic."

"Non-alcoholic champagne?" he snorted, acting like she had offended him and millions of his fellow Frenchmen.

"Yes, and I'm in a hurry."

The bartender reluctantly made the sale and then used his hands to shoo them away.

With the bottles in hand, the two women were about to leave the bar when Alexandra made a beeline to the ladies' room. Once inside, she started unwrapping the bottle of champagne. She popped the cork off and poured the contents down the sink.

"What are you doing?" Gisella asked.

"I have an idea." She washed out the bottle more than once and then filled it with water before jamming the cork back in. It may have been non-alcoholic, but she wasn't taking any chances. Plus, she didn't care for the taste of champagne, especially now with her stomach on edge. "Okay, let's go."

They headed toward the main elevator, which was guarded by three Russian security agents. The men took notice as the women approached, having a hard time not ogling the eye candy that was coming toward them.

"Let's hope this works," Alexandra said.

Alexandra had gone with her little black dress, dignified yet appropriate for a night on the town. Gisella had brought only one other outfit with her—a yellow mini-dress that looked like a thin sheet of rubber had been shrink-wrapped around her. It was tight and short enough that little was left to the imagination. Every bit of her was magnificent.

Alexandra took the lead with the man in front.

"We need to see Minister Balakin."

"He's busy."

Alexandra noticed that the man didn't dismiss them out of hand. He could have told them to get lost or have them escorted off the premises. But it was obvious that he had been approached by beautiful women destined to see Balakin before.

"I know he is, but I think he'll want to talk with me and my friend. It's very important. Tell him Alexandra Julian is here." She showed him her identification and let it be known that she worked for the White House.

The man studied the ID and then her.

"And show him a picture of this," Alexandra said, handing the bottle of bourbon to Gisella.

The security agent looked at Alexandra, appearing to admire her moxie, and then Gisella with her high-end bourbon. He smiled. "You know Minister Balakin well," he said, raising his phone at Gisella to snap a photo. "Wait here."

The wait took five minutes. Long enough that Alexandra began to worry. What if she couldn't get up there? There was no Plan B. This was it. It was up to her.

The elevator doors opened, and the agent from before waved them forward. "You have to be patted down."

Alexandra nodded, expecting it.

The man took his time running his hands over their bodies, lingering on places that no weapon would ever be found. Once the groping ended, he pointed toward the open elevator.

When the doors closed, Alexandra gripped the bottle of champagne hard. This was her moment. This was what she had been telling her husband she could do. This was her chance to change the world for the better.

Breathe in . . . breathe out.

At the sixth floor, the doors opened, and the security agent led them down the hall to the Ambassador Suite. Two more agents were stationed outside. They looked on but said nothing. Both had seen beautiful women ushered in on numerous occasions. The lead agent swung open the door to Balakin's suite and motioned them inside before shutting the door behind them.

They were in.

Now all Alexandra had to do was find the card.

CHAPTER 32

Air Force One over Illinois

"Mr. President!" Secretary Javits said. "Our satellite intel shows the Russians are opening their missile silos. They are preparing to launch."

"How reliable is that intel, Russ?"

"Good enough not to take it lightly."

The President ran a hand over his head, the information coming in from all corners.

"Where is General Cummins?"

"He's at Site R. He's seeing the same intel I'm seeing."

"Is the Pentagon ready?"

"Yes, the Director of Operations, General Ricks, is in the war room and ready to relay your orders to the combatant commanders."

"Okay."

The President told an Air Force staffer to get General Cummins and General Ricks on a video chat so he could see who he was talking to.

"Russ, tell everyone to standby."

CIA Director Parker appeared on another screen.

"Go ahead, Bill," the President said.

"Mr. President, the FBI is reporting there is smoke coming from the Russian Embassy in D.C. They might be destroying their classified documents. I think this is it, sir."

"Do we know the whereabouts of Ambassador Grigorov?"

"He left D.C. this morning to return to Moscow."

The President cursed.

"Sir," Agent Clark said, interrupting the President's video call. "Director Defoe believes you should skip Offutt and head to Colorado Springs and Cheyenne Mountain."

"Why?"

"It can withstand a nuclear blast better than the bunkers at Offutt. You can run the war from NORAD."

The President looked at Javits and Parker and then the phone. His mind was trying to do two things at once. More like five things at once. He picked up the phone and hit the number for the cockpit. "Colonel."

"Yes, sir."

"Cheyenne Mountain."

"Roger that."

That's all it took. The President hung up and told Javits to put all American forces on the highest alert.

Paris, France

"Minister Balakin," Alexandra said. "Thank you for meeting with us."

Upon glancing at the women, a visibly agitated Balakin stopped pacing near the windows. "Now is not a good time, Alexandra."

She scanned the suite, trying to keep her head still as her eyes went back and forth in search of where the card might be hidden. Balakin was wearing black dress slacks, a white shirt, and a black tie. His suit coat was off, and she didn't see it anywhere. The fireplace was lit, and he had a drink in his hand.

Even though he said now was not a good time, he had allowed them to come up. Alexandra saw the opening.

"I was worried about you when you didn't show up at the meeting tonight. I thought something might be wrong."

Balakin turned toward them, giving a longer look at the two. Alexandra could read the tell he gave off, his eyes flickering with excitement at seeing the two beautiful women. He couldn't help himself. It was a part of who he was. He downed the contents of his glass and set it down. He then focused on Alexandra and a surprised look crossed his face.

"Alexandra, are you drunk?"

Perhaps he saw that she was shaking or the fact that her cheeks were red. She shifted her weight ever so slightly, as if she might be a little tipsy. "Not yet. Are you?"

"It takes a lot for a Russian to get drunk. I'm surprised at you, though. I would have thought with the seriousness of our situation that you would want to stay sober."

"Given the seriousness of our situation, Dmitri, sometimes a drink is the only thing that can keep us going. We've only had a little." She pointed at Gisella, who was holding the bottle of bourbon in front of her. "I brought you a gift."

Balakin walked toward the woman, eyeing her more than the bottle. "And who might you be?"

"I'm Gisella. It is a pleasure to meet you, Minister Balakin."

Balakin took immediate interest in her, what with the tight dress, the ample breasts, and the Italian accent. "You don't sound American."

"Italian. I'm from Milan."

"Milan? And how do you know Alexandra?"

Gisella looked at Alexandra, as if wanting to know what she should say. They hadn't prepared a backstory. "I met her during one of my previous modeling jobs."

While Balakin ogled Gisella, Alexandra eyed everywhere she could. *Where is that suit coat?* The closet doors were shut, and a suitcase sat closed on the floor outside of the bedroom. Coming up empty, she knew she had no other choice but to snoop around.

"I thought we could discuss business, Dmitri. Our meeting was cut short last time, and we might be able to come to an agreement better than our respective diplomats. You know how stuffy they can be."

Balakin offered a wry smile. "And you thought bringing your model friend would help?"

"I figured it certainly couldn't hurt. Would you like for me to send her away?"

He reached out a hand toward Gisella, gently grabbing hers, the ladies' man coming out in him. "No, of course not. That would be rude."

"Perhaps we could open her bottle."

Balakin took the bourbon and read the label. "Oh my. You definitely have good taste in bourbon, Gisella. Let's open this up."

That was all Alexandra needed. "Let me find some glasses."

She didn't wait around for Balakin to stop her and offer assistance. With the champagne in her hand, she went straight toward the door on the left, hoping it was the bathroom. It was.

With her heart rate shooting through the roof, her focus failed her. Her eyes darted left and right, forgetting to even take in what she was seeing.

Calm down. Breathe. Look for the card.

She found the glasses upside down in the corner of the vanity. "Found some," she announced. She grabbed two, clinking the glass. A closet off to the left of the vanity was closed. She hurried to open it, eyeing the rack inside and the cubbyholes full of unused bath towels.

Nothing.

Alexandra was coming up empty. The only other spot for a suit coat or a pair of pants was on the back of the door. She prayed one of them would be there. She couldn't stay there much longer. Her hands were shaking, and a fleeting thought flashed through her mind as to how she was going to rifle through the pockets with a bottle of fake champagne in one hand and two glasses in the other.

Her eyes looked behind the door, and her heart suddenly felt like it was going to explode. A black pair of dress pants hung from the hook. *Were they his dress pants destined to be worn at the meeting? Had he taken them off to keep them from getting wrinkled? More importantly, did he leave the card inside one of the pockets?* She wondered how her husband kept from shaking like a leaf in these situations.

Holding the champagne in her right hand with the two glasses stacked on top of each other on the bottle's cork, she reached up with her left hand and plunged it down into the pocket.

Empty.

She went to the right, sliding her hand down the fabric that enveloped her up to her wrist. Her fingers felt something. Plastic. Shaped like a rectangle. It was the only thing in there.

The card.

She got it. She had to bite the inside of her lip to keep from screaming with excitement. She actually got it. She wanted to run, to grab Gisella by the hand and get the heck out of there and back into the company of the Secret Service and Vice President Stubblefield. They would be safe.

More importantly, the world would be saved.

She had it out of the pocket when she jumped at the sound of Balakin's voice.

"Need any help?"

Palming the card in her left hand against the bottle, she looked around the door. His eyes were focused on hers. She wondered if he could see her heart beating through her chest. Had she been found out? What would he do to her? To them?

"Can I give you a hand?"

"Yes, yes," she blurted out. "Could you take these two? I need to get another one."

Once he took the glasses and turned around, she steadied herself against the door. Then she went back to the corner of the vanity for another glass. She felt like she was going to vomit, the exhilaration of the moment bubbling up inside her and ready to explode.

She couldn't believe she had done it. She could only imagine what her husband would think of her spy craft. She needed to stash it somewhere. Her dress was tight enough that she thought she could stick it underneath the fabric and leave it there.

But she had to do one thing first. Unable to resist the temptation to know what the Russians' nuclear authentication card looked like, she took her palm off the bottle and read the words on the card.

Park Hyatt Paris-Vendôme.

Grunting, her stomach felt like it was about to hit the floor. She looked at her reflection in the mirror, her face red, feeling like it was on fire. She gritted her teeth, realizing she had not stolen the Russian Defense Minister's nuclear authentication card but his hotel room key.

She cursed under her breath.

Seeing a folded towel on the right side of the vanity, she slid the card underneath. Taking a breath to regroup and refocus, she walked out to see Balakin and Gisella seated together on a love seat. She sat down on a chair nearest to Balakin and poured some champagne into her glass.

"No bourbon for you, Alexandra?"

"I'm not much of a bourbon drinker. Plus, we're in France," she said, holding up her bottle of champagne but keeping the label away from him. "When in Rome."

She raised her glass and took a sip. Even though it was mostly water, it still tasted like champagne—alcoholic or not. She kept from making a face.

"So, I hope you didn't bring your friend up here to try and seduce me, Alexandra. That's one of the oldest tricks in the book. We're quite familiar with it in Russia." The smile he gave her indicated he knew what she was doing.

"Of course not, Dmitri. I was wanting to make sure we would get a meeting, however." She winked, telling him she knew how to play the game.

"Well, we're here."

"I'm worried about the rising tension between our countries, Dmitri. I'm not sure I've seen it this serious in my lifetime."

"Your country might be to blame for a large part of that, Alexandra. When you try to assassinate a country's leader, they might not take too kindly to it. A response is to be expected in such situations. President Volkov has a right to defend himself."

"But war, Dmitri? Nuclear war? President Volkov has threatened the entire world. That cannot stand either."

Balakin shrugged. "I guess we'll have to let it all play out then."

Alexandra didn't care for the way things were going. The man didn't seem intent on backing down or intimate that a negotiated peace could be in the cards. She decided she had to play her husband's card. Duke might not like it, but she, at that moment, was the one with the man who could stop nuclear war from starting.

"Would you care for more bourbon, Gisella?" Balakin said, leaning forward to reach for the bottle on the coffee table.

It was then that Alexandra saw it. The black suit coat on the back of the love seat. Balakin had had his back up against it, the pocket end draped behind it. She made quick eye contact with Gisella, the nod telling her what she needed to know.

Gisella held out her glass and let him pour. "Thank you, Dmitri. It is wonderful bourbon."

"That it is."

They clinked glasses and took sips, enjoying the moment as the liquid hit their throats.

"You seem tense," Gisella said, her fingers reaching out and touching his arm.

"If you knew what I know, Gisella, you'd be tense, too."

"You could probably use a massage, Dmitri," Alexandra said. "It might help."

Although the suggestion was directed at Balakin, Alexandra was hoping Gisella would take the hint. Gisella did, and Alexandra was beginning to think the woman was a natural.

Gisella ran her fingers up Balakin's arm. She then got up and walked behind him. "Here, let me see if I can help. I know a thing or two about getting men to relax."

"I bet you do, Gisella."

She started with his shoulders, and her touch immediately sent waves of relief through his body. He rolled his neck and let out a low groan. When his head went down, Gisella looked at Alexandra, wondering what she should do next.

Alexandra nodded several times, telling her to keep it up.

"Wow, are you a model or a masseuse?"

The suit coat was within Gisella's grasp. Her hands dug harder into his shoulders, and then began moving down his arms.

"Lean forward," Gisella said softly into his ear.

Balakin complied, fully content to let the tension leave his body, and he let out another groan as her hands went down his back.

The move left his suit coat exposed on the back of the love seat. Gisella gave a wide-eyed look at Alexandra. It was right there for the taking.

Alexandra's mind worked in overdrive. Should she join Gisella in a two-person massage? Should she sit next to Balakin and try to go through the coat's pockets? Should she suggest Balakin and Gisella take it into the bedroom?

She stood and walked to the love seat, sitting down next to him. He gave her a look that wondered what she was doing, but Gisella's hands soon dug deeper into his shoulders. The fact that two beauties were so close was throwing off his senses.

"Dmitri, I want to bring peace between our two countries," Alexandra said, her left arm going to the back of the love seat. She could feel the Armani fabric in her fingers. First the collar and then the lapel.

"I want peace, too," he said, not even looking at her.

Alexandra struggled with her reach. She could feel the flap of the pocket. Adjusting her seating position, she had to lean closer to him, allowing her hand to reach further. She could almost drape a leg over his thigh, she was so close. But it was enough to reach the pocket. Finally, she opened the flap. Her fingers were inside, searching for the card, going as far down as she could go.

Until she reached the bottom. The pocket was empty, and her hand came out.

Gisella saw the look and then the empty hand. "Here," she said to him. "Let me move your jacket out of the way. I don't want it to get wrinkled."

She flipped the jacket over and set it on the back of the love seat, closer to Alexandra, before resuming the massage. It wouldn't take long now.

The pocket was well within Alexandra's grasp. All she had to do was open the flap, grab the card, and toss it to the floor. Gisella could get it then.

Alexandra's fingers grabbed the flap. She was right there. This was her moment.

As soon as her fingers went inside, the doors to the suite burst open and two agents rushed in.

"Minister Balakin! President Volkov needs to speak with you immediately!"

With the two women and Balakin startled at the intrusion, Alexandra's hand never made it into the pocket.

"We must get you to the secure room. Now!"

The agents grabbed Balakin off the couch, but not before he reached behind him and snatched his suit coat off the love seat. The three then hurried out of the suite without another word to the women, both of whom were left behind stunned. Alexandra sighed when she saw Balakin pat the pocket of his suit coat on the way out.

And she knew right then that her plan had failed.

CHAPTER 33

Air Force One over Kansas

"Mr. President!" Secretary Javits said. "Our signals intelligence indicates Volkov has given the order to launch."

"Lieutenant Commander Black!" the President yelled. He then added, "Somebody get the Secretary of State on the phone."

Thirty seconds later, Mike Arnold came on the line. "I'm here, Mr. President."

"Where are you?"

"I'm at the Embassy. Talks broke down. It doesn't look good."

"Mike, I need you to let our NATO allies know what's going on. Get on the horn to the Brits. Tell them to be ready and have them spread the word. Call the Japanese and South Koreans and have them be on alert for any joint movement from China and Russia."

"I'll get on it."

"And make sure you get the word out to all of our enemies that now is not the time to mess with us."

"Yes, sir."

When Lieutenant Commander Black appeared in the doorway, the President motioned for him to approach. The man entrusted with the nuclear football had only opened it one other time for the President—when they were on their way to China and the North Koreans had launched a missile. That was nothing compared to this.

"Open it up," the President said, taking out his card.

Black unlocked the briefcase and handed him the book, oftentimes referred to as the Denny's breakfast menu for nuclear war. Open it up and pick three options—the target, the weaponry, and how do you want those eggs—over easy, sunny-side-up, or scrambled beyond recognition.

The President had studied the menu for the past three weeks, but with the decision at hand, he struggled with his focus. Small, medium, or large. How massive and deadly did he want it?

Option A was all-out nuclear destruction of Moscow and every major city across Russia. It would cripple Russia back into the Stone Age. Hundreds of thousands of Russian citizens would perish.

Option B was a targeted strike on Russian military sites—airfields, ports, and missile silos. Tens of thousands would die, mostly military but some civilians.

Option C was a strategic strike on essential military assets—airfields, missile silos, radar installations—all in hopes of preventing Russia from launching or retaliating. Hundreds or thousands would be killed.

He could mix and match if he wanted—it was all up to him. All he had to do was give the order, and General Ricks in the Pentagon's war room would, after confirming the President's identity, take it from there.

The nuclear football also contained instructions for the President to initiate the Emergency Alert System, which would allow him to speak with the American people over radio and television. The corresponding Emergency Action Notification would inform Americans that the United States has been subjected to a full-scale nuclear attack and that NORAD has detected the launch of missiles, whether any have been intercepted and if a second wave has been launched, and the location and time of expected impacts. The attack warning would also include instructions on seeking a fallout shelter; gathering food, water, and a battery-operated radio; and what to expect from the bright flash, the blast wave, radiation, fire and heat, the electromagnetic pulse, and the accompanying radioactive fallout.

In other words, it would scare the hell out of every American.

Along with the ominous EAS Tones, the automated voice was ready to say, "The first wave of nuclear missiles is expected to strike in approximately eight minutes."

As the President thought of the destruction he wanted to unleash, he spoke to Secretary Javits without even looking at the screen.

"Russ, contact the FAA and initiate a national ground stop. Clear the skies. I want all commercial air traffic on the ground if the missiles start flying."

"Roger that, Mr. President."

The President ran his finger down the list. He knew what he wanted to do.

"Russ. I've made my choice. I want—"

The screen showing Secretary Javits suddenly turned to snow.

"Did we lose him? What's going on?"

The President kept looking at the screen. *Did something happen to Javits' Doomsday plane? Had it been shot out of the sky?* The fog of war was rolling in thick and fast.

"Russ . . . Russ, can you hear me?"

"Standby, Mr. President," someone said.

"Come on, come on," he snapped, pounding the desk with his fist. "We've got a hundred different ways to communicate with the bombers and subs up here, let's get one of them working. Why don't we have General Cummins at Site R or General Ricks at the Pentagon on the screens yet?"

"Working on it, sir."

The President stood and pointed at another airman. "What about the trailing wire antenna? We can use the very low frequency communications to contact the subs."

The man shook his head. "We're having problems with the antenna's spool, sir. We're attempting to fix it."

The President cursed and pounded the back of his chair with his fist. "I should have stayed at the White House. Come on, people, let's go. I don't have time to wait. We gotta get something working."

Two Air Force staffers left in a rush, and then National Security Advisor Harnacke appeared at the door. "Sir, the Vice President is going to be contacting you on video conference. He says it's urgent."

The President looked to another screen on the wall and saw Stubblefield appear. "Ty, I've lost contact with Russ. What's going on?"

"Balakin didn't show up at the meeting so I sent Alexandra to meet with him at his hotel."

"And?"

"It didn't work. He was rushed out of the room by security before she could get the card. I think Volkov might have given the order. That's why they hustled him out of there."

"That's the intel we're getting, Ty. Is he going back to Moscow?"

"We don't know yet. Sir, we're running out of options."

The President stated he understood. The screen dedicated to Javits went from snow to a test pattern. No one could give the President an explanation other than to say they were working on it.

At that moment, the President knew he had one option remaining, one card that he hadn't played yet. He still didn't want to do it. It was the last option short of launching missiles and starting World War III. He knew it was time. He just hoped he wasn't too late.

Grabbing the desk phone from the cradle, he made two calls. First, he called Colonel Hauser in the cockpit and told them there had been a change in plans. They were going to bypass Colorado Springs and head to Edwards Air Force Base in California.

Once he hung up, he picked up the phone again and waited for the E4-B's communications officer to answer.

"Yes, Mr. President."

"Get me Duke Schiffer."

Beverly Hills, California

Seated in the front passenger seat of the Ford Explorer in the parking lot of the Beverly Hills Hotel, Duke Schiffer was showing his tablet to Segel and Wolfson, scrolling through pictures of Katia Balakina's mansion and grounds.

"Once you get beyond the pool, there are fourteen steps to a landing and then another twelve to the patio. There is some cover on both sides. Once we get into the back entrance, it's only fifty feet inside to the curved staircase on your right. Then it's up to the second floor. Master bedroom will be on your left."

Wolfson nodded, his mind memorizing it all.

"There's a wine cellar and theater room on the lower level. The master bedroom is our best bet."

Schiffer's phone vibrated. Seeing the number for the Air Force's communications system, he said, "This might be the call we've been waiting for."

He tapped the screen and put the phone to his ear.

"Yes?"

A female voice came shortly thereafter, "Please identify yourself."

"Duke Schiffer."

"Please hold for the President."

The wait was only a few seconds, but it gave Schiffer plenty of time to wonder why the President was calling. Had something happened? Was there a change in plans? He would soon find out.

"Duke?"

"Yes, Mr. President."

"Where are you?"

"I'm in L.A."

"Is the package able to be picked up?"

"Yes, sir. I can do it right now."

There was a silence, but what the President said next was firm and to the point. There was no wavering, just a direct order.

"Grab the daughter."

CHAPTER 34

Los Angeles, California

With the Holmby Hills neighborhood of Los Angeles only a mile from the Beverly Hills Hotel, Schiffer, Segel, and Wolfson were in sight of Katia Balakina's mansion within minutes. The President told Schiffer that he would have assets in the air from Vandenberg Space Force Base and Edwards Air Force Base to assist with pickup. They were on the way and would respond to Schiffer's orders.

"Get her to a safe location so we can talk to her" were the President's last instructions.

"We're gonna have to make this quick," Schiffer said to the Israelis. He plugged his phone into his comm unit and hoped Dustin at the NSA was ready to roll. "Dustin, you copy?"

"Yes, sir. I'm here."

"Okay, standby. We're heading to Katia Balakina's mansion. We might need you in about ten seconds."

"Need me? What?"

"We might need you to help us. Copy?"

"I . . . what? I don't . . ."

Schiffer mouthed a curse. "Dustin, is this your first real-time op?"

"Y-y-y-yeah."

"Just calm down and breathe. You're going to be fine. You did well when we were in Palm Springs. Now I need you to step up. And don't worry, nobody's going to be shooting at you where you're sitting. They'll be shooting at us."

"Okay."

"Standby."

Segel drove slowly past the main entrance to the mansion, the gates shut, the ominous signs of security systems and snarling attack dogs still outside the walls. Schiffer's check of his phone app revealed that Katia's phone was located inside. The plan was a go.

As Schiffer and Wolfson suited up, Segel drove around the block again.

"Looks clear," Segel said. "All appears quiet."

Schiffer pulled the black balaclava over his head and then checked his mic with Wolfson. Both had their suppressed Sig Rattlers with Aimpoint red-dot sights and magazines with .300 Blackout subsonic rounds, quiet but plenty lethal. Their spare mags had supersonic rounds in case they wanted to go long and hard.

They accessorized with night-vision goggles and a backpack full of flex-cuffs, gags, duct tape, and hoods. They even had a rope with a retractable grappling hook in case they needed to scale the side of the house to get to the balcony off the master bedroom.

Duke checked the magazine in his Glock 19 pistol and holstered it on his thigh. "You ready, Wolf?"

"Ready."

Similar to their earlier recon, Segel drove on the north side of Katia's mansion heading east, the high wall visible on their right. As they were going slightly downhill, Schiffer and Wolfson opened their right-side doors and let gravity keep them open. Segel made a quick turn into the neighbor's driveway and slowed before the closed gate.

"Let's go," Schiffer said.

Schiffer and Wolfson were out of the vehicle before it even stopped, nothing but their shadows in the faint light could be seen crossing the driveway. Within three seconds, they were in the neighbor's tree line and up the berm fully concealed. Segel backed out and began making loops around the block.

"Watch the sensors on top of the wall," Schiffer whispered.

The two men crouched as they walked beneath the canopy of leaves until they had a view on opposite sides of the pool house and into Katia's backyard. There was no one in the pool, and Katia was nowhere in sight.

"We've got two bodyguards on the patio," Wolfson whispered.

"Armed?"

"They're not carrying anything in their hands, if that's what you're asking."

Schiffer moved to his right to get a better view. "I see them now." He scanned the grounds, looking for movement. "Where's the third guy?"

"He could be inside. Maybe in a security room. Or he could be out front or off duty."

"We better figure on him being somewhere around here." He lowered the volume of his whisper. "Dustin, you copy?"

"Yes."

"I need you to scramble the security cameras."

"I'll try."

The wait took thirty seconds, but it was worth it.

"The security feeds are all snow, sir."

"Roger. Keep them that way." Schiffer whispered over his mic to Wolfson. "Security cameras are down."

"Copy."

"Segel, you copy?"

"Loud and clear."

"We're heading over the wall."

"Roger that."

Schiffer looked to his right but couldn't see Wolfson. "Let's move."

Both men navigated the top of the wall, avoiding the sensor. Once on the ground and hidden behind the trees and ficus hedges that ringed the property, Schiffer took the left and Wolfson went up the right. Although the pool area was lit, the trees provided dense cover and the goggles helped the men's progress.

They were level with the end of the pool closest to the mansion when Schiffer whispered over his mic. "We've got company."

A third bodyguard had appeared on the patio, walking with purpose to the two men. He was talking loudly in Russian, his arms gesturing like he was fed up with something.

"Can you make out what he's saying, Wolf?"

Wolfson translated as best he could. "It's the security cameras. He says there's something wrong with them." He paused before saying, "He's telling one of them to check the perimeter."

Schiffer kept the curse inside him. He didn't want someone snooping around the trees and alerting the others. A subsonic round from his suppressed Rattler might not reach the ears of the men on the patio, but the falling dead body of their comrade would.

"He's coming your way," Wolfson whispered. "He picked something off the patio table."

"What is it?"

"Rifle with a sling. Looks like he's right-handed."

Schiffer found a hedge that jutted out and tried to vanish into the shadows. This was going to get real in about twenty seconds.

He could hear the man's footsteps as he crossed the grass into the landscaping. Four steps and then a stop to look around. After a few seconds, four more steps, the decorative red rocks crunching underfoot. Even without seeing him, Schiffer could hear the man pulling a package out of his pocket. The package was opened, one of its contents removed, and the package closed. It was returned to his pocket. Schiffer then heard the scratchy click-click of a lighter, and for a split second through the leaves of the hedge, he could see the glow of the flame as it lit the cigarette.

When a gust of wind blew through the trees, rustling the palm tree leaves, Schiffer pounced. Startled, with his mind focused on his cigarette, the man's lighter fell to the ground before he could reach for his rifle. Before he could even yell out, Schiffer spun the man around, put a gloved hand over his mouth, and then choked him out. His body went limp, and Schiffer silently lowered him to the ground.

Taking a second to watch the two bodyguards still on the patio, Schiffer dragged the man into the shadows. After hurrying through his backpack, he used the flex-cuffs to bind the man's hands and feet and then duct taped his mouth. The gardener would find him in the morning. He took the man's rifle, ejected the magazine, and cleared the chamber. He then plunged the barrel of the rifle into the dirt and threw the magazine on top of the ten-foot hedge.

"Wolf, we got one down."

"Two to go."

On opposite sides of the spacious backyard, Schiffer and Wolfson moved silently along the tree line, hidden amongst the foliage and darkness.

"I've got movement on the second floor," Wolfson said. "Master bedroom. Looks like the target."

"Copy. I see her. Give me a few more seconds and I'll be in position to move."

As soon as Schiffer said it, the heads of the two bodyguards exploded in a fine bloody mist and their bodies crumpled to the patio.

"Wolf, what the hell are you doing?" Schiffer whispered into his mic. "That wasn't part of the plan."

"It wasn't me. I thought it was you."

Female screams could be heard from the second floor of the mansion. There was a struggle in the master bedroom. Two men and Katia. Schiffer cursed.

"What the hell's going on?" Wolfson asked.

"We're late. Somebody beat us to her. We gotta move!"

With his Rattler raised, Schiffer sprinted across the grass toward the back of the house. He soon saw Wolfson emerging from the tree line and charging toward the patio.

"Segel, we've got a problem," Schiffer said, taking the steps up the patio two at a time. "Somebody's beat us to the target. What do we have out front?"

Shots rang out, breaking the glass in the sliding doors, and Schiffer took cover. "We're taking fire!"

Wolfson raced to the opposite side of the patio and took up his position behind a pillar. He fired at one of the shooters through the busted glass.

"Two downstairs, Duke!"

Female screams were heard followed by angry men barking orders.

"Segel! Anything out front?" Schiffer asked. He ejected his empty magazine and went with the supersonic rounds. No sense being quiet now.

"I'm taking fire near the front gate!" Segel radioed. "The front gate is open. Heavy fire!"

"Wolf," Schiffer said. "We gotta get to her. Cover me!"

"I got you."

Wolfson laid down a barrage of bullets and Schiffer hurried inside and took cover. "Get in here, Wolf!"

With Schiffer providing cover, Wolfson ran and took up position on the side of the staircase.

"They're coming down the stairs!"

Schiffer was pinned down behind the kitchen wall. He peeked around and saw a man firing down from the second-floor landing toward him. "He's right above you, Wolf. Right in line with that chandelier."

Wolfson took a step out and saw the man. He fired twice, both shots hitting the man underneath the chin and exiting out the top of his skull.

"Segel, status?" Schiffer said.

"I've had to take cover, Duke! The vehicle is shot to hell!"

Schiffer could hear yelling from the men upstairs. It sounded like people yelling in Russian.

"I gotta get into position to take the staircase, Wolf."

"Go!"

Schiffer took two steps from behind the wall and the second-floor landing lit up, the hail of bullets forcing him to the other wall.

The yelling increased, and the bullets took a more level direction. Schiffer could tell the gunmen were making their way down the stairs. He knew he couldn't fire blindly at them, not wanting to hit Katia. Wolfson would have a better shot from his vantage point.

"Wolf, they're coming down with her! Watch the target!"

Schiffer could hear rapid fire from a different angle, most likely Wolfson picking someone off. But the response was quick, and Wolfson had to take cover.

"Duke! They're down the stairs! They're going out the front!"

Schiffer peeked around the corner, his eyes catching two men carrying a hooded female by her armpits. One gunman followed behind, covering the rear.

"I'm moving, Wolf."

Schiffer rounded the corner and shot the man in the shoulder then the chest. The man tumbled hard to the floor. "Another one down, Wolf."

"I'm right behind you."

Schiffer sprinted through the foyer toward the front door. The door was open, and he could see the two men putting Katia into their vehicle. He fired off a shot, taking out the passenger side window. The man pushing Katia in dove on top of her, and the driver floored the vehicle through the front gate.

Schiffer and Wolfson gave chase, but the vehicle was around the corner and out of sight.

"Segel, where are you?" Schiffer said, his chest heaving.

"I'm right behind you," Segel said, himself out of breath. "What the hell happened?"

Schiffer cursed in frustration. "They got her." He looked west and then east, trying to think of something. Powering up his phone, he prayed for a miracle. He soon got it.

"She's got her phone on her. They're heading west." He looked toward the mansion. "We gotta go."

"We don't have any wheels," Segel said.

"We'll have to take one of hers. Ariel, check the garage. Wolf, come with me. We need to see if those guys have their phones on them."

Air Force One over Colorado

"I told Duke to grab the daughter, Ty."

"Copy that. I haven't heard anything from him."

The President was in the E4-B's conference room. The Vice President was in his hotel suite in Paris. Both were standing. The President paced back and forth.

"Neither have I."

When the jet began to lose altitude, the President's pacing stopped. It was a noticeable fast descent, enough that he reached out to the chair to steady himself. This wasn't turbulence. They were going down. He looked toward the door, as if expecting someone to come in and give a reason. He then waited for the plane to level off. When it didn't, he called out for Agent Clark who was standing post outside the room.

"Yes, sir?"

"Why are we descending?"

"Cheyenne Mountain, sir. We're preparing to land in Colorado Springs."

"I told Colonel Hauser that I wanted to go to Edwards."

"It's not safe, sir," Clark said, shaking his head. "You could be in serious danger in California if Volkov wants to light up the west coast."

The President smacked the leather chair with his fist. "Mac, I told him I wanted to go to Edwards."

"It was determined that the best plan would be to divert and head to the Cheyenne Mountain complex. It can withstand a nuclear blast, and you can run the war from there."

"Mac, I'm the President. I make the decision. We're going to Edwards!"

"Mr. President, the Vice President is out of the country. He is not at a secure location. If you're in harm's way and he's still in France, the fate of the country could be in jeopardy."

"The fate of the country could be in jeopardy if I don't get to Edwards, Mac." When Agent Clark held out both hands like he was going to try to stop him, the President cursed and said, "Get out of my way."

"But sir."

After hurrying up the stairs to the flight deck with Agent Clark trying to keep pace, the President headed straight for the cockpit.

"Colonel, I told you I want to go to Edwards. Why are we descending?"

Shocked to hear the President's voice in person behind him, Hauser turned in his seat and said, "Sir, I was told by the Secret Service that it's not safe to go to California. They said Colorado Springs."

"Colonel, we're going to Edwards."

"Sir," Agent Clark said. "It's not—"

The President raised a hand to silence him and then pointed his finger at Hauser. "Colonel, we're going to Edwards. And that's an order."

Looking over the President's shoulder, Colonel Hauser made eye contact with Clark, who said nothing. Hauser then looked at the President and nodded. "Yes, sir."

"Colonel, if we don't land at Edwards, you and I are going to have words."

"Roger that, sir."

"How fast can this thing go?"

"Max speed is six-hundred-and-two miles per hour."

"Well, Colonel, with the fate of the Western world hanging in the balance, I suggest you push it to the limit."

The shock having worn off, Colonel Hauser smiled and said, "Yes, sir."

CHAPTER 35

Paris, France

"Mr. Vice President, we've got a problem," Duke Schiffer said.

"Go ahead."

"The Russians got to Katia first."

"They what?"

"They've taken her."

"Taken her? Is she still alive?"

"Affirmative. As far as I can tell."

Stubblefield held his hand over the phone and told Alexandra what was said. When he put it back to his ear, he could hear Duke breathing hard like he was running all out. He hit the button for the speakerphone and set the phone on the table. "Duke, are you sure they're Russian?"

"We heard yelling in Russian from Katia and the gunmen. And these guys were highly trained, too. They got in without us knowing it. Fully automatic weapons. Probably mercenaries. I think they were going to keep her in the house until we showed up and surprised them. My bet is they're going to use her as bait. Get her dad to do what Volkov wants or they'll kill her. I'd bet good money Balakin's going to hear from them real soon."

"Where are you now?"

"We're getting ready to go after her. We can track her with her phone. They're heading west toward the Pacific."

"I'll let the President know. Do whatever it takes to get her back."

Stubblefield ended the call. Things were falling apart faster than he could do anything about it.

"Volkov is going to claim we kidnapped her," Alexandra said. "He's going to blame the United States and give Balakin no other choice but to carry out his orders."

Stubblefield let fly an expletive.

"What are you going to do?" Alexandra asked.

He rubbed a hand over his bald head. "I think there's only one thing I can do. Go talk to Balakin."

Air Force One over Utah

The communications officer appeared in the cockpit doorway after the President gave his order to Colonel Hauser.

"Mr. President."

"Yes?"

"You're needed in the conference room for a video call. We've got Secretary Javits back online. He says it's urgent."

The President growled under his breath. *What now?* He hurried back down the stairs to the conference room and saw Secretary Javits on the screen.

"Russ, what's going on?"

"Sir, we have spotted the *Belgorod*! It has risen to launch depth."

"Black!" the President yelled for the Lieutenant Commander standing outside the door.

The man with the nuclear football stepped in and toward the President.

"Get it ready," the President said pulling out the card from his pocket. "Russ, I have to do something before it's too late. I've made my decision. I want to bomb the *Belgorod* out of the water."

"I concur wholeheartedly, sir."

"And I want to take out the Russian radar installations. Hopefully that will blind them."

Next to the screen showing Secretary Javits, the President saw separate screens with Chairman Cummins and General Ricks ready to act.

"General Ricks, this is Anthony Schumacher." The President felt a tingle up his spine as he prepared his next statement. "I'm ready to launch."

"Yes, sir," Ricks said. "I must confirm your identity with a challenge code."

"Go ahead, General."

"Romeo Whiskey Tango."

The President looked at the biscuit and ran his finger down the card to the letters *R W T*. He moved his finger to the right and the corresponding letters. He responded, "Foxtrot Oscar Lima."

"Authentication complete, sir. Mr. President, I need your launch order."

Once the President gave the order, the Pentagon would send an encrypted message to the launch crews around the world—in the air, on the ground, and under the sea—as well as the Alternate National Military Command Center at Raven Rock and to Javits' E-6 Mercury. Thereafter, locked safes would be opened, sealed codes compared with launch commands, and target data entered into launch computers. In a matter of minutes, the missiles would then be armed and ready. Once launched, there would be no turning back.

Before the President gave the targeting details, the phone buzzed.

Over the speaker, the communications officer said, "Sir, it's the Vice President."

"Put him through." The President yanked the phone off the cradle. "Ty, I'm about to give the order. The *Belgorod* has risen to launch depth. I have to take it out."

"Mr. President, I'm going to try to meet with Balakin. I need a little more time."

"I'm running out of time, Ty! The *Belgorod* is getting into position to launch. I can't wait any longer."

"Just give me a few more minutes to see if I can talk to him."

Paris, France

From the back seat of his armored limo, the Vice President ended the call. Alexandra was seated next to him as the security convoy approached the Park Hyatt.

"The President's about to give the order," he said, moving closer toward the door. "We're going to have to hustle."

The Vice President's Secret Service detail was on high alert. Against all protocols, the agents had had no opportunity to make a security sweep of the Hyatt. There were no magnetometers at the entrances and no snipers on the roofs of the surrounding buildings. None of the people inside the hotel had been wanded or searched. The entrances weren't locked down. They were going into an unknown environment, with possible hostile forces inside, and it set the dozen agents swarming the hotel on edge.

"Sir, I have to advise against this," Special Agent David Rose said from the front passenger seat as the limo came to a stop.

"I know you do, David. Now open the door."

Once outside, Stubblefield didn't wait for the agents to get into formation, and they had to pick up the pace to keep the Vice President surrounded.

When the flurry of activity billowed in from the street, the Russian security agents took immediate notice. All that did was ratchet up the tension. Radios started squawking and eyes widened. Hands reached for hidden weapons, ready to be drawn.

There was about to be a face-off with heavily armed men and women who were trained to take any and all steps to keep their protectee safe.

The Vice President and his entourage headed straight for the elevator.

"I'll do the talking, David," Stubblefield told Agent Rose.

The lead Russian security agent stepped forward into Stubblefield's path. When he held out his hand, the Vice President stopped.

"I need to talk with Minister Balakin."

"He's busy."

"Tell him it's an emergency. It has to do with his daughter."

The security agent locked eyes with Stubblefield. It was clear the man knew who he was. He took a few seconds to consider what Stubblefield said.

Stubblefield tried to move things along. "Her life might be in danger. I need to talk to him . . . now."

The agent used his wrist mic to radio upstairs. He turned away, put his hand to his mouth, and mentioned twice that it was "Vice President Stubblefield" who was asking for the meeting. He listened to the response in his earpiece and then turned around. He looked at Stubblefield and said, "They're asking him. Now we wait."

Stubblefield gritted his teeth and then looked at his watch. *Well, tell 'em to hurry up.* He eyed the elevator, wondering if they were going to have to barge through the line and do things the hard way.

The doors opened.

The security agent held up a hand and then pointed at the Secret Service agents surrounding Stubblefield. "Not all. Just one."

"Mr. Vice President," Agent Rose said, offering an objection.

Stubblefield shook his head and then pointed at Alexandra and Agent Rose. "These two are coming with me."

The Russian agent considered it and then nodded. He pointed to a fellow agent and motioned toward him before looking at Stubblefield and saying, "Follow me."

They headed into the elevator and the doors closed. No one moved. No one spoke. The two Russian agents on one side were armed. Stubblefield and Rose on the other side were armed. Alexandra eyed both sides from the middle. All five of them realized this could end badly if someone took something the wrong way. World War III might start in an elevator at the Paris Hyatt.

On the sixth floor, the doors opened, and the lead Russian security man motioned for the Americans to follow him toward Balakin's suite. Three Russian security agents, all of whom matched Stubblefield in size, were standing in front of the door.

Balakin's head of security stepped forward and held out his hand, stopping the Vice President.

"I need to see Minister Balakin."

"Mr. Vice President," the man said, respectfully but strongly. "Minister Balakin says he will meet with you. But there is one thing I have to do before letting you in."

"And that is?"

He pointed at the left side of Stubblefield's chest. "You and I both know that you are armed. You also know that I can't allow an armed man inside the suite with my protectee." He then pointed at Agent Rose. "Your man would not allow it either if the situation were reversed."

Stubblefield eyed the man, the muscles in his jaw clenching. The man wasn't wrong, but it would go against Stubblefield's every instinct to willingly disarm himself. He simmered in silence. *Desperate times . . .*

His left hand slowly pulled open his suit coat, revealing the Glock 19 in his shoulder holster. He pulled it out, holding it up long enough to get everyone's attention. His thumb hit the release button, ejecting the fifteen-round magazine. He handed it to Agent Rose.

"Hold out your hand," Stubblefield said to the Russian.

The Russian agent squinted slightly as if not understanding.

"What?"

"Hold out your hand."

Not sure of what Stubblefield wanted, the man held out his hand.

Stubblefield turned the gun on its side and racked the slide back, ejecting the bullet. It hit the Russian in the chest, bounced off, and landed in the palm of the man's hand. The man looked at the bullet and then at Stubblefield. The wide-eyed Russians all knew Stubblefield had had a live round in the chamber. The big man didn't mess around.

"Keep it as a souvenir."

The Vice President secured the gun and handed it to Agent Rose.

The Russian agent held out his hand and said, "I need to pat you down."

Stubblefield had enough. He pointed a finger at the man. "That's all I have. Now let's go."

When the sea parted for Stubblefield to move, Agent Rose made one last attempt to stop him. "Sir, I don't think you should go in there alone."

"I think I can handle myself, David." He motioned for Alexandra to follow him, and the Russians didn't object.

Once they were in, the doors closed behind them. A red-faced Balakin spun around and glared at them.

And right then, Vice President Stubblefield knew he had only one shot to save the world.

CHAPTER 36

Paris, France

"What the hell do you want?" Balakin snapped.

Stubblefield stepped forward with Alexandra three steps behind him. "Minister Balakin, I imagine you're going to receive a call here shortly."

Balakin, his eyes flashing daggers, held up his phone. "I'm already receiving calls! President Volkov is ready to launch and I have to follow his orders! I'm about to start nuclear war, so yeah I expect lots of calls! What are you doing here?"

The agitated Balakin looked like he was ready to throw the phone at Stubblefield, and Alexandra noticed the man had the nuclear authentication card in his hand. He looked like he was two seconds away from throwing them out of his suite so he could do what needed to be done to launch.

"Sir, I have information about your daughter."

Upon hearing the word "daughter," Balakin's eyes narrowed, his nostrils flaring, like a bull ready to charge. "What about my daughter?" he hissed, his chest rising and falling. He took three steps in anger toward Stubblefield. "What have you done? What have you bastard Americans done!?"

"Your daughter has been kidnapped." Upon dropping that bombshell, Stubblefield raised his hands in defense. "It wasn't us." He noticed how the verbal blow struck Balakin hard in the chest. "I'm going to be totally honest with you, Mr. Minister. We were going to pick her up. We had three men on the ground in Los Angeles who were ready to grab her and hold her to keep you from executing the launch orders. We were ready to do it. But someone got to her before we could."

Balakin's rage turned to fear, and he had to steady himself against the back of the love seat to keep from collapsing. "Katia," he whispered. "Who would do this?"

"Sir, we believe the kidnappers were Russian."

"Russian?" Balakin looked like his mind was on overload. The rage returned. "You are lying. You are making this up. You Americans always lie. You tried to kill President Volkov and now you have kidnapped my daughter!"

"No, I'm not lying. Our man on the ground said he heard Russian being spoken when it all went down. He thinks they were mercenaries. There was a gunfight and they took her."

"My darling Katia," Balakin whispered again, falling in and out of anger and despair.

Alexandra stepped forward. "Dmitri, we believe President Volkov is behind it. We think he is going to either kill her or hold her until he gets you to launch."

"Is she okay?"

Stubblefield wasn't sure, but he wasn't going to say it. "Yes. For now. Our men are trying to get her back. But we need time. If you launch nuclear weapons against the United States, it's all over. If L.A. is a target, you'll never see your daughter again."

"Katia," he whispered.

Balakin's phone rang. He turned the screen toward him. It was President Volkov. He looked at Stubblefield, as if trying to determine whether this was all a ruse. *Did the Americans really kidnap Katia? Was this a trick? Would President Volkov really do that? To his kotenok?*

"Please, Dmitri," Alexandra said. "You have to believe us."

Balakin swallowed, trying to regain his composure. He eyed Stubblefield wondering if he should do what he was about to do. He decided he would and tapped the screen for the speakerphone so they could all hear.

"Yes, Mr. President."

"Dmitri!" Volkov spat out. "I have terrible news! The Americans have kidnapped your daughter!"

"My daughter?"

"Yes! They have kidnapped my *kotenok*! They are going to kill her! This is an act of war! Russia must respond with overwhelming force! We are ready to launch. I have sent the order and my codes to General Dernov. He has the targeting details. Now you must act. It is time to destroy the United States for what they have done to us!"

"Yes, sir," Balakin said reflexively.

"Do it now!"

Stubblefield could tell Balakin's mind was spinning, not knowing who to believe—his old friend or his country's enemy. The Vice President stepped forward and put his finger to his lips, motioning for Balakin to mute his phone. To his relief, Balakin did so.

He lowered his voice and said, "Sir, we don't want to harm your daughter. You have to know that. If you want us to get her back, you have to stall for time."

"How do I do that?" He held up his nuclear authentication card. "You heard him. All I have to do is get the *Cheget* and send in my codes."

"Tell him you must get to a secure location to execute the orders otherwise American intelligence will learn of it and launch first. Just give me a little more time."

Balakin was shaking his head. "I don't know if I can trust you. I don't know if I can trust anyone."

"You're going to have to trust me now. It's your only hope. I know you love your daughter, and you wouldn't have let me in here if you didn't want to put off making the hardest decision you'll ever have to make in life. Let me contact my man on the ground. He's the only one that can save your daughter now."

The Vice President's words made him think. He gripped his phone in silence.

"Please, Dmitri," Alexandra said softly. "Give us a little more time."

The hope of seeing his daughter again won out. Rubbing the back of his neck, Balakin nodded in response. He took a breath and unmuted his phone.

"Dmitri! Are you there?" Volkov screamed.

"Yes, I am here, Mr. President."

"Execute the launch orders! Now!"

Balakin stared at Stubblefield. It had come to this. The order had been given. The fate of the world and that of his daughter rested on his shoulders with his next decision. If Balakin said he was ready to launch, Stubblefield was prepared to bolt from the suite and tell the President to act. It all depended on what Balakin decided.

"Sir . . . ," Balakin said. "The Americans must pay for what they have done. But I have to get to a secure location to use the *Cheget*. The enemy could be listening."

Volkov cursed. "We don't have time for that, Dmitri! Send in your codes!"

"I must get to a secure location, Mr. President. We must maintain complete secrecy to maximize the destruction."

Volkov cursed again, and Balakin mouthed the word "where" to Stubblefield and Alexandra.

"The embassy," Alexandra whispered.

"Let me get to the embassy," Balakin said. "It is not far. Once I give the order, I will head to the airport and return to Russia."

Volkov cursed something indecipherable before yelling, "Hurry up!"

Balakin ended the call and glared at Stubblefield. "Get my daughter back, Mr. Vice President. Otherwise, I have no choice. I either launch or I'm a dead man."

CHAPTER 37

Los Angeles, California

After commandeering Katia's Range Rover, Segel had picked up Schiffer and Wolfson and took off in pursuit. He made a left at the gate and then a right at the stop sign. Once on Sunset Boulevard, he put the Range Rover's V8 to good use, the luxury SUV's five-hundred horsepower roaring to life. At that hour, the streets were nearly deserted, and Segel had a clear road to make up some time.

"Where are they?" Segel asked, gripping the wheel hard as he made the curves leaving Holmby Hills into Bel Air.

"They're still heading west on Sunset," Schiffer said from the front passenger seat. "Let's hope they're not familiar with L.A. It'll slow them down."

"Where do you think they're going?"

Schiffer looked at his tracker app. Katia's phone was on the north side of the UCLA campus and south of the Bel-Air Country Club. "If they want to get her out of the country, they'd have to make a run for the border or go by boat or air. They might be going west toward the Pacific or south toward LAX. But if they want to make contact with Balakin, they're going to need to stash her somewhere. And who knows where that could be."

"It's sounding like we're looking for a needle in a haystack," Segel said.

"As long as she keeps her phone on, we can find her." Schiffer turned in his seat. "You get anything, Wolf?"

Wolfson had his head down in a phone he took off one of the dead gunmen. He had forwarded pictures of the two men to Tel Aviv and was waiting for a response. He came across a voice message and played the fifteen-second clip.

"You understand it?" Schiffer asked.

Wolfson shook his head. "My Russian is rusty. Something about a sleeping cat."

Schiffer's phone buzzed. It was Stubblefield. "Yes?"

"Duke, I've got you on speaker with Alexandra and Minister Balakin. Talk to me, buddy."

"We're getting close. She has her phone on her and we can track it."

"I bought you some time, Duke. But it's not a lot. President Volkov has given the launch order. We need to get her back."

"We took the phone off one of the men we bagged at Katia's mansion. It's Russian. There's a message on it." He motioned for Wolfson to play it.

Knowing those on the other end were going to struggle to hear the message being played with the hum of the Range Rover's engine in the background, Schiffer raised the volume.

"What's he saying?" Stubblefield asked Balakin. "What does he mean by '*kotenok*'?"

"It's Russian for kitten. He's saying they've been ordered to put the kitten to sleep."

"Is that a code? What does that mean?"

"*Kotenok* is the nickname President Volkov gave to Katia when she was a little girl." Choking up, he added, "He told them to kill my daughter."

"Duke, did you hear that? Minister Balakin says the order has been given to kill his daughter. You gotta get her back."

Segel took a corner with too much speed, and Schiffer and Wolfson had to grab something to hold on to.

"Duke?"

"We're trying, sir," Schiffer barked, stating the obvious. "I'm going to have to call you back."

Paris, France

"They're going to kill her," Balakin mumbled over and over again.

Stubblefield thought the man was going to start sobbing. His eyes were starting to redden, and he looked like he was nearing collapse. It was not a good mental state for someone with the authority to launch nuclear weapons. Stubblefield needed to think of something.

"Dmitri, how much power do you have over your military?"

"I have some. Obviously General Dernov has some, too."

"Do you trust each other?"

"We're Russian, Mr. Vice President. We don't trust anybody."

"Can you convince Dernov to stand down?"

"I don't know. There would have to be something in it for him."

"Perhaps you should think of something to make it worth his while."

The door to the suite opened and Balakin's head of security walked in. "Sir, it's Mr. Roznak. He is here to see you."

Balakin's face went white, like his whole life flashed before him as the world was crumbling all around him.

"Who?" Stubblefield asked. "Who is it?"

"Oleg Roznak," Balakin said weakly. "He's—"

"Volkov's mercenary leader."

"Yes."

"What is he doing here?"

Balakin took a deep breath. He looked at the door, as if expecting it to blow open at any moment with Roznak marching in. "He is here to kill me. They are going to kill me and my daughter if I don't go through with the launch orders."

Stubblefield glanced at the door. He flinched when his hand almost reached up to pat the butt of his gun that was no longer there. *Over my dead body.* "Dmitri, I need my security man in here."

Balakin nodded and gave the order. His security man went outside the suite and then let in Agent Rose.

"David," Stubblefield said, gesturing him over. "There's a man downstairs named Roznak. He can't come up here."

"Okay."

"You need to secure the hotel. Do whatever you have to do. Lock it down and harden up. Get the French Protection Service in here if you have to and see if you can get a Marine detachment from the Embassy over here. We may have to evacuate."

"Roger that," Rose said, beginning to move.

"David," Stubblefield called out, stopping him. The big man stepped closer and lowered his voice. "You got my gun?"

"Yes."

"Give it to me." Once the loaded Glock was safely tucked in his shoulder holster, Stubblefield nodded toward the door. "Now go."

Pacing the floor, Balakin was rubbing his head with his hand, looking like he was on the verge of a breakdown. "He's here to kill me," he said again. "They are going to kill Katia."

"Not if I can help it," Stubblefield said. "Where's your nuclear briefcase?"

Balakin looked at him, blinking his eyes trying to understand the question. He glanced down at the card in his hand.

"Dmitri, you and I need to work together if you want to see your daughter again and prevent the start of a new world war. You need to secure the briefcase. Get it in here."

Balakin gave the order. The military officer carrying the briefcase arrived, his face white thinking he was about to take part in world history—the start of nuclear war.

"Corporal," Balakin said. "The *Cheget* stays with me from now on. If something happens to me, no one else must use it."

The man held up the briefcase, still handcuffed to his wrist. "Yes, sir."

Stubblefield wasn't done. His mind was moving fast, his eyes looking around the spacious suite.

"Minister Balakin," he said. "Let's get you away from the windows."

"What?"

"Get away from the windows."

They moved to the bathroom with its walk-in dressing room providing plenty of space and, more importantly, thick walls to keep any Russian snipers from taking out Balakin.

"You need to start thinking about getting into contact with General Dernov," Stubblefield said.

Balakin either didn't hear or didn't care. He could do little more than shake his head. "Katia," he cried. "My darling Katia."

CHAPTER 38

Los Angeles, California

"They're going south on the four-o-five," Schiffer said.

Segel rounded the bend on Sunset Boulevard and the green signs for Interstate 405 appeared above them. He veered right, took the on-ramp, and then mashed the gas when he hit the five lanes of the freeway.

"How far behind are we?" Segel asked.

"No more than a half mile." Schiffer pointed to the right. "Use the shoulder if you have to."

Segel pushed the Range Rover to near a hundred, weaving in and out of the traffic, thankful it wasn't rush hour.

"What are we going to do if we catch up to her, Duke?" Segel asked. "If they're going as fast as we are and she's not restrained, it could be the end of her if there's a wreck."

Schiffer didn't have a plan, just an objective. His mind raced through the possibilities. Shoot the driver. Shoot the tires. Crash the vehicle. None of them were great choices at the moment.

"Let's just catch up to her first."

Once Schiffer and Wolfson switched out the old magazines in their rifles, Schiffer checked his phone.

"They're getting off the interstate!"

"Where?" Segel asked, gripping the wheel.

"Interstate Ten, heading west."

"What's near there? Where they heading?"

"It heads toward Santa Monica. There's a small airport there. And it's a straight shot to the Pacific. They might have backup waiting to get her out by boat."

Less than sixty seconds later, Segel veered right on Interstate Ten. "Can you see them?"

Schiffer gave it one look off into the distance and then checked his phone again. "If they're heading to the beach, we'll wait until they get out and take 'em when they're on foot."

"Watch for shooters from any boats out there," Segel said.

Another check of the phone. "They're getting off!"

"Toward the airport?" Segel asked.

"No, they're going north. They're probably going to stash her and make contact with her dad." He pointed at the upcoming exit. "This one! This one!"

Segel veered right and then screeched to a stop at the bottom of the off ramp. "Now where?"

All three men were breathing hard, their chests rising and falling, their ears straining to hear any sounds in the surrounding area.

Schiffer eyed his phone. "They've stopped. Either that or they've tossed the phone. Go left."

Segel made a left, and all three men had their heads on swivels.

"Coming up on it," Schiffer said. "On the right."

The nondescript building was dark, save for a light shining over the sign that read *Trident Industries*.

"Looks like a warehouse," Segel said, making a slow right turn. "Not a lot going on. You think they could be in there?"

"Pull in over there," Schiffer said, pointing across the street. He checked his phone again. "That's the address it's showing. This thing is supposed to be accurate within fifty yards."

The three men looked around. The warehouse was the only structure nearby. There was a large garage door in the middle and a windowless door to an office on the right. There was no movement, and no vehicles in the lot that was surrounded by a chain-link fence. The gate was open.

"What do you think?" Segel asked.

"Like I said, unless they tossed her phone, that's where she is. I think we have to assume that's the case."

"There looks like there's light coming from under that garage door. Do we go in with guns blazing?"

Schiffer scanned the surroundings. There were so many things he wished he had now—a small cadre of Navy SEALs being one of them.

"Dustin," he said into his mic. "You still with me?"

"Yes, sir."

"Do you see the location of Katia Balakina's phone?"

"Yes, sir."

"Can you shut the power off in that warehouse?"

"Sir, it would take me time."

"How much time?"

"Half hour."

"You've got five minutes, Dustin."

"I . . . I . . ."

"Dustin! I need you to focus, bud. This is gut check time. If you do this for me, I'll set up a meeting with you and Katia. She might even throw in a big kiss for you. Agreed?'

"Yes, sir."

"Attaboy. Get to it."

Once the call ended, Segel asked, "Should we call in reinforcements?"

"We don't have time to wait. We gotta go now." Schiffer then turned to Wolfson. "You got anything in that bag of toys?"

Wolfson opened his backpack and rummaged around. He had rope, the grappling hook, a drone, some duct tape, more magazines. "Thermal imager," he said, pulling the device out. He handed it to Schiffer and reached in for more. "How about this?"

Schiffer smiled at seeing the breaching explosive. "You do have nice toys."

The plan quickly came together. Schiffer and Wolfson would do a fast recon with the thermal imager to make sure Katia and the three Russians were inside. Depending on their location, the breaching explosive would be readied on the opposite side. Once they were ready, Segel would use the Range Rover to barrel through the garage door with Schiffer and Wolfson rushing in behind. Speed, surprise, and as much firepower as they could bring was the best they could do under the circumstances.

"That okay with you, Ariel?"

Segel responded without hesitation. "Let's do it."

Schiffer and Wolfson hurried across the street, keeping to the shadows. Once they got to the west side of the building, Wolfson fired up the thermal imager. He pointed straight ahead toward the east. "Opposite side. Four of them. Three of them are moving. One looks to be seated."

"Okay, that's Katia. They're probably getting ready to get her on camera. How good are you at close quarters battle?"

Wolfson snorted. "I'm the best."

"I knew you were going to say that. You ever do any hostage rescue?"

"Just your wife and Ariel's in Cairo."

"Good enough." Schiffer pointed to the right. "Let's put the explosive on the side wall. We blow it to distract them and then barrel through the garage door. Shock and awe."

Wolfson nodded and took off to place the charge.

Alone, Schiffer whispered into his mic. "Dustin, how you coming on the power?"

"Two more minutes."

"Copy that. After I tell you to cut the power, I want you to call the local nine-one-one and have the police and an ambulance sent to this location just in case. You got that?"

"Yes, sir."

Wolfson hustled back. "It's ready to go." He showed his hand to reveal the trigger to blow it.

The two men hurried back across the street to Segel and the Range Rover.

"You guys ready?" Schiffer asked. After getting nods from both of them, he said. "Here's the order. Dustin cuts the power. Wolf blows the charge. Ariel rams the door. I go in on the right, Wolf goes in on the left. Three tangos at the rear. We take 'em out. We save the girl. Just like John Wayne. Any questions?"

None.

"Ariel, watch yourself. Veer left once you get in the door. It'll give you a little cover and us a clear shot."

Segel nodded.

"Dustin?"

"I'm ready."

Schiffer took a breath. "Let's do this."

CHAPTER 39

Santa Monica, California

Wolfson and Schiffer took up position on both sides of the garage door, twenty feet back. They'd get a running start once Segel roared by. Both of the men readied their weapons and lowered their night-vision goggles.

Schiffer got a thumbs-up from Wolfson and then Segel at the entrance to the driveway. He motioned for Segel to gun it.

"Dustin . . . cut the power."

The light underneath the garage door went black as Segel accelerated the Range Rover toward the door.

"We're dark. Blow it, Wolf!"

The explosion on the south side of the warehouse echoed off the surrounding buildings but only until the Range Rover crashed into the door and barreled inside. Segel veered left, the tires screeching on the floor. Smoke from the blast and the burning rubber filled the warehouse.

Schiffer and Wolfson were sprinting straight in when the Russians' automatic weapons lit up the rear of the warehouse.

The two men charged forward. The red dot of Schiffer's scope landed right above the man's nose and Schiffer put a bullet in the man's skull.

On the left, Wolfson gave two quick trigger pulls and a second Russian went down with two in the chest.

The last Russian fired blindly, a bullet whizzing past Schiffer's ear. Schiffer flinched but got a shot off. It hit the man in the knee, and he went down hard. He fired from the ground and got off two shots before Schiffer pumped a round in the man's chest and then in his head.

Three tangos down.

"Aaagh!" Wolfson yelled.

Hearing Wolfson in his earpiece, Schiffer turned to his left and through the heavy smoke saw the man on the ground.

It was Wolf. Schiffer's stomach dropped. He could see blood, but it was difficult to tell how bad it was.

"Wolf! You okay?"

Wolfson cursed and then grunted again in obvious pain.

"Wolf!"

"Duke, she's running!" Segel yelled. "She's running! Grab the girl!"

Schiffer had no time to help Wolfson as he saw the female figure of Katia Balakina bolting for the open door. She was running for her life. He took off in a dead sprint and grabbed her from behind. She screamed.

"Let go! Let me go!" Her legs flailed, trying to kick at Schiffer and stomp on his feet. The screams were louder this time.

"Katia!" Schiffer yelled into her ear. "American! I'm an American!"

She put up quite a fight, trying to scratch and claw her way to safety. Schiffer finally had to kick her legs out from under her and take her to the ground.

"Katia! Easy now! I'm an American! I'm here to help!"

With his weight on top of her, she stopped squirming. He turned her over but stayed on top of her, both of them breathing hard. Schiffer took off his goggles, their eyes meeting.

"I'm here to take you to contact your father, Katia."

Pinned down by him, she struggled to catch her breath, her eyes showing her fright.

"I'm here to get you in contact with your father. Do you understand?"

Her chest heaving, she blinked twice and licked her lips. She could do little else than nod.

"I'm going to take you so you can talk with him. You have to trust me. Okay?"

She nodded again.

Schiffer got off her and held out a hand. After a few seconds of thought, she took it and he helped her to her feet.

"Segel! We need to move!"

Schiffer turned in time to see Segel attending to a bleeding Wolfson, who was still on the ground in obvious pain. Schiffer cursed. Escorting Katia by the arm, they hurried over to the two Israelis.

"What happened?" Schiffer asked.

Wolfson let out a Hebrew expletive, something akin to a female dog, his right hand grabbing his crotch. "She elbowed me in the face and then kneed me in the nuts." His rudimentary knowledge of Russian slang was good enough to fire off another curse at her. "I think she might have broken my nose."

Schiffer somehow managed to restrain from laughing. He looked at Katia. "You did that?"

She shrugged. "I didn't know who he was."

"I don't think I've ever seen a guy get his ass kicked by a girl before," Schiffer said, ribbing Wolfson.

"Screw you," a wheezing Wolfson spat out. He grunted again, got to his knees, and wiped some of the blood off his face.

Schiffer smiled at Katia. "I've been wanting to do that to him for years now." He gestured to Segel. "Get the vehicle. We need to move. They might have backup." He gave Wolfson a kick to the leg. "Get up. We have to move."

The four piled into the busted Range Rover and took off, blowing past the police cars and the ambulance heading their way. Segel drove with Wolfson in the front passenger seat. Schiffer and Katia were in the back.

"Where we going?" Segel asked.

"Head west toward the Pacific."

While Segel hustled onto the interstate, Schiffer worked his phone and then activated his comm unit. The ninety seconds it took felt like a lifetime, but he finally made contact with the Air Force coming from Edwards.

"We need pickup," he said to the chopper pilot.

"Give me a location."

Schiffer looked out the left passenger window. "Santa Monica Pier. Look for the Ferris wheel. North side on the beach. We'll be there."

"Roger that. We're three miles out."

"You're going to have four passengers."

"Roger that."

"And then we're going to have to haul ass back to Edwards."

Near Edwards, California

"Edwards Tower . . . this is Air Force One," Colonel Hauser said over the radio. "Request immediate clearance to land."

"Air Force One . . . Edwards Tower. You are cleared to land on Runway Five Right."

"Runway Five Right. Wind check."

"Wind one-eighty at fifteen, gusts to twenty-eight. Be advised you have one helo inbound."

"Copy that."

The President was standing over Hauser's right shoulder as the runway lights to Edwards Air Force Base came into view. He sure hoped this worked.

"Colonel, I don't know how long we're going to be on the ground but be ready to move. I have no idea what's going to happen next."

"Yes, sir."

With the Mojave Desert surrounding them to both horizons, the wheels of Air Force One touched down on the concrete of the 15,000-foot runway. Hauser brought the plane to a stop a hundred yards from the chopper, where two people were heading their way.

Schiffer walked Katia up the airstairs and into the President's office.

"Mr. President, I have a special delivery. This is Katia Balakina."

The President took a few seconds to look the woman over. He had seen her in some movies and he had to remind himself that this wasn't one. Her hair was mussed a bit and there was some bruises beginning to appear on her face, but they did little to hide her beauty. She was taller than he expected.

He reached out his right hand. "Katia, I'm Anthony Schumacher."

She looked at him and then his hand, almost afraid to take it. She finally did and softly said, "It's nice to meet you, Mr. President."

"Are you injured?"

She shook her head, but the movement caused her to wince in some pain. She reached up and touched her head.

"Katia," he said, motioning to his left. "This is my wife, Danielle. I would like to have one of our service women look you over. You've got a little blood on your forehead, and I want to make sure you're all right."

Her head drooped, and the President could tell she was tearing up. The First Lady reached out to hold her hand.

"Katia," the President said. "You are safe with me. Nobody's going to hurt you."

She looked up at him, the tears running down her golden cheeks. "And my father? What has happened to my father?"

The President smiled, thankful to give her good news. "He's safe, Katia. He is with the Vice President of the United States right now at the American Embassy in Paris. As soon as we have someone look you over, I'd like for you to speak with your father. I'll get it set up right now."

She held in her sobs and nodded before being led away. Once the Air Force medic checked Katia's vitals, gave her a butterfly bandage for her forehead, and a bag of ice for her hand, she was brought back to the conference room.

The President was seated at the table looking toward the screen.

"Minister Balakin, can you see and hear me?"

"I can see and hear you, Mr. President. Where is my daughter? I need to see her. I need to speak with her. I must make sure my Katia is safe."

The camera angle widened, and Katia Balakina appeared on the screen on the President's right. To her right sat the First Lady.

Balakin's hand covered his mouth. He choked back tears and blurted, "Katia, are you okay?"

"I am okay, Father. I am okay. Thanks to President Schumacher's people. They have treated me well."

"Minister Balakin," the President said. "I have had my medics check your daughter over. She has sustained some bruising and a few cuts, but they expect her to make a full recovery. She is okay. Do you understand?"

"Yes. Yes. Thank you, sir."

"Your daughter is being well taken care of. But there's still someone out there that wants to do her harm, to do you harm, and to do the whole world harm. Minister Balakin, I don't know you. But I think I know enough about you that you are not of the same mind as President Volkov. I don't want war, Dmitri."

As if something clicked, or as if a director had yelled "Action!", Katia looked at the camera. It was like she realized she was playing the role of a lifetime. It was time to say her lines. Her hand reached out to the President and he told her to feel free to speak.

"Father, I know you don't want war. The Americans don't want war either. They are the ones that rescued me. Please, Father, let us have peace."

"Minister Balakin, I know there's talk about you becoming President. I don't have anything against you, and I won't stand in your way. Maybe you can make General Dernov see the light and let him know that war is in nobody's best interests. And someday, perhaps we can all meet and enjoy a new friendship together."

Balakin blinked the tears from his eyes and then nodded. "I can do that, Mr. President."

"Thank you, Dmitri."

"No, thank you, sir."

The President reached over and patted Katia's hand. The blonde hair reminded him of his daughters—his beautiful daughters that he loved as much as Minister Balakin loved his.

"And Dmitri, from one father to another," the President said, trying to keep it together. "Your daughter is safe with me."

CHAPTER 40

Near Mineral, Virginia

Duke Schiffer and Alexandra Julian were back at home, back in bed together after too many days apart. Both were exhausted with their travels, and they were content to hold each other close and make up for lost time. Little was spoken about what had gone on—with Alexandra in Milan and Paris and Duke in Los Angeles. They figured there would be time for that later.

The TV on the wall was tuned to the national news. The pictures on the screen showed a chopper's view of President Volkov's residence near Gelendzhik, Russia. The outskirts of the property were ringed with Russian military hardware. A Russian warship was anchored offshore in the Black Sea.

Unconfirmed reports indicated Volkov was under house arrest, being on the wrong end of a military coup led by Defense Minister Balakin and General Dernov. Leaked intelligence indicated Volkov's cancer had become "shockingly aggressive," and it was believed he only had a few days left to live if he didn't end it on his own beforehand.

Balakin and Dernov were both in Moscow, having worked out a truce that would keep both of them in power for the foreseeable future. Neither trusted the other, but they were used to that. Both would spend the next few years looking over their shoulders and keeping each other at arm's length. For now, the first official order they agreed on was to call the *Belgorod* back to port in Severodvinsk.

Russian mercenary leader Oleg Roznak was nowhere to be found. Having seen the buildup of American and French security at the Paris Hyatt, he vanished into the Parisian night, allowing himself to fight Russia's fight, or what he believed was Russia's fight, another day. He had plenty of violent men willing to follow him.

Back at the White House, President Schumacher, with Vice President Stubblefield at his side, praised the work of his National Security Council staff and all the members of the military who stood ready to defend the United States. He hoped the new leadership in Russia would lead to a promising and peaceful relationship between the two countries, one that would never again bring the two rivals to the brink of war.

Along with the videos from Russia, every news outlet was gushing about the exploits of Katia Balakina, the superstar Russian actress who some claimed might have saved the world. Glamour shots were shown interspersed with a few recent photos showing the aftermath of her ordeal. Those latter photos may or may not have been released by her agent and publicist. The biggest names in news were promising a big payday for her first exclusive interview. Oprah's people were even said to have reached out.

For now, Katia was keeping out of the public eye. After having been flown to Washington on Air Force One, she had an emotional reunion with her father. They reconnected until he had to return to Moscow, but not before he promised to return to the United States so she could show him southern California.

Before she returned to L.A., she granted a special request from Duke Schiffer, who said it involved someone who had a hand in saving her life. The picture of her kissing Dustin on the cheek would be on the NSA man's bedroom wall for the rest of his life.

"I know you think she's cute," Alexandra said, snuggled in her husband's arms, a video of Katia playing on the screen.

Schiffer chuckled silently. She just wouldn't leave it alone.

"Noah said you were on top of her."

"Oh my goodness," Schiffer said, looking toward the ceiling. "I can't believe he—"

"He said for a long time. He thought you were enjoying it a little too much."

"That son of a . . ." He envisioned Wolfson laughing maniacally at the thought of getting back at Schiffer for the wisecracks. "That guy wouldn't know what was happening because he was on the ground holding his nuts in pain after getting beat up by a woman."

"But you don't deny you enjoyed it."

Schiffer sighed. "Oh, babe." He reached his hand out and lovingly massaged her belly. He wasn't stupid. He knew how to play the game when the subject needed to be changed. "I can't wait to have this little one. You're going to be such a wonderful mother."

Her eyes met his. "I'm sorry again for spilling the beans over the phone. I was mad, but I should have told you in person."

"It's okay," he said. "I've already forgotten about that. I'm too excited anyway. I've already started thinking of names."

"You have? So have I." She rattled off a few—for both a boy and a girl. "What about you? What do you want to call him if he's a boy?"

He thought for a second and gave her a couple. "Andrew is a good one. Or Jacob."

"What if she's a girl?"

Schiffer bit his lip. He knew he shouldn't, but he couldn't resist the chance to give it back to his wife. She might get ticked. She might even give him a sharp elbow to the ribs. But she'd forgive him. Someday. Maybe.

"Huh? What do you want to call your daughter?"

He shrugged. "I don't know. Katia's a pretty name."

THE END

For those who might be interested

As of November 2023, there are over 2,700 stars on the Hollywood Walk of Fame.

Gene Autry, the "Singing Cowboy," is the only person to be awarded a star on the Hollywood Walk of Fame in each of the five categories—film, television, radio, music, and live performance.

John Wayne's star on the Hollywood Walk of Fame is located at 1541 Vine Street.

Near the former Bob Hope residence, the Elrod House in Palm Springs, California was once used for scenes in the 1971 James Bond film, *Diamonds Are Forever*, starring Sean Connery.

Edwards Air Force Base in California witnessed Chuck Yeager's 1947 flight breaking the sound barrier for the first time and the first Space Shuttle landing in 1981.

Brigadier General Chuck Yeager, who shot down 13 enemy aircraft in World War II, including five in one mission, drove the pace car for the Indianapolis 500 in 1986 and 1988.

Rob Shumaker is an attorney living in Illinois. *Doomsday in the Capital* is his twelfth political thriller. He is the author of the Capital Series, which includes *Thunder in the Capital, Showdown in the Capital, Chaos in the Capital, D-Day in the Capital, Manhunt in the Capital, Fallout in the Capital, Phantom in the Capital, Blackout in the Capital, Justice in the Capital,* and *Firestorm in the Capital*. A standalone thriller, *The Way Out*, was published in 2019.

He is also the author of the Huron Cove Series, a collection of Christian romance novels, including *The Angel Between Them, Turning the Page, Christmas in Huron Cove, Learning to Love Again, The Law of Loving You, The Fire of Love,* and *Love on the Diamond*.

Did you enjoy *Doomsday in the Capital*? Readers like you can make a big difference. Reviews are powerful tools to attract more readers so I can continue to write engaging stories that people enjoy. If you enjoyed the book, I would be grateful if you could write an honest review (as short or as long as you like) on your favorite book retailer.

Thank you and happy reading.

Rob Shumaker

To read more about the Capital Series novels, go to www.USAnovels.com

... .—

Made in United States
Troutdale, OR
11/14/2024